William Joseph Roberts

Presents:

Misfits of Magic

Three Ravens Publishing
Chickamauga, GA USA

William Joseph Roberts Presents: Misfits of Magic Anthology
Is a collective work of contributing authors and Published by Three Ravens Publishing
threeravenspublishing@gmail.com
P.O. Box 851 Chickamauga, Ga 30707
https://www.threeravenspublishing.com

Credits:

Cover art by: J.F. Posthumus

William Joseph Roberts Presents: Misfits of Magic by William Joseph Roberts /Three Ravens Publishing – 1st edition, 2022

Trade Paperback ISBN: 978-1-951768-52-2

Contents

Introduction

This fantasy anthology started out as a fun idea to bring together a bunch of great authors for a collection of stories that would take the reader on all sorts of adventures.

But inspiration is one of those things that can come at you from left field with a squirrel brained idea and send you spiraling on a whole new tangent.

While grabbing a bite with Toni Weisskopf at a local pizzeria here in Chickamauga, she told me some of the backstory of Jim Baen and Baen books.

And while working with his buddy Tom Doherty at TOR, Jim started a series entitled "Jim Baen presents". There wasn't anything magic or special about it, but still, something about it stuck to the back of my brain pan and just hung there. That's when I decided that I wanted to do something similar through Three Ravens.

Out of respect for Jim, I tossed the idea at Toni, since she was the closest I'd ever get to asking Jim himself, and she gave me her blessing.

So here we are at the first volume of "William Joseph Roberts Presents." A fun collection of fantasy stories that I'm sure will whisk you away to new worlds and adventures.

I hope that you find this collection from a great group of authors as enjoyable a read as I have, and that you'll be looking forward to the next installment in the series.

- William Joseph Roberts

Acknowledgements

Without the help of a number of people, and the team that is Three Ravens, this collection would have been even harder to put together than it was. Between an editor shift and some major life events going on here at Raven Central, this collection was unfortunately delayed.

I'd like to take a moment to call out a few folks that were instrumental in getting this collection complete.

Kristina Barnes
Jenny Wren
Philip Booker
And of course, Meg,
(My rock and the Three Ravens Word Witch.)

I would also like to extend a special thank you to Piers Anthony for taking the time to write a small piece about his experience with the Fantasy Genre. Without creators like him paving the way and inspiring the next generation, Fantasy wouldn't be what it is today and may have taken a few steps back in the process.

Thank you, Mr. Anthony.

Dedication

In the last few years, we have lost a number of great authors and mentors. Without their contributions and guidance to the writing community at large, a lot of us wouldn't be where we are today.

This collection is dedication to the work and influence of

Ben Bova
David Farland
Eric Flint
Mike Resnick

Each and every one of them will be missed. I can only hope to see them again at the great convention in the sky.

Opening Words of Wisdom

My history with fantasy has been mixed. My first fantasy novel, *Hasan*, was an adaptation of a prominent *Arabian Nights* story. As I recall, it was rejected twelve times by publishers, but then sold five times, in part because it was once bought but then written off unpublished. You know, the New Editor syndrome. So yes, it seemed to be a misfit. So I stayed clear of fantasy for a decade as difficult to place. But later I wanted to work with an editor I had admired, Lester del Rey of DEL REY BOOKS, and he was their fantasy editor, so I wrote a new fantasy novel, *A Spell for Chameleon*. In effect I turned Florida into the magic land of Xanth. That did not make instant waves, but it was the start of the Xanth series that now runs forty-seven novels. The fifth novel, *Ogre Ogre*, became my first national bestseller, putting me on the map as a novelist. Other fantasies followed, such as the Adept series and the Incarnations of Immortality series, and I was a bestseller through much of the 1980s, appearing on the national bestseller lists a total of fifty-two times. It has come close to being a movie several times, but canceled before quite getting there, maybe a magic jinx. So fantasy, having originally been a drug on my market, became my fortune. I can't guarantee that it will do the same for other writers, but the potential is there. With magic, anything is possible.

Piers Anthony

A Whisper on the Wind
By Megan Higgins

The sun-dried planking of the dock scraped Hodger's back through his travel-worn cotton shirt as he fell in front of the sailor that shoved him. That little corner of his being churned in anguish thinking about the dead wood underneath him, trees killed only to be trampled upon instead of standing tall and proud as they should have.

And he meant to get on the ship moored behind the sailor, the *Sea Whisper.*

"We don't 'ave any room for a freakish whelp without a copper to his name on board," the sailor said with a sneer.

Hodger scoffed at the man's insult as he stood. Whelp? He was easily older than the ragged sailor, a man whose face wore the high tide years of living, and anyone else on board. It came with being a Salket, one of the descendants of *luvior*, the tree spirits of old, which is why he was a growing man at 92. But he wouldn't mention that. He needed to get onboard to continue his journey across the Theris Ocean to Tatheria and punching this man for his ignorance would not get him any closer onto the *Sea Whisper*'s decks.

"I'm a good worker, worth any three men you already have on board," argued Hodger.

"Oh, so I'm to kick three other boys that got here before you so you can get on, am I?" The wrinkled sailor stepped forward, his right fist tightened again.

"Oh good, you haven't departed yet," said a new voice.

A man strode up to the sailor with familiarity, and Hodger felt a distinctive prickle on the back of his neck. The stranger looked normal, brown hair, average height for a Crafter, a brown cloak, brown trousers, a white linen shirt, and a single leather pack slung over his shoulder. Hodger had seen hundreds of the same since he left home five years ago. He watched the man as he spoke to the sailor.

"Good ta see you, Rick," the sailor patted the Rick's shoulder. "We've got a full house this trip, so be ready for some hard work. Quite an interesting crowd, if I do say so meself."

"All the better, Sav," Rick said. He glanced over his shoulder at Hodger, confirming Hodger's suspicion that even the man's eyes were a normal brown, but a shiver trickled down his spine. Rick's eyebrows rose when he looked at Hodger--although that was nothing new, people had found Hodger's amber ringed eyes a novelty, it was the only thing that distinguished him from Crafters--and he smiled. "What about this boy? Is he coming along?"

"He asn't got the money for the trip, and we've enough men working for their fares. He'd just be another mouth to feed."

"Wouldn't you let him on? Call it a feeling, but I'd say he's worth the food," said Rick. "What's your name, boy?"

"Hodger Bungleton," he said. He didn't understand, but if the man could get him onto the ship, he would ignore the uneasiness the man's presence caused.

"I don't know…" Sav scratched his stubbly chin.

"If he isn't worth his weight, I'll be responsible for his fare from my own pocket," Rick promised.

Scratch, scratch.

"Alright, he can come onboard, Rick," Sav said in resignation. "And you!" He pointed a hard finger at Hodger with a sharp look, "Rick here's a good man, stickin' his lot in with you. I'd best see you workin' twice as hard as the others, and if you start retching 'cause you ain't got any sea legs, by Ocean himself, you'd best work four times as hard! I won't have Captain Laros complainin' I allowed dead weight on."

"Yes, sir!" Hodger responded, gulping anxiously. *What were sea legs?* he wondered.

"Great!" Rick clapped his hands and headed up the single wooden plank onto the *Sea Whisper.* Sav jerked his head at Hodger, and Hodger rushed onboard as well.

Up on the deck, people of all walks milled about, different Speakers from different lands. Senron, where they were departing from, was one of the major port cities on this side of the continent, after all. Crafters poor and rich were mixed in with what seemed to be an envoy from a tribe of Tamers.

Despite Crafters and Tamers being the two Speakers that worked closest together, they were easy to differentiate. Crafters had simple brown, blue, or green eyes, and a startling lack of presence. They made up for their diminutive existence, however, by being the center of all trade around the world and building with their Skill what the others could not. It would not be a stretch to say the weakest race was in fact the true ruler of the world.

Tamers, on the other hand, were feline hunters on two legs. Their gait suggested stalking predators, and their slitted cat-eyes watched with the intensity of a lion. Add their tipped ears, claw-like fingernails, and the thin layer of hair all over their body that was more than peach fuzz, and a Tamer was immediately distinguishable from a Crafter.

Oddly enough, he noticed two Crafter children among the Tamers, standing quietly by the Tamers' feet with their heads down. They wore clothing of a similar sort to the Tamers, tan linens and worn leathers, meaning they did not wander over from one of the many groups of Crafters.

"Come on, Hodger," said Rick, pulling his thoughts away from the children. The mysterious, average man led him down into the hull of the ship. Down below was a dark nest of hammocks and bustling men, sailors and passengers alike.

They searched for somewhere that was not claimed, which was of course impossible, so they settled for a corner clear of barrels and dripping water. Hodger startled when he saw three enormous figures cloaked and hooded in black huddled in the dark corner close to their spot. Miners.

Hodger had never seen a Miner without the trademark hooded cloak, but he had heard stories they were like large moles with bulging black eyes suited more for the depths of their caves than the sunny world above. Their claws would be the most interesting to see, though. A Miner's Skill was all in their claws, which could dig through rock and stone like they were butter. It was the closest he had gotten to one, let alone three.

"Hello," he said, offering a wave to the three figures. Obscured faces under hoods and cloak of darkness made it impossible to tell if they were awake or listening.

One head shifted up toward him. "Hello," came the deep voice. A meekness emanated from the voice that clashed with the owner's size. Based on their huddle, Hodger bet they would half double his size of five-foot-seven. The head tilted back down.

No more conversation there then.

"So where are you headed, Hodger?" Rick asked.

"Tatheria," Hodger said, although with some hesitancy. There wasn't much hiding where he was going, though, since they were both headed there. "Why did you vouch for me like that?"

Rick smiled a secret smile, "Because I knew you would have an interesting story to tell. That is my price for covering your passage."

"Story?" Hodger huffed. "How is that worth the price of a voyage to another continent if I don't work enough to satisfy Sav?" He had heard prices for the trip. It was several pieces of gold to get to Tatheria. He'd never *touched* a piece of gold.

"Money is all the same. Coppers, silvers, golds. One gold is like the other. It comes and goes. There's little value in it aside from what people put on it. But stories… Stories are unique. They are knowledge. They give insight into an experience that the listener never had. They enlighten, they teach, they bring thrill and joy. To me, a good story is worth more than a few gold."

Hodger considered the man in front of him. Rick's words were filled with gentle passion, a sincerity that would be hard to fake. That sensation was still there, although Hodger could not say if it was his instincts yelling, *"Danger!"* If anything, it reminded him of the Venor trees back home. The ancient titan tree bodies of the *luvior* occasionally gave him a similar feeling, beings that were more than the environment surrounding them, shaping it rather than it shaping them. This person Rick was not a person you meet and forget.

"Alright, I'll tell my story."

Three weeks on the *Sea Whisper* crossing the Theris Ocean and Hodger was more than used to the swaying sight of open waters dancing over itself. Dolphins leapt out of the water with their friends and clicked at the deck-goers in some game they only knew, and sea gulls called overhead as they dropped their white gooey gifts on unsuspecting victims.

He was tired of it.

Sure, it was beautiful and majestic, but he missed his rich soils and sturdy trees. He had never been away from trees for so long in his life. He wanted nothing more than to get on solid ground and spend a night up in the first tree he found.

There had been some comfort when he managed to take up residence in the crow's nest when he wasn't anywhere else cleaning and tying ropes, or even scraping barnacles off the exposed portions of the hull. Convincing Sav, the quartermaster, to let him keep night watch was easy since their previous man had fallen on his way down and broken his foot and none of the other crew were willing to stay up or available.

Most days were grueling work, just as Sav demanded. However, Rick made sure to sweat and strain right along with him, all the while listening to his adventures. Hodger neglected to tell Rick about who he was and where he came from, but he gladly told the man about the discovery and hardships after leaving home.

Rick was a perfect audience. He let Hodger talk and talk and talk without interruption, only asking questions to pick up the story ends when they were stopped by work and expressing a range of reactions to each story beat. It made the days go by quicker, even if it left him desperate for a drink of water and honey if he had it.

According to Rick, there was another five weeks if the winds favored them. Food was rationed from day one in case of a tedious voyage. When possible, sailors cast nets into the water for fish.

Pulled taut into the depths, nets creaked on wood railings against the ocean's effort to drag it farther down, the momentum of the ship fighting through the water's resistance. Right before wooden railings seemed about to break, ten men heaved the nets out of the water to reveal their catch. They went through this arduous routine at least three times a day.

Ignoring his blistered hands, Hodger lent his strength to pull the frayed rope up. Today was his turn to cast and pull, just like every other day. Other men were on a rotation, but Sav made sure Hodger was paying his due. When the net came up bare and empty the third time that day, every man groaned.

"It is an embarrassment to watch these Crafters try to fish," said one of the Tamer tribesmen in a thick accent Hodger had to pay close attention to understand. He was the youngest of the five that had boarded, Shaza, and he spoke to his four companions with arrogance in his slitted green eyes. "They have no way with the art of capture."

"My children could read these waters better than them," chuckled another of the tribesmen. He was far more mature than the first, gray beginning to touch his brow, although no more dismissive than his younger counterpart.

The demeaning commentary continued. The Tamers had not been discreet with their insults, and many a Crafter sailor glared at the pair. Yet, no one made a move to rebuke the Tamers. It was drilled into every single working man onboard that they could not start fights with the paying passengers. It was a long journey for anyone, and they all needed to get along, so people weren't throwing others overboard. Especially since a fair number of passengers carried weapons with them. Each Tamer had a spear hitched on their backs at all times.

But Hodger was not in the mood to suck it up. He was tired, overworked, aching, blistered, and hungry. And he would jump overboard before he let some arrogant Tamers walk over him.

"Then come over here and do it yourself!" he barked at the Tamers.

"What was that?" asked Shaza.

The other sailors were sending alarmed glances at Hodger. He was stepping into dangerous territory. When a stone is cast, though, it's easier to throw another than to grab the first. "What, aren't those pointy ears of yours for hearing better? Couldn't you hear me when I told you to stop wagging your tongues and do it yourself? Do you need one of those children you always drag around to pass on my message instead?"

With a stride that put any feline to shame, the young tribesman approached Hodger in measured steps. Up close, the Tamer towered over him by half-a-foot. A self-satisfied grin crept onto his chocolate gold skin. He was close enough that Hodger could see all of the fine hairs, the exact color of his flesh, in exacting detail. "Ringed gold eyes… ringed gold eyes… Interesting for a Crafter. If only you were younger, and I would have loved to tame you just like these children."

Unease filled the air as they bore witness to the scene. Hodger's thoughts stuttered. He could not understand what the young brat of a Tamer was talking about. He did not want to understand. Those two children, a boy and a girl no older than ten years, did not flinch under the sudden scrutiny of everyone on deck as they stood at the legs of the Tamers.

"What do you mean, you've 'tamed' them?" Hodger demanded.

"Simple. They are slaves we are training. Just like any other animal, we pick up Crafter orphans, feed them, clothe them, teach them, and train them so eventually, they can be sold as premium slaves for whoever is willing to pay."

"You can't just tame other Speakers like that. They're people, like you!" Hodger yelled. His arm ached from work, yet it ached more so to tear Shaza's face off.

"Don't forget, Ring-eyes, we're all just animals, whether we can talk or not," Shaza proclaimed.

That can't be possible, can it? Can a Tamer use their Skill on other Speakers? Bend another person's will forcefully so they become master in that person's eyes? Override their free will? Hodger's anger fizzled a bit as it trickled into a pool growing at the bottom of his gut, feeding a new emotion. Fear.

"Eyes like yours, you would fetch quite a price, even if you may be a little old," said Shaza. Hodger wanted off that ship and as far away from these Tamers as possible.

Sav came stomping in between Hodger and the Tamer. The old, weathered man that did nothing but berate and increase his workload became an iron bastion against the Tamer. "Enough of that talk 'ere! Payin' customers or no, you won't be acquirin' any of my men for your business. Get on, now!"

With a final slitted-green-eyed glance directed at Hodger, the Tamer stalked back over to his group.

"Thanks, Sav," Hodger said, and he meant it every bit.

"Go keep watch, Hodger," gruffed Sav. The man shoved through sailors, barking orders to any man unfortunate enough to pass him. The harsh commands held none of the bite Sav's words usually delivered. Hodger's discontent toward Sav lessened a bit. As much as Sav worked him to the bone, the man did have a moral code.

Rick leaned toward Hodger, whispering, "I would learn to sleep with your eyes open if I were you."

"Why didn't you step up and do anything?" Hodger said, rounding on Rick, indignant fury roaring back to life in his chest. The man had not moved an inch when Shaza was a few steps away from putting a leash and collar on him. Yet Rick had stood by the entire time, the person Hodger thought was at least his friend after all the time he spent telling his stories and working side by side with him. He did not know who Rick was, or why his hairs stood on end every time the man came within three feet of him when no one else seemed bothered, and he had no clue whether Rick was any good in a fight, so he did not know what he expected of him. He expected *something*, though.

"I like to watch how people react to situations. And I prefer to let others sort their problems themselves if they can. Just because I can step in all the time does not mean I always should," Rick answered as though it were a fact as normal as the sun rising in the east. Not a single trace of regret existed in his being.

"Right," Hodger said, the 't' snapping, "well, maybe I should leave you to your observations, then."

As Rick helped bunch the net back up to cast it a fourth time, he called over his shoulder, "And Hodger, I mean it when I say you should watch out for them."

Hodger stormed away to clean something, frustration making him no more than a petulant boy. He had no words to say to Rick that were not a scathing hot retort.

Later that day when he slept next to the shadowy corner of Miners, before taking his night watch, his dreams were plagued with Tamers running after him, leashes in hand, as they pulled him into the ocean's black abyss, muffled and drowning under their control. Rick watched from the ship's decks, his face pensive.

Nerves splintered like a tree ravaged by bear claws, Hodger could not walk around a corner or into another part of the ship without searching the area for the Tamers for the next week. Whether they really could use their Skill on another Speaker was yet to be clarified, but he had no desire to wait for them to call him to heel.

Days of work passed more slowly, now that he was loath to recount any more tales to Rick. And, for the Crafter's part, he seemed to realize this and did not ask for any.

Stars consumed his view. Up top in his crow's nest, the cool salty breeze clearing away the musky smell of unbathed sailors, Hodger felt like he could breathe. No one could get up here without his notice, and he was away from unfriendly folk.

All he had to worry about now was watching for sea serpents.

Captain Laros had summoned all passengers and crew on the *Sea Whisper* up to the deck for an announcement that morning. Depending on the winds, they would be entering the Snake Nest, territory of the sea serpents, before the next day was out. Notorious for crushing ships en route to other continents and devouring its passengers, sea serpents were every sailor's nightmare. Vessels only managed to get by infested waters by coating the hull of the boat with a special substance that warded the serpents away--a trade secret according to Sav--and ceasing all possible noise. No one would be allowed in the hull for fear the steps and sounds would echo through the water more clearly than above deck. A boat that creaked too loudly could be a death sentence.

Four days minimum they would have to travel like that and pray to whatever god they had that the right winds fill their sails. Captain Laros instructed all crew members, whether they were seasoned permanent sailors or men working for the voyage, on the hand signals they used while passing through the Snake Nest. No man on duty was to become distracted or lose focus, lest he miss the signs. If someone did miss the signs and the man next to him saw, it was the second man's responsibility to make the first aware. If a course correction needed to be made, they had to act without a moment's hesitation.

His line of sight reached the horizon on all sides from his perch. The wind swirled his hair in front of his face, and he hurried to push it out of the way. Calm waters of midnight blue rippled away from the bow of the *Sea Whisper*. The water undulated like liquid glass; it was so calm. Captain Laros, Sav, Rick, and every other sailor on deck were waiting for his signals on bated breath. More than sixty lives depended on his keen eyes and quick reaction.

It was a good thing he had volunteered for the night watch early on. He was one of the best archers back in the Dunic, so he knew his eyes were sharp enough. Besides, he had noticed along his journey that Salkets had night vision, whereas Crafters became helpless without their lamps and fires. Out in the middle of the ocean in the twilight hours, where the waters gulped up any light, a few lamps did little to aid a Crafter's sight. He would rather be the one up there, knowing that he at least was not limited by the cloak of darkness.

A new ripple broke the water surface ahead of them, mere yards off from the starboard side. A row of spines slithered through the waveless waters parallel to the direction the *Sea Whisper* was sailing. He pushed down his reaction at the length of spines stretching twice the length of the ship, pointing with his index finger and thumb right. Right. Right.

All at once, the still crew, statues frozen into readiness, burst into hushed motion. The watcher on the deck followed Hodger's line of sight to the ridge running adjacent to the ship. He held up ten fingers to the men at the riggings, and then a hand pointing to the left. Multiple sailors jumped to adjust the masts and sails, while the helmsman steered the ship ten degrees portside.

Hodger gripped onto the railing while the *Sea Whisper* tilted out of the direction of the sea serpent. First one down. The ridge of spines remained in the side of his vision as he turned his attention to their altered course where he spotted an outstretched shadow submerged yet shallow under the surface. This one was diagonal from the front portside of the *Sea Whisper* and heading straight toward them.

He signaled left forward. Left forward. Left forward.

The watcher on deck searched for the shadow. He scrambled his telescope open, the tinny sliding of metal against metal on the tubes echoing like clashing sabers on the deck. His telescope swiveled around, trying to locate a shadow underwater at night, and Hodger pointed fervently as best he could from his perch.

A looming figure in a black cloak stepped up beside the watcher and pointed a claw where Hodger had been looking. *Of course! Miners have better vision in the dark than anyone,* thought Hodger.

His bearings found, the watcher jerked his hands in rushed movement. The helmsman cranked at the wheel, and the eight sailors rushed to adjust. But it was too late. Hodger watched in trepidation as the shadow enclosed on the portside of the ship.

Ten feet.

Eight feet.

Five feet.

Four.

Three.

Two.

One.

In the darkness, the shadow of the serpent touched the ship's. It touched…

Then it faded downward into the abyss, a fan of spikes webbed with glossy skin kicking above the surface before disappearing with the shadow.

It just left? Was that because of the stuff they coat the ship keel with?

Either way, he didn't allow himself to celebrate the close call. A mile ahead, there was more choppy water that he had no intention of getting close to. When every other spot of water was smooth, he could not trust the disturbance. He flashed ten fingers twice, then five, then pointed starboard. The captain had given Hodger the authority to direct the ship if he felt it absolutely necessary since his position was the only one that could see all that was happening at a given time. Although he was leading them on a bit of a detour, it would continue to take them forward. No matter what, he wanted to avoid going around in circles in those waters.

They passed within range of the frothy area, and he saw two slick, scaly bodies wrestling with each other. It was hard to make out more than a dark aquamarine body and an indigo body. However, both sea serpents were lined by that single ridge of long spikes, yet none of the spikes punctured the opponent's body despite scraping against it.

Sea Whisper's bow glided through the dreaded nest, swerving with the point of Hodger's fingers, a zigzag so convoluted they lost an hour traveling what could have been fifteen minutes in a straight line. Sailors swapped with each other in quick succession after dodging around several times in a row. Most of the time, Hodger was successful in avoiding a run-in with the sea serpents. The two times he was not, the sea serpent would get close enough to scrape the ship, then would dive as though running away from a monster more frightening than they.

No wonder people could cross the ocean in spite of the Snake Nest. Whatever mystery coating they put on the ship, it worked.

And as much as Hodger wanted to be the lone hero guiding the crew that he had worked with for weeks and make Sav indebted to him so he wouldn't have to pay after the voyage was done, the Miners had taken up positions around the ship to watch on all sides, including behind them where Hodger had not bothered much to look.

Night waned with close call after close call. Terrified passengers grew too tired to stay awake, numbed to the passing of the monsters that never did more than make a few splashes. If only they could see what Hodger saw. Outlines of beasts that could wrap the *Sea Whisper* in its grip twice over and break it like a twig. Heads so large that it dwarfed a person. Children would be no more than snacks.

One sea serpent on the port side was slinking away from the ship, while another approached from starboard, the very tips of its spikes above water. He signaled. The Miner on the starboard bow directed the watcher on deck, and the song and dance repeated once more. However, this one had more speed to it, and Hodger doubted they would get out of the way on time to clear it.

He watched the silhouette come closer to the ship, waiting for it to dive down.

It touched.

Then disappeared down.

Hodger let out the tiny breath he had been holding. He could never be too sure.

The water swirled about where the portside sea serpent had been swimming away. The spikes curled into an elongated "u". Hundreds of spikes turned from heading away to heading toward them.

Hodger's heart sank. Not a single serpent had changed course like that.

He didn't waste a single moment to point hands emphatically toward the approaching sea serpent. No one could see the panic scrawled over his face. No one could hear his heavy breathing as he restrained a cry to tell the crew to *MOVE!*

The crew was not slow to move, no, they had not grown complacent. And the wind would not have allowed a greater speed than the one they were at. He knew these things, yet he almost could not resist the urge to yell. He wanted to yell at the Miners pointing at the oncoming terror of the ocean, to yell at the Tamers to use their Skill, to yell at the sky to give them stronger winds, to yell at Captain Laros and Sav to drop the oars and start rowing as fast as possible, to yell at Rick to do something instead of standing there again.

SSSSHHHHHHRRRRRKKKKKK! The ship rumbled and creaked as countless spines scraped the underbelly from portside to starboard. A scaly, dark blue head that was almost black rose out of the water on the starboard side. Shorter spikes donned the crown of the sea serpent's head, a line of them stopping right where Hodger expected a pair of eyes to be and found none. There was simply a nose, flat smooth head, and an extensive tongue hissing at them.

The rumbling screech clawed out of the sea serpent's mouth as it faced its sightless gaze toward them and drew up a dozen more heads like it. Soon, those dozen others were slithering their way over to the *Sea Whisper*.

"I wondered why that other fellow ssssuddenly retreated like a coward," hissed the sea serpent in a coherent voice that was indistinguishable as male or female.

Sea serpents are Speakers, too? he thought.

"Clever, I'd say," the serpent went on, "mixing shed dragon skin in with whatever you put on your ship. Crafters truly are innovative."

Hodger did not like the tone of the serpent. He was no expert on gigantic marine reptiles or their speech patterns, but he heard the universal pitch of sarcasm in its voice.

"However, you should have done what those other little sailors do. They bring a whole flock of livestock. We do love the warm, deliciousss meat of you land-dwellers. Then one of us will essscort you to sssafety," it said.

Captain Laros stepped up to the railing. Hodger admired how the captain did not tremble one step. "We don't have any livestock to be giving to you now, but on the return journey back, I can make sure to bring plenty for you. Captain's promise."

The serpent chuckled, which came out in a mangled sound between a hiss and a screech. "No livesssstock? I beg to differ. There are plenty of people on your boat."

"I mean no disrespect, but no one on my ship is mere food," stated Captain Laros. As he spoke the words, nervous glances stole across the deck. Many Crafters' eyes landed on the Tamers, who had not done anything to make friends since the voyage began.

"If I let you go now," the sea serpent argued, "what are the chances I will run into you again? And even if you do bring delectable meats for me, you will give them to the first of my kind that you run into to save your skins. That would leave me with nothing. I am no fool."

"Take the Tamers!" screamed one Crafter, a wealthy nobleman accompanied by two of his retainers.

"Quiet, you!" shouted the captain.

"What did you say, you overgrown swine?" started the oldest tribesman, advancing in dangerous strides. "You would fill the serpent's belly faster than us."

"Enough!" said Sav as he pushed passengers away from one another. "Enough!"

Order was lost and Hodger stared in horror as the eyeless beast's grin widened, hundreds of small white teeth catching what little light the lamps made. "It ssseems none of you can decide. That's not very ssselflessss of you. Not one person is willing to offer their life for sssso many others?" it sneered. "Ssssuch sssselfish people invading our territory with foul-smelling dragon ssskin and not one gift in return, I'd sssay you all deserve to be eaten, hm?"

From the other side of the ship, the serpent's dark blue finned tail rose high above the water and hooked itself onto the *Sea*

Whisper's portside railing. Hodger's world turned sideways as the boat tilted farther and farther, until salty sprays of water sloshed onto the deck. Many desperately hung on to whatever was near them, masts and ropes and railings and grates.

Four figures did not. Where the Tamers had been, one remained with the children underarm and gripping a railing. The other four, however, had drawn their spears and slid down to the partially submerged railings. They prepared a heavy thrust at the serpent's tail, aiming for the thick flesh covered in slime and scales.

The spearheads came down as sure as could be and… slipped off.

"You can't hurt a sea serpent's hide, you idiots!" yelled the captain. "That damnable slime is their Skill! Nothing except dragon fire can get through it!"

Before the Tamers could follow up on their ignorant bungle, the fin swatted at all four, sending them careening through the wall of the captain's quarters. The sea serpent dove its head into the crowd of passengers that were staggering about along with the swaying ship. For a head without eyes, it struck very close to a sizeable group of Crafters, all of whom screamed in terror.

The snake head turned to the screams, drawn by the sound. At sea, a dozen more heads ducked into the water and sped toward the besieged *Sea Whisper*. The passengers and sailors scrambled like frantic ants before the hungry beast.

Invisible to the sea serpent in his perch above, Hodger took in his surroundings with a calm eye while battling the adrenaline that urged him to move. The fear buzzed in his hands as he leapt out onto the sail beam just outside the crow's nest. Directly below was the sea serpent's head playing its game of hide-and-seek with the frightened Crafters.

I may regret this later, but I won't get to if we're all dead, he thought, and then he gave a resounding *STOMP!* on the white oak beam, a wordless command of Skill delivered in the same moment his boot landed.

The two-foot-wide beam cracked under his single stomp. Twigs fell like rain, and the beam, held by a few ropes, jerked downward as each rope snapped under its weight. Fifteen feet of oak beam slammed onto the monster's spiky spine.

A bone-chilling howl erupted from the serpent, drowning out the snapping of dozens of spikes, and the force of the cry flung the beam off its back. "DAMN YOU, CRETINS!"

The ship groaned and snapped beneath the tirade as the serpent thrashed about. Hodger tried to grip onto the crow's nest edge as best he could, but the shockwaves through the poor ship shook him free. His hands flailed for the mast, the tingling gravitational pull in a Salket's hands toward wood guiding him to stability. Like a spider on a wall, he stuck to the mast without rope or ladder.

It was a small victory, though. The *Sea Whisper* was damaged wherever he looked, more sea serpents were swimming closer, some already lifting their spiked snakeheads out to taste the air.

"Warm meat," they hissed among themselves. "Fake dragon," crooned others.

"They. Are. MINE!" snarled the first.

"Don't be rude. Share," an emerald green one said, breathy and light.

"I found them while all of you ran away from the stench of dragon. They're mine." By then, the first serpent removed his head from the deck to face the others.

The ship finally turned back upright, battered and beaten, but floating yet. Hodger took the respite to climb down. Passengers raced down below deck as though it would protect them. A few limbs peeked through the rubble in the captain's quarters where the Tamers had been thrown.

Who knows? Being knocked out when they died sounded the least painful way to go, in Hodger's opinion.

Speaking of dying, he thought as he searched for his new and estranged friend. *I should apologize before we die. It was nice getting to tell him stories.* He searched the deck for the brown hair and worn brown coat, half-expecting the tingle to not work with the current threat flooding his body with fear.

He had not seen Rick on deck before breaking the beam, so he checked in the hull. Children huddled with their parents, grown men cowered against the walls of the ship, but Rick was nowhere to be seen. Their corner by the barrels and the Miners' spot was empty. He searched the crew's quarters, where men prayed to the mighty Ocean to be delivered safely from his servants, the sea serpents.

Still no Rick.

Hodger went back onto the deck to where Captain Laros and Sav sat, watching the beasts fight over who would eat them with a listless gaze and a bottle of rum. When they saw him, Captain

Laros nodded out at the debacle and asked, "My bet's on that silver one there. Sav's betting on the one that attacked first. What's your bet?"

More massive than any of the other sea serpents, a sleek silver serpent was encroaching on the first serpent's space and the ship. Unlike the others, the silver one had a mouth big enough to swallow a Miner whole.

"You might be right about the silver," Hodger said, to which Sav waved a dismissive hand. "Have you seen Rick?"

"Rick?" Sav asked. He grabbed the proffered rum flask and took a swig. "Think I saw him in the captain's quarters. Checkin' on the Tamers."

"Thanks," he said and rushed to the torn crumbled wall. The four Tamers were indeed knocked out cold under the rubble, one of them being the cocky youth. The whole confrontation seemed so silly to him now in the face of imminent death.

He moved past the pile of bodies and debris to head farther into the dark room. In the captain's chair, nailed down to the floorboards, Rick sat static, fingers steepled together in his lap.

"Rick?" he called, afraid to disturb him. He was no less than ten feet away when he felt his hairs stand on end worse than ever before, his gut ringing in alarm.

Rick drew a deep breath. "…I'm ready." He rose to his feet. "Yes, Hodger?"

Hodger bit back his question. The man was probably preparing himself for death. "I wanted to apologize for being a petty brat, and for not talking to you because of it. You've been a good friend these past few weeks. I'm glad I was able to meet you before I died."

The Crafter's footsteps sounded dim in the quiet room as the serpents screeched and growled at one another outside. Rick stopped in front of Hodger. "Thank you, Hodger. I loved your stories. You have quite a knack for telling them."

And then he patted Hodger's shoulder once, a motion so simple, yet it drew such a reaction from the Salket. In that instant when Rick's hand touched, it was as though lightning had struck him in that one spot, muscles contracting involuntarily, and dancing lights blinded his vision. The next moment, it was all gone, and Rick was out the broken cabin wall.

Hodger knew he needed to follow. To see what was about to happen. To see something greater than him. He rushed onto the deck where Rick planted himself squarely toward the sea serpents. They were less so arguing by that point, and more focused on enjoying their catch. As the captain had predicted, the silver one led the way while the dark blue one with the broken spikes attempted to repel the poachers.

"Out of the way, and I'll save you a morsel or two for your hard work, Iyal," growled the silver serpent.

"Olishk, you thief!" Iyal said, but Olishk whipped his tail at Iyal.

Olishk, now right where Iyal had been beside the *Sea Whisper* yet dwarfing it all the more, slithered his tongue out to taste the air. The broad, silver snakehead, a sword stark in the night rising from the ocean, propelled forward as though a master swordsman's strike straight at Rick.

Rick directed his hands to the floor and drove them upward, arms shaking under some imaginary burden he carried in his hands. "I think that's enough, now," he said.

Waves surged upon Olishk, Iyal, and the next two closest sea serpents to the *Sea Whisper.* The water defied gravity, defied the stillness of the water surface, defied the beasts as it swirled around them as snakes free of solid form. The serpents reared back, but the water bindings held them, dragged them closer.

Rick's arms, elevated high above him, crossed over into an 'X' and he pushed them down and away like twin swords slashing a single target. The water bindings all the way to the ocean surface froze. Icy columns encircled the serpents, tables of ice thick enough to walk on spanning between each column, all of which created a tableau of a frozen field of imprisonment upon the open ocean waters.

"*SssShaed…*" hissed Iyal.

Hushed whispers echoed through the remaining people on deck at the sacred word. All eyes, and eyeless gazes, focused on the average-looking man that commanded the attention of these colossal beings that were only known to fear the ferocious dragons.

Shaed. The rarest race of Speakers. Born once every thousand years to a Crafter family immortal and invincible. Their Skill transcended every other. The ability to bend any energy to their will made them akin to gods in the flesh. Created by Nature itself, Shaeds were the wise shepherds to guide the younger, mortal races toward harmony and knowledge. No sane nation opposed the advice of a Shaed.

"I never would have dared attack had I known you were on this vessel, Master Shaed," Iyal said, the ice allowing just enough movement for speech. "May I ask for your name, Master Shaed?"

"Ralan is fine." A larger ripple of whispering broke out, more active than the first and with a bigger audience since the frightened passengers and crew had been drawn out of their hiding places by those on deck. "And I know you wouldn't have attacked. That isn't the point. You should not be eating passing ships *at all*. It saddens me that we still need to remind the marsen on this matter."

"Great Master Ralan, we apologize for our misconduct. There are no excuses for our behavior. Please, accept our apology and know we will pass on your word to all of our kind within the depths of the Theris Ocean when you consider our punishment," said Iyal.

Rick, or Ralan, threw a grin at Hodger. "Your punishment has already been met, as far as I am concerned, Iyal. The spikes on your back will not grow back. And I do expect you to relay my request on to all the marsen you meet." His right hand waved at Iyal as though he were wiping away the ice in a single sweep, and it all melted away. Iyal prostrated a dark blue scaly head to the Shaed.

He went on. "Olishk and the two that so eagerly waited to consume the occupants on the *Sea Whisper*, you three will be met with the same punishment." Another wave of his hand and the ice snapped a couple dozen spikes clean off the three serpents' backs. Screeches shook the air until the ice still holding them began to crack. One last wave released them back to the ocean where they curled in on themselves in pain.

Even so, the three hissed out, "As you bid it, Great Master Ralan."

"Good," Ralan said. "You may go." His tone held no inflections, nor did he yell or plead. He dismissed the sea serpents as a teacher dismisses a classroom of children. None of them reared up in protest. None of them said a word. None of them let out a hiss.

Over a dozen Sea Serpents all dove out of sight, as far away from the Shaed as they could.

There was a surreal moment after the serpents departed that had to sink in for those on the *Sea Whisper*. A second later, a cheer rang out among the crew and passengers. Happy tears of relief flowed freely. There was no shortage of people lining up to admire Ralan, the Great Master Shaed.

"Rick, why'd you never tell me you were a Shaed?" Sav said, although a huge grin adorned his face. "We wouldn't have made you work for your fare all these times. Heck, we wouldn't have charged you fare if we knew a Shaed would be on board!"

"Honestly, I'd like to hire you for every voyage, but even I know that's not possible. Who would have thought I had the ever-wandering Shaed Ralan on my ship not once, but four times!" Captain Laros said.

"Don't worry about it, Captain, Sav. I personally prefer doing manual labor to get my basic needs. I have to stay humble somehow," laughed Ralan.

Laros scoffed his reason away. "Humble? Bah! You're one of only three survivors from the War of Madness, the biggest war the world has ever seen. How many people get to claim they're living war heroes from 10,000 years ago? Wasn't it just you and the two eldest Shaed against the third eldest that had gone rogue and started the war?"

"Yes, but I was barely older than 100 back then. I knew next to nothing compared to the others," Ralan said, humble yet not sheepish. Whatever insecurities he had back then, the flow of ages had worn away as a river wears away the rocks in its streambed. "Before we get caught up in my past, though, we should worry about the state of everyone onboard." Ralan headed back to the captain's quarters, where Hodger had remained rooted just outside. As he passed, he whispered, "I'll need a Salket's help to get those Tamers out safely."

"You knew?" Hodger asked. He had not told anyone in a long time that he was a Salket. His kind had gone into isolation four hundred years ago for a reason that he did not know, but he respected it all the same and pretended he was a Crafter.

Ralan tapped his temple, right next to his eyes.

Of course he knew. A Shaed would know that Salkets have ringed eyes, unlike Crafters, Hodger thought. He should just assume that Ralan knew everything and get on with it. He went back into the wrecked cabin where the pile of bodies lay.

The fifth Tamer that had kept the children slaves safe the entirety of the attack was there, removing the debris from his companions with the children. Three of the Tamers were awake and waiting to be uncovered. The young, snide one had his eyes clenched and mouth open panting. Hodger helped remove debris until one large board required him, the fifth tribesman, and Ralan to move.

"Be careful," the one next to the youth cautioned. "I think he was more than knocked out.

As soon as they lifted the final board, the three Tamers that could move dashed out from under the board. They crab-walked out of the way of the unconscious tribesman, revealing a square stick of wood that was one-inch wide protruding a foot from the front and back of his gut.

"Hodger," Ralan said loud and clear for all those present, "I am going to need you to hold the stick from both ends, right at the entry and exit points, while I sever the wood and heal him." The Shaed looked pointedly at Hodger, and then it clicked why Ralan had said he would need a Salket's help.

Miniscule chunks of wood dug into his knees as he knelt on the messy cabin floor, hands positioned on the stick next to the young Tamer's flesh as blood leaked over them.

"Get ready, and…" Ralan said, holding his own hands above the mess of hands, flesh, wood, and blood, "now!"

Concentrating on the stick, Hodger thought about every fiber of dried pulp within the stick. He thought about the white oak trunk it came from, and how the knots and grain of the wood melded together. Very carefully, thinking of each of those dried fibers splitting away and holding to either side of the stick, not leaving one splinter behind, he sent the familiar sensation of a command through his arms, to his hands, into his fingertips. In that command, he said, "*Break in two and only two.*"

Snap! The stick came apart, although Hodger waited for Ralan to give the go-ahead to remove it. With a nod from the Shaed, he carefully removed the pieces and inspected his handiwork. Covered in blood and as jagged as they were, one would have expected dozens of shards to get caught in the Tamer's flesh. However, Hodger matched the hundreds of jagged lines and brought the stick together. The seam encircling the stick was nearly invisible except for the blood that sank into the cracks. He could have put some wood glue in that, and it would be as good as new.

A meek, strangled gasp drew his attention away from the stick. The young Tamer panted, his hand reached for his wound and Ralan allowed it, and he stared at Hodger holding the bloody stick. "You…"

"He helped me save your life a moment ago," said Ralan. "You should be fine, although you will want to get proper medical treatment to be sure when we reach Tatheria. However," he adopted a cold expression while addressing the Tamer, "I trust you'll leave your Crafter wards in my care at that time."

"What-!" the youth yelled, then fell back in agony.

His tribesman that had been caring for the children and witnessed the ordeal with the sea serpents put in his own opinion before his healthier companions could argue the point. "Speak with respect, Shaza. It is an honor to have the Great Master Ralan in our presence."

The boy, Shaza, stared at Ralan wide-eyed. His thoughts cascaded over his face. He settled on deference. "Thank you,

Great Master Ralan, for saving my life and those of my brethren. It would be an honor for me to leave the children under your protection."

"Perfect!"

Like that, Hodger no longer feared the presence of the Tamers, and Ralan asked that the children be allowed to play with the others on the ship for the remainder of the voyage. Sav did not demand as much from Hodger, claiming his debt was more than paid. Personally, Hodger was convinced that Sav did not want to collect money on a person that Ralan had vouched for from the moment he boarded.

Although, Hodger ended up utilizing his skills with carpentry quite a bit in the next few weeks as he helped fix up the *Sea Whisper*. Thankfully no one except Ralan realized that Hodger had broken the sail beam, but he still made sure to put in the extra effort to repair it.

For the next four days, the *Sea Whisper* sailed straight through the Snake Nest with nary a fin or spike in sight.

Solid dirt and pebbles crunched under his feet for the first time in ten weeks. He delighted in his body not rocking back and forth every other second. Sadly, there were no trees in sight in the city of Tatheria, but he would find one soon. Maybe forego the inn and camp in a tree. The idea sounded heavenly.

"Hodger," Sav said as the others were offloading, "if you need a ship back and we're in port, we'd be glad to have you again." He offered a gnarled hand to Hodger.

Chuckling as he thought about his initial attempt to get on the *Sea Whisper* weeks ago, Hodger clasped the man's hand in a firm grip. "I'll keep my eye out for you guys when I do."

A good number of the other crew members bid him fond farewells, too. After so many harrowing experiences, they had all bonded as a big, sweaty, stinky, foul-mouthed crew.

That's right, I need a freshwater bath, Hodger dreamily thought. So many things to do now that he was back on land where he belonged. There were tons more places for him to visit, lands to explore, new cultures to experience.

The tingle on the back of his neck jostled him from his daydreaming, though he was used to the feeling by now. "Glad to see you planning your next adventure, Hodger," Ralan said. He held the hands of the two Crafter children as he approached Hodger.

"Well, I got on that boat for a reason, Rick." Hodger and the others had gone back to calling him Rick at the Shaed's behest. He did not like to stand out so much, and the name "Ralan" was a beacon for attention. "I'd say meeting you is going to be one of my biggest stories, though."

"Fine, I'll let you tell that one to your folks back home. I'm sure they miss you, so make sure to live through your adventures. If fortune favors it, we may run into each other again someday."

"Heh. Yeah, that would be nice. And then, you can talk until your throat goes dry next time while I get to listen," Hodger teased.

"I don't think that's what my immortality is meant for," Ralan said.

"Hey, before you go, Rick."

"Hm?"

He thought about asking Ralan why his hairs stood on end whenever Ralan was nearby, something he had not mentioned to anyone in the ten weeks on the *Sea Whisper.* He debated asking. And then he decided not to ask. He did not want to say goodbye to his friend right after telling him his presence was unnerving.

"Never mind. Goodbye, Rick. I hope your days are happy."

"The same to you, Hodger Bungleton. I hope we meet again."

Hodger shook his hand and turned eastward. He checked over his shoulder as he got on the busy port street, thinking to spot the brown-haired man with a brown coat holding hands with two young children. A stream of strangers walked through where Ralan had stood.

Hodger marched through the streets of Tatheria, imprinting memories of his time on the *Sea Whisper* in his mind, as he sought out another adventure to stumble over.

END

The Wraith and the Wizard

By Jennifer Brinn

The crowd in the tavern was perfect. Loud, happy. Just in from harvest market with pockets full of coins. The time was right for a tale.

"No shit, there I was--"

"Were you captured again?" Constan's bored tone expertly derailed my thunder. He lurked in his chair, his broad shoulders giving a slight shrug. Constan swigged his watered-down ale. It didn't quite hide his smirk.

It was my turn to glare. Even if Constan had heard my stories a thousand times—and he'd even been there for most of the events that had become my go-to get-free-drinks-tales—there was no need for his ruining my fun.

Especially in front of the lovely young brunette I'd spent most of the evening trying to convince that women were more her thing.

She giggled, leaning forward to give everyone an even better look at her cleavage. I didn't mind that. I did mind that she was poised by Constan's side as if her entire life's happiness hinged on his notice of her.

She was in for some disappointment if that were true. Constan was loyal to his wife and a devoted servant of Thress, the goddess of the hearth and hater of fun.

"Now, now, you know getting captured--"

The tavern door banged open so hard the building shook. A tall reedy man with a nose that hinted at something orc or troll in his ancestry stood framed in the doorway, wringing his hands. Small town drama started this way. Farmer's cows run amok. Someone sleeping with the wrong spouse. That man's mutt got that man's prized hound pregnant. I leaned back to watch.

Silence fell, which was good because his voice came out in a choked whisper.

"The Wraith has been kidnapped!"

While everyone else gasped, I laughed. Attention swung to me, and not the pleasant kind. I think they assumed I didn't care. Well, I didn't, not really, even if kidnappings were often lucrative business opportunities for people like us.

"Look," I said in my most diplomatic voice. "That's impossible. You can't hold a Wraith captive. Much less run off with it. It's in the Mandate from the Gods. Wraiths are Wraiths. Servants of Bishal. Chosen mortals for his mission of making people talk to each other, raised up to semi-great power. His holy couriers. Those Wraiths." Communication to connect the Three Lands was so protected that the best thief in the world couldn't steal a package from one.

Just don't ask how I know. That's not a fun story.

Murmurs more in my favor ran the room. Constan, though, stood up and pushed past his adoring farmer's daughter to approach the doorway.

"We will--"

Cursing under my breath, I jumped to my feet and spoke over Constan before he volunteered us for anything. "Good sir, do tell us more of what you know."

Constan grunted but let me take over the negotiations. It would have been much better if Lylle was with us, but she was still sleeping off our last job. I crossed the room, my bright blue robe fluttering around me, the light fabric catching the breeze that blew in through the doorway.

"You say a Wraith has been captured. Kidnapped even. We need a few more details to figure out what happened."

"Who are you?" He stared at us both, as if just realizing we were strangers to town. Given the presence of the coaching inn, and the town's position halfway between two actual places people wanted to be, I was a little surprised at how surprised he was.

"I am Trinakalax, Wizard of the Violet Order of the Golden Throne. This is my companion, Constan the Wise."

"Have I heard of you?"

Constan answered with a bit more diplomacy than I was capable of. "Only you can answer that, my friend."

He took the man's hand and led him to the nearest table. I inspected said table, pronounced it clean enough, and sat down upon it without using a minor spell to deal with any residue I couldn't see. It would have distracted our messenger from getting to the point.

"A man in a red cloak rode up to the Waystation. I saw him get down from his horse, a silver gelding."

"You checked?" I asked before I could stop myself. "Never mind, keep going."

"The waystation only has one Wraith right now. One that stays here, not travels." He took a deep breath. "The man rang the bell to summon the Wraith. She came out, and he just grabbed her. He put a string around her wrist. Then pulled our Wraith up behind him on his horse. Then just rode off!"

I glanced at Constan. It was possible to get a Wraith onto a horse willingly. Yet Wraiths didn't ride horses. Not normal horses, anyway. They had to be specially trained to carry a Wraith. Being touched by a god slipped them just a bit sideways of normal.

“Anything more about this man you can remember? Was he of local stock or from the king’s road, a traveler? Did he wear a sword?”

The man shrugged. He grabbed the nearest drink and downed it, but it didn’t soothe his shivering, which was getting worse. Was it just a matter of having seen the impossible happen? Or did he have greater reason to fear. I shifted just a bit so my face wouldn’t be so obvious to Constan because he hated it when I got interested in something where the money was incidental. It meant trouble.

I knew it, and I couldn’t stop myself.

I touched my pouch that held my readied mana, meaning I could cast without the incantation and gestures that would give away what I was doing, but paused to consider. There was no way this man wasn’t going to tell us everything we needed to know without magical charms, if I were patient enough. I hated being patient, but we'd ride this one out.

"I didn't see a weapon. His cloak though, it shimmered in the light, catching the sun in a way that almost blinded me. I'd never seen him before, or someone with a shiny cloak that color."

I wanted that cloak now. It sounded glorious. I had no idea what it was either, as cloaks in general were made out of fabric, which wasn't shiny without a lot of metal threading. Metal thread was expensive, which added to the allure, but it would have shone as gold or silver or even copper, and a yokel would have noticed that right as it blinded him with reflected sunlight.

"Wait, sunlight? It was nighttime, wasn't it?" I hadn't been partying enough yet to miss an entire evening.

He stared at me, confused. "Yes, it's night."

I put my hand to my forehead to rub at the headache that wanted to appear. "When did this happen?"

"Just now? I saw this, then ran here, didn't I?"

"Did he hold his hand like this once he was leaving?" Careful now not to touch my mana pouch, I held up a hand and quirked my fingers through 3 symbols while I silently recited a few lines from a bawdy drinking song from Laothain to prevent myself from doing the spell.

He frowned, then nodded. I cursed three times, because once or twice didn't seem enough. More than three seemed repetitive.

Constan, for only the fifth time in the years since I'd been traveling with him, also cursed. "By Parli's leafed ass!"

Parli was one of the more minor war gods. Not really known for leaves on his ass or anywhere else, but Constan didn't get much practice at being profane.

The tavern was staring at Constan and myself, which was difficult as he was not next to me.

It was too late to pretend I didn't know the spell, but thankfully no one here seemed to realize that knowing the spell was dangerous outside the Order of the Blessed Scourge. They'd been a holy order once, but now were filled with renegade mages. And even that branch was thought to have been wiped out. Thoroughly. In a not-so-holy crusade kind of way.

"All right, you've convinced me." I hopped up to my feet and stretched my arms out.

"Convinced you of what?"

"We'll take the job."

"Job?"

These villagers, always so slow on the uptake. "A Wraith's been kidnapped. Kidnapped people, even Wraiths, need rescuing. Rescuing's one of our available services." Damn, Lylle was much better at this than I was, and she was a lizard. I continued on, as I stepped back to grab Constan's arm. "Rewards will follow, I'm sure."

But we would do this one for free.

Lylle was none too happy to be woken up. Kinfolk might look like humanish lizards, but they moved quick when roused. Using a broom to poke Lylle was the reason I didn't have a knife in me.

Her tail lashed, and she did her sub-vocal growl for at least half of my hurried explanation. Constan was no help at filling her in, as he focused on what weapons we had available. We didn't have nearly enough. A rogue wizard, a kidnapped un-kidnappable, and who knew what else awaited us.

I normally didn't get fully kitted up in my Order's colors. Not that violet and gold didn't suit me, but these were hard to keep nice when adventuring. And while robes looked impressively wizardly, they were hell to tromp around in for long wilderness distances.

This was going to make me a huge target, which was good. Because I guess someone needed to be, and I had no chance of defeating said rogue wizard by myself. And my companions didn't have built-in spell defenses the way I did.

"I have a question," Lylle said as she strapped additional knives onto her belt as if there weren't enough already.

"I'm sure I don't know but ask." I opened a long black case. I pulled on my gloves and drew out the stick carved with tiny runes. A blood wand, the runes had sharp edges designed to nick the skin and fuel its power. I examined it under an appraising eye to make sure the magic hadn't gone sour. Sometimes these things did, if you didn't use them enough. Seemed fine.

"Why a Wraith?"

"To prove you can? To get at whatever message or letter or package it had?" Wondering to myself hadn't gotten me anywhere on that answer. Lylle snorted at me with disappointment.

"Not obvious enough. And too obvious."

I considered her words. "If you wanted to prove it could be done, you do it in front of more than one witness, so that it will be believed. And if it is about the mail, then it's too easy to get at it some other way that didn't involve making you an instant target the moment the Wraiths and their god found out about it."

She nodded, a quick bob up and down of her head on her long neck. She settled into a pose that allowed her to focus, and set about changing her scales to salamander red. It appeared if I was going in regalia, so was she.

I couldn't think of any other reasons someone might want a Wraith. I guess we'd have to track our rogue wizard and find out. Tracking probably wouldn't be hard, at least not for us. It was what we were going to find that worried me.

"These people are crazy. That spell is banned for a reason. It locks the target in a moment in time, for a short while. They then reappear wherever they were as if no time had passed. Not good if something else is there when they return."

"The sickness is worse." Constan shuddered.

He was right. That poor villager was going to go through the worst sorts of symptoms while his body tried to re-align itself with the universe. A few hours adrift wouldn't kill him, probably, unless he was weak of constitution. Worse I'd ever seen was someone who'd lost two days. Not a good way to go.

"And if they are using that spell, what other magics are they doing?"

We'd just have to find out.

The way station itself was standard. Lots of chains draped over the windows, and the door was hung with ropes tied into complicated knots. The bindings showed how all peoples are connected through language and communication.

The flower beds were less symbolism and more tradition. The Wraiths seemed to enjoy tending them. These seemed wilted though. Perhaps an after-effect of being caught in the lock spell, but maybe this Wraith was just not a good gardener.

I left Lylle and Constan to do the tracking detective work. I went into the waystation instead, looking to see what had been disturbed. A small town like this probably didn't have much work for a local courier. Yet the station office was a disaster of paper strewn all about.

I'd done my share of room tossing, and this all appeared too casual, without any form or reason. As if papers came in the door and were tossed wherever. Not a search, just casual disregard for things like stacks and piles.

I picked up a few pages. No directions on where they were to go. Carefully folded once, with neat crisp lines that still marked the paper. The writing was gibberish. I dug out my spellbook and flipped the pages until I found the spell for deciphering languages. I drew the rune in the air and started the incantation.

A moment later, as my vision was clearing, and I hurt from where I'd been thrown back against the wall, I remembered that the Wraith waystations were also protected against any arcane magics. Along with the Wraiths themselves. Bishal was annoying that way.

Lylle stuck her head in the door and snickered at me once she saw I'd live.

"Trin, you're an idiot." When I didn't argue she sighed dramatically, flared her neck spines, and helped me to my feet. I retrieved my spellbook as she lectured me on paying attention to my lessons, as if my mentor had been big on world politics or the mail system's anti-arcane magic protections.

"What this means, Lylle, is that whatever the wizard did to get the Wraith to leave with him, it wasn't arcana. And don't look at me that way."

"You should've known that already."

"Did you?"

"No, but I'm a thief, not a wizard."

I shook myself dramatically and returned to the contents of the floor. The letters were still gibberish. Another protection, or was this place filled with nonsense? I tentatively tried to take a letter out, then picked myself up again. This was starting to sting.

Figuring out that the kidnapper had needed the Wraith if he wanted anything from the waystation was not particularly new or helpful. So I trundled outside again.

"I have the trail," Constan said.

"I don't want to do this anymore." I said. "I know we have to at this point, but I'm pretty sure this is now a god vs god situation."

"I hate zealots." Coming from Constan, that was kind of funny but I refrained from laughing.

We retrieved our horses but left the pack animals behind. We were already well behind the kidnappers. No need to make it a greater head start by moving slow.

As we rode, we bounced ideas off each other. Who was he working for? What god did he serve? Was that church the actual culprit, or was he using his powers without their knowledge?

A thousand possibilities. No real answers.

We were all a little grumpy by the time the sun rose. No sleep and we didn't even get a full night's carousing for it. I'd had to juggle a cloaking spell to keep us from being a target for bandits, a light spell so we could see where we were going, and a warming spell to keep Lylle awake enough to ride.

Cold-blooded bitch, I call her. When she can't hear me.

Bandits we could have handled easily, but they would have slowed us down even more.

The trail ended at a small hut, like the kind used by woodcutters. It hunched in a tiny clearing, and in the lean-to was a silver gelding.

Yes, I checked.

Constan prowled the outside of the place while I looked for magical traps. I didn't find any, which made me even more suspicious. The gelding was still in full tack, and while he had water, he had only a little hay to munch on. Either the kidnapper was coming back soon, or he'd left his horse in a tiny stall to die. If that was the case, I was going to consider doing something very bad to him.

Like use the time lock spell on him for three days.

Lylle trotted up to me, shaking her head. "Something's not right here."

"Understatement."

"No, I mean, as far as Constan can determine, the wizard and the Wraith both vanished. And this place looks like any other woodsman's hut we've seen, except there's no food stores, no hearth laid ready. And no protections of any kind."

"Woodsmen aren't known for their dedication to home safety."

"They are known for their devotion to Illatri. Not a single blessing or shrine anywhere."

"That's...that's...just wrong." I peeked in the building myself. Not even a single carved rune above the cot to keep meddlesome forest sprites out of your dreams. "Yeah, no one who actually works in the woods uses this place."

The little huts throughout the forests of this area weren't as safe as a waystation, but they were known to be a place to go if you need a mostly safe place to sleep. It should be dripping with charms against bears getting you in your sleep and from bedbugs in your bedroll.

"Horse, you're my only clue. What can you tell me?" I slipped into the stall. The horse whickered at me and snuffled at my belt looking for treats. He was the kind of all grey you didn't see often and was well kept. His coat looked silver from careful brushing and good feeding. Even I could tell he was expensive.

"Hey Constan, come tell me where he got this—"

As I called out, I set my hand upon the saddle. That's when the world got very loud and very bright.

I awoke to the sensation of choking. Only long habit and too much practice did my body not fight it. Even if a healing potion ended up in your lungs and not your stomach, it still worked. It tasted like bitter acorns and not-quite-rotten eggs and burned my mouth as if it was southern spices without any of the fun flavors you could taste before your taste buds melted.

Once I was aware enough not to throw up, I allowed myself to try to breathe. I immediately began coughing. I opened an eye. Lylle was covered in blood.

"Did I miss a battle?"

She hissed at me. I mostly saw rather than heard. I guess whatever had blown up had taken my eardrums and the potion hadn't caught up to them yet.

Or I was hurt worse than I thought.

Oh, something had blown up...

"He rigged a spell into his saddle? That bastard! The horse…"

Lylle flicked her tongue at me, maybe to hear my words better or maybe to mock me. I couldn't always tell, so I usually assumed mocking. She shook her head.

"He killed that horse. I am going to geld him."

"Not kill?" Constan stuck his head into my field of vision. He must have been farther away because he wasn't splattered with gore. I kind of hated that he skipped worst of the commotion.

"Oh, we're going to kill him. But gelding first. Proper order and all that. That's a nasty trap."

"You didn't get a hint of anything?"

"I wasn't looking. What donkey sucker sets an exploding rune on the saddle on his horse?"

"The one we're hunting. Took out the whole shed. Flattened some trees."

I ran a hand over my magical protections. Shit, he'd burned through most of them. Of course, that meant I was still alive and not like the poor horse. I couldn't tell how many surge stones burned out on my collar, but I probably didn't have enough for a real fight.

"I hate it when it comes down to dodging. Not my best skill."

Lylle helped me sit up. I wasn't sure how much of the blood on her was horse, me, or her own. She'd downed a potion herself though, the empty vial tossed next to mine. And dodging was her skill.

The warm fuzzy feeling of the potion made me more sure of being able to stand than my legs agreed with, but they held me upright. I pulled out my spellbook. I flipped to an unused spell for detecting magic on the wind.

Not useful in many scenarios. Magic had a tendency to collect everywhere people did, including us. But I had a feeling there would be a really big indicator pointing me in a direction. I stood on tiptoes, waited until the wobbling stopped, and traced the rune as high as I could reach. I was glad my companions couldn't really see it. It was as wobbly as me. But the command word worked.

The pull was strong, leading deeper into the forest.

I pointed that direction. "Lylle, you good enough to climb a tree?"

She gave me a throaty growl as if my question was ridiculous. "What would I look for? A path?"

"Nope. You're looking at the sky. For a fucking castle."

"No one uses those anymore."

"People who blow up horses do it seems. I can feel the magic's pull."

She left a bloody trail up the tree and back down.

"Black and gold. Not too far, really."

A rogue wizard. A kidnapped Wraith. An exploding horse. And now a floating castle.

Everyone took inventory of what we had. Besides the healing potions we'd drunk, four of the remaining six had shattered when the saddle exploded and Lylle was sent flying. Probably why she wasn't dead. Even on her skin, the potions would have helped.

Because the spell had been set off on my hand, my magical protections had surged. A clever trick, in most cases. One shielding spell to prevent enemy magics powered by empowered gems. Problem was, unless I was awake to monitor it, the surge was less than precise. Not that it mattered. I'd been in bad shape even still.

The shielding spell had eaten up some things not meant for it though. Including my favorite "I'm just a rock, don't look here spell." Along with some more deadly tricks. Because casting spells in combat was hard, I'd pre-set some of the nastier ones. Gone.

Fire spark? Gone. Levitation? Gone. Ice wall? Gone, gone, gone.

"Oh, not even my swarm of bears spell. I never even got to use it."

"Because it was stupid, and we wouldn't let you?" Constan asked.

"Not real bears. No real bears would have been harmed in the making of my swarm."

"Then what would be the point?"

"I like bears. And that took me an entire fortnight to enchant."

The rest of our equipment had fared well enough. No weapons were harmed in the explosion. Except mine.

Lylle asked the next important question.

"So how are we going to get into a floating castle?"

"We need a really big rock," I said. "And some rope."

They stared at me. That was fair. It was one of my stranger ideas.

"Floating castles take a lot of magic just to stay afloat. The kind that needs to be renewed on a regular basis. So you keep it semi-anchored somewhere, so you can add wood to the fire, so to speak."

I paced. Tried not to think about horse blood getting sticky as it dried. Very sticky. Moving kept my body busy and let my mind work on dredging up information from classes I'd taken a long time ago and paid not enough attention to. Plans didn't float. They walked up on you while you were distracted.

"Are you going to tie it down to a big rock?" Constan asked.

"Sort of? How to explain the magic..." Pace, ignore sticky, pace. "This little shack was in a place the castle returns to, right? Somewhere nearby is a wellspring of some kind, some ripple in a ley line the castle is tethered to. We're just going to cause some interference when it swings back this way."

"That could take months, Trin."

"Got any better ideas? And probably not, since the wizard left his horse ready to ride."

Constan shook his head. "He left his steed to die."

"Yeah, that." Lylle was pacing now too, her claws raking splinters from the shed out of her way as she strode. "Can you interfere if they are far away?"

"Well, technically yes, but—"

"I assume your plan was to annoy the rogue wizard until he came down to challenge you to a spell duel."

"Yes," I admitted, a little sullenly because she'd summed up my plan as if it were stupid.

"Why not just levitate up to it?"

"They broke my levitate spell stone. It isn't one of the spells I've bothered to learn myself."

She sighed. "How low might the castle drop?"

"Within fifty feet possibly, if picking up or dropping off a wizard."

"Wait, what about our horses?"

Constan shook his head. "Two are dead. I'm sorry, Trin."

I tried valiantly to push myself back up, but I think bones were still knitting in my arm because it hurt so bad, I couldn't see for a moment. I paused until the bright light cleared enough that it was only the sun again.

"You don't want to see it."

"Like hell I don't. Get me up, Constan." I ignored Lylle's protests and crawled my way up Constan's arm to my feet.

The area around us had some flattened trees from the blast. One of them had been where we'd tethered the horses. Lylle's specially trained red roan had been crushed in the fall. Mine. Oh my pretty palomino. I first noted that her throat had been cut, then saw what had happened when the tree landed on her hindquarters.

"Thank you, Constan." I let myself sink back down to the ground again. "Thank you."

He nodded. I took my grief and transmuted it into rage. Then a few painful deep breaths and I'd built a cage around that so I could think straight.

"I never cast levitate straight. It requires a bird as the component unless I bind it into a bird replica first."

"We can catch you a bird."

I winced. "No, see, the bird doesn't just provide a sympathetic nature of flight. It...it...well, it takes the full weight on itself."

"Ugh. Does it have to be alive?"

"It starts that way." I avoided being too specific, because technically I could kill it first, but it was less effective that way. Plus, I had to kill the bird myself. I couldn't use just any bird.

Magic kind of sucks.

"Fine." I had a feeling Lylle knew what I was avoiding. "Fifty feet is within easy bow shot. Lock in a grapple, I climb up, send a ladder down for the human folk."

Constan shook his head. "They might have defenses against just such a thing."

"We're assuming it."

"This guy blows up innocent horses. He has defenses on his stupid castle."

It takes a lot of magic to hold a castle in the air. Well, to launch it. It doesn't take nearly as much to keep it up, but it does take some. And that some is based on the way it was lifted and how it is tethered.

I hadn't studied it nearly enough, because it is considered a ridiculous extravagance these days. Not that magic will run out or anything, but the dangers were so high.

Ley lines shifted over time. Wellsprings stopped functioning, popping up somewhere else the way an underground stream might change course. Or so it was explained to me.

And someone, an enemy, could cut your tether line so the wind moved you out of position from the magic line, and then you run out of power like an exhausted songbird.

My plan to duel the sorcerer wasn't very good anymore, since most of my defenses and best offenses were ruined. Poor swarm of bears. I'll build you yet again.

"How do they get normal supplies up there?" Constan asked. "Don't they have a portal or something?"

"Of course they do," Lylle responded. "The servants and deliveries don't just fly up there."

"The portal will be in the courtyard, if this is a normal flying castle." I thought about the examples I'd heard of, the ones I read about when I dreamed that this was the height of luxury, not stupidity. "There's only a few passphrases that will trigger the portal, but they need to be said in the courtyard."

"So tell me what they are," Lylle said as she readied her bow. "I'll climb up and over the wall. Any defenses will be aimed at the normal ways to get in. I'll trigger the portal, you come up, and we do this thing."

Neither Constan nor I had a better idea.

We waited as Lylle did her thing. We trudged along the castle's shadow in silence. I ran over and over the possible ways things could go horribly wrong. What if Lylle was caught and he used a time spell on her? I tried to convince myself that would be stupid of this wizard. Lylle would still be in his courtyard at the end of it.

Eventually, we got the shimmer that showed the magic interacting with the ground. There was a moment, then the castle stilled in the air. A beam of bright light struck the ground and music chimed in the air.

I'd forgotten that it might not be subtle.

Constan and I jumped into the glittering light and squinted. My stomach did a flip as the portal pulled us through. Even if we were technically going up, the portal was on the ground and pulled down. Meaning if one wasn't used to it, one's composure might not arrive at the same time at the other end.

I was blinking away portal blindness and testing my legs to see if they were still attached when Constan shoved. I toppled with a muffled meep into a pile behind some crates held together by dust and sadness.

Voices bounced around for a moment before I could make out words.

Constan's voice was strong and confident in a way mine wouldn't be able to be for at least another quarter-hour. "We are here on behalf of the Temple of Bishal. You will release what you have stolen."

A gruff man snapped out an order to "take them."

I crawled until I could see past the pile of rotting pallets that had once held food nicely organized.

Great. Constan and Lylle were using my signature move. Weapons were removed, hands were bound. I felt left out.

There were only four guards that I could see from my vantage point, but I heard at least two others clanging around. They weren't looking for me, which means that Constan had shoved me into hiding before they took stock of the courtyard. I didn't jump out and scream for them to take me too. Just barely. I wasn't quite sure how to work the plan from the other side of the ropes.

All the guards – seven of them – escorted their captives. From behind, I couldn't fully assess them, but I could tell a few things. Their livery didn't fit. The colors were faded. Their weapons were real spears. I notice the important things.

They didn't look back, so I didn't even have to be Lylle to follow them. Inside, the castle was much like any other floating monstrosity. Tapestries hung on the walls. Sconces for lanterns hung at regular intervals, though none of them were lit except one that bounced along with one of the captors.

I ran a finger along the wall. The stone was cold, smooth. I patted a couple of tapestries. The wool kicked up a lot of dust. I collapsed onto my knees and held my breath to try to stop a sneeze. It worked, but my eyes were watery, and I was wearing a century of dirt. Not that it would be different from the more recent dirt. Still, I liked to look my best for a proper confrontation.

The trick was going to be keeping our enemy from using the time-lock spell. He might not have it prepared, but I had to assume it was the main threat. If he used it once he was likely to use it all the time.

I pulled myself to my feet. I was sticky, dusty, and my friends were captured by a madman who blew up horses and stole Wraiths. I had a plan.

I pulled out the blood wand. These things were tricky. Great boost to my power, but they meant I needed to be extra careful. I was planning on not being careful.

I never said it was a good plan.

There were two guards stationed outside the throne room. I knew what it was because it was where guards tended to be. Also, it had a sign. I walked out of the shadows straight towards them.

Both of them took long enough to figure out I wasn't supposed to be there that I was almost able to come right up to them.

I shook my head. "If I were a bad guy, you'd be dead now."

They jerked to attention. Spears pointed at me.

"Hold!"

They were young, but not that young. Might one day have careers in mercenary work if they survived working for their current employer.

"Trust me, you are not being paid enough to be between me and my friends. I can either tell your boss you put up a good fight, or you can actually put up a good fight. Either way, I'm going through those doors. Just depends on how many bruises you—"

The one on the left stabbed forward with his spear. I wasn't expecting it, but I had been on the adventuring circuit for many years now. Instinct took my feet and moved me to the side. The spear tip nicked my elbow.

"Bruises it is."

Magic was energy plus a focus plus will. I was in a castle tethered to a ley line. That was the energy. The blood wand I pressed into my palms was the focus. Will? That part was being played by the annoyed wizard who'd just been cut by a spear tip.

I didn't bother with an actual spell. Just energy pushed outwards. The obstacles in my way, both guards and closed doors, parted before me. The whole castle shook. I was barely able to reabsorb the energy that bounced back at me before I was crushed by it.

I'm not the subtle one. That's Lylle's job.

I stalked into the room as if I was sure my legs would listen to me. Lucky for me, they did.

On the lord's throne sat a middle-aged man in a silver robe. On the lady's, sat a Wraith. The one we were looking for, I assumed. Like all Wraiths, she was pale and ageless. A tiara had been set on her head. Her hair was long and stark-white but braided in an intricate style. Wraiths kept their hair short, and she hadn't been gone that long, so it was a wig or grown by magic.

A red-gold chain was around her neck, like an over-sized necklace, though it had more of a look of shackles than jewelry. A thin cord ran from the chain to each wrist.

"Oh, that's how you did it. Clever, actually." At this point everyone but the Wraith reacted to my entrance. Constan said three curse words I didn't even know he knew. Lylle's scales flickered from regalia red to a violet shade I'd never seen before. And our rogue wizard? He raised his hands ready to inscribe a rune into the air.

"Who are you?" He demanded.

He hadn't stopped me yet, so I kept walking forward. It was a big throne room.

"I'm Trin. And you are? Oh never mind, I'll just forget it."

"His name is Verl," the Wraith said. She rotated slowly as she spoke so she could look at him.

"Verl. Nice. Using demon chains. Forbidden magic, but it is the one thing Bishal can't pierce through. Though, what did you do with the demon?"

His face blanked for an instant. Long enough. He didn't know what he was doing.

"Stop or I'll have my men kill your companions here."

"These? I barely know them. Did you find the tome of forbidden magic and the chains in here? What else are you playing with?"

The guards had frozen. Holding prisoners they could handle. Cranky sticky wizards talking about demons facing off against their boss who was also a wizard short on sense? Not in their job description.

Lylle dropped the ropes that had tied her hands. They'd taken her knives but hadn't bothered to see how sharp those claws were. She whipped around and hissed at her captor, her neck spines at full attention. He bolted.

"Lylle, you're so dramatic."

"Me? You're the one dripping blood everywhere." She leapt into the air and tumbled to a landing next to Constan. In a moment, he held his captor's spear, and Lylle was flicking her tongue rudely at the man's back.

"Not my fault. That's how it works."

Verl locked his fingers together and twisted. Wind roared in my head. Screaming, calling down minutes and days, blotted out the courtyard. Time twisted in on itself, spiraling like a tornado into my chest. One breath became one from sometime in the future. The next wanted to be years from now, decades. I threw the blood wand at the band of energy whipping towards us and said a prayer to Thress that it would work.

Hey, even I get sentimental.

Blood wands draw in energy when covered in the user's blood. The user in contact with the wand can control that, direct it—in fact, it was crucial to the operation. Because otherwise the blood wand would overload.

Verl and I had the air ripped from our lungs as the wand sucked in a huge amount of energy the moment the time-lock spell hit it.

Unable to speak, I waved towards the Wraith to direct my companions. They'd been with me long enough to know that I had done something monumentally stupid that would save us all. Or blow us up. Chances were usually about even.

The time-lock spell and wand hovered in the air between me and Verl. I could see the distortion. I still couldn't breathe, but I did my second or tenth stupid thing for the day. I reached out my mind and grabbed a hold of the ley line energy.

I stepped around the tangled magical mess in the air.

Verl was scribbling runes with his hands in front of him. He was very lucky he wasn't able to stabilize the magic long enough to cast any of the spells he was inscribing. They were sloppy enough to cause blowback on their own—this is how war wizards usually died. But also, he was playing with some truly nasty stuff he didn't fully understand.

Constan and Lylle pulled the Wraith from her seat. She yielded, trotting behind them in silence. Demon chains will do that.

Once on the other side of the spell, I took a ragged breath.

"What kind of monster sets a trap on his own horse?" I wanted to yank the time-lock onto him, have him feel his body twist, muscles contracting and stretching as the living flesh tried to catch up with when it was supposed to be. Musical snapping of bones that couldn't keep up, guts wrenching as it tried to deal with foods it should have already digested. "You are so lucky I'm me."

I stomped up the stairs to the dais. I wasn't a fighter, but Constan had taught me a few things.

I punched Verl in his stupid face.

Unknotting the time-lock and putting things to right took longer than expected. Constan and Lylle removed the Wraith's chains. Once free, she set off to return to her post or whatever it was that Wraiths do.

Lylle said I missed the part where Verl had explained that he and the Wraith had been lovers before she'd been given to the temple of Bishal. Noble intention. Might have made him the good guy except for the whole blowing up of horses and playing with dark magics.

An idiotic good guy, because even doing things right wasn't going to wrest a devoted from her god. The moment we untangled the chains, she headed towards the nearest waystation. Divine power wasn't bothered by things like floating castles. Verl cried out for her to stop, but the bright light faded before he could finish the words.

If it wasn't for the horse, I might have felt sorry for him.

The dark magic was also a problem. He admitted he'd found the wrong books while searching the castle for a way to save his lover. He'd spent time studying them. Time lock had been the one he'd thought harmless enough to use. Unlearning forbidden spells was not pleasant. So we bound him up so he couldn't try anything else. My Guild would send the right people to dismantle his ability to cast the spells and clear the castle.

The last problem was now Lylle wanted to be the one to get kidnapped. We argued over it all the way back to town.

Fire with Fire

By: Benjamin Tyler Smith

Quentin grasped Rina's chin and jerked her head upward. She gasped in pain and tried to pull away, but her fellow student's grip was unyielding. He glared down at her, his normally blue eyes glowing with green and brown light. "You stupid little nit! You're channeling fire magic!"

Rina opened her mouth, but her voice failed her. She clenched at the half-empty waterskin Quentin had just returned to her. She looked away from him, focusing instead on the rainforest canopy high above them.

Quentin doubled over in a coughing fit, his face turning red from the exertion. His hand fell from Rina's chin and grasped her shoulder. Grimy nails dug into the crimson fabric of her robe, and she whimpered.

"Douse. Your. Spark," he demanded between coughs.

Rina's chest constricted. If she released her elemental power, she would no longer be immune to the smoke surrounding them. Worse still, she'd be vulnerable to the wildfire at her back. A familiar, searing pain seeped up her legs from her toes, stopping below the knee. And the odor that wafted up from the darkness of her memory…

Quentin tightened his grip on Rina's shoulder and shook her violently. "At once!" he shouted.

Rina cried out, and the remembered agony in her legs dissipated. "Yes, Master! At once!" She closed her eyes and concentrated on the spark of flame that burned inside her chest. She had yet to perfect the ability to quickly ignite or douse her spark, so she worked through the exercise she'd been taught.

She imagined she was in Master Elis's office back in Alphard. Elis was there as well, towering over her slight, thirteen year-old frame. He looked majestic in his courtly robes, his white beard seeming to blend in with skin pale from too many days sequestered in the academy's library. One hand stroked at that long beard while the other held out a long-handled douter made of shiny brass. Rina took the douter and turned toward the table against the wall, where a single candle rested in a silver chamberstick. Most of the candle's wax was brown, but its base was milk-white and lumpy.

With trembling hands Rina held the douter's cup over the candle and gently lowered it, extinguishing the flame. A thin wisp of black smoke rose from around the douter's beveled edge and tickled her nose. She sniffled. More smoke boiled out from under the cup, and she began to cough like Quentin had.

Rina opened her eyes. No more was she in the comfort of the royal palace of Zele. Instead she was back in Shentef il Sewet, the "Walking Forest of Rain." This magical place was Zele's southern neighbor.

And it was on fire, as it had been for days.

Rina turned her head to the left and saw distant red light shining between the thick boles of trees. The roar of the blaze was dulled by the sound of branches clacking together and the piping hoots of the trees themselves. The forest was afraid. *Very* afraid.

Rina's hands shook, her breathing became erratic. She tried to remind herself that the fire was far away, but it was hard to keep down the panic welling up inside her. She shook her head to clear it.

It was only then she realized that Quentin was there, his back now turned to her. Rina retreated from him, and then thought of the wildfire and its relative proximity. She was afraid of the young nobleman, but he was still a welcome distraction from the blaze. She took a deep breath to steady her nerves.

As she did so, Quentin's low mutterings reached her sensitive ears. "-will never understand why Master Elis wanted to bring a fire mage along. It only makes the Maurians nervous and suspicious." Quentin wiped a green sleeve across his forehead and cursed. "Seer's Myrrh! These saplings won't remain still!"

Rina spread her booted feet apart and leaned to the side until she could see around Quentin. Ahead of them both was an area Master Elis had deemed *The Copse,* the holding area for many of the Shentef's immature trees. Elis had suggested to the Maurians who called the forest home that the saplings be moved into a central location, and they'd complied.

The saplings in the Copse numbered in the thousands, ranging from wrinkly cork oak to thorny kapoks to broad-leaved sky fruits to fragrant teaks to trees Rina did not recognize. They were as varied and dynamic as the population back in Zele's port capital of Alphard.

And they were sick. Their trunks sagged, their bark was cracked, and their branches were not full of the shiny, grooved leaves of the older trees of the forest. They looked malnourished, or diseased. According to the Maurian shamans, this had been going on for many months, and dozens of saplings had already perished despite their best efforts.

This dire situation had prompted the Maurians to request help from Zele. Master Elis had organized a contingent of water and earth magi, and they had spent the last fortnight in the Shentef, trying to determine the cause. In the midst of this problem, the wildfires had begun. One day a loud boom had echoed through the forest, and within hours smoke filled the air. The fire spread rapidly, and it was all the company of magi could do to keep it marginally contained.

One of the saplings, a Shentef nut tree, hooted as its thick, shallow roots broke free of the muddy earth and it started forward. Quentin snarled, and his eyes flared with power. The mud beneath the escaping sapling rose and coiled around its roots and trunk. The young tree shuddered to a halt, its whistles of pleasure turning into hisses of fear. Its branches groaned and cracked as they scraped at the mud in a futile attempt to escape.

Rina felt a pang of sympathy for the frightened sapling. It was used to roaming free in a forest of ever-shifting canopies. To bind and corral such a creature was a horrible thing, but it was for its own safety. She hoped it would understand that one day.

"Stupid tree," Quentin said. He wiped his face again and then staggered backward. Rina dropped her waterskin and reached out to keep him from falling. His weight crashed into her and almost bowled her over, but she spread her legs wide and held her ground. When he straightened, he glowered at her. "Are you still here? There are others on the cordon that need water, too. Begone!"

Rina bowed her head and snatched up the waterskin. Ten other skins hung from a belt at her waist that slapped against her thighs as she walked away from Quentin. Their contents sloshed, and the noise reminded her of water striking the breakers in Alphard's harbor. She looked forward to returning there when they were finished with this dirty, sweaty, and scary business.

The smoky haze caused Rina's eyes to water and her lungs to burn. She was sorely tempted to call upon her spark again, but she dared not. For days she'd drawn just enough power to maintain her fire immunity. The amount had been so little that her green eyes barely changed color. Still, she couldn't fault Quentin for his admonishment. She'd been forbidden from using even a little of her spark. The Maurians were fearful of fire, and it was only because of Royal Magus Elis's assurances that she'd been allowed into the Shentef at all. If the Maurians found out what she'd been doing, it would greatly embarrass Master Elis. She couldn't disappoint him like that.

Rina had to stop several times to get her bearings. The smoke was thick, and without her elemental power she could not see through it. Very little sunlight penetrated the forest's high canopy, and that added to the difficulty. She glanced at the Copse, where warm light from above bathed the sick saplings. It brought into sharp detail the unnatural hollows on their thin trunks and the brown splotches covering otherwise green leaves. She did not let her gaze linger.

She eventually found Harlan, the next earth mage in the cordon. The tall man was one of her teachers back in Alphard. He had a habit of running his hands through his wild red hair when frustrated, which served to make his hair even wilder in appearance. He was doing that now, but he stopped when he saw Rina. "Lass! Fancy meeting you in so fine a place as this."

His lazy grin was infectious, but Rina could not bring herself to return it today. Wordlessly she unhooked one of the full waterskins and handed it to him.

"My thanks," he said as he uncorked it and drank deeply. When he was finished, he wiped his mouth and sighed in contentment. "That hits the spot."

He cast a critical eye over Rina, his smile fading. "Did Quentin say something to you?"

Rina felt heat rise in her cheeks, and at once she was thankful her tan skin hid such blushes. She shook her head.

Harlan continued to stare at her.

She hesitated, then ducked her head in an affirmative. *What was it about teachers and their ability to read minds?*

Harlan grunted. "I thought as much." He handed back the waterskin and gently placed a hand on her shoulder, the same shoulder Quentin had dug his fingers into moments ago. Rina fought back the desire to shy away from the touch. "Don't let him bother you, lass. You're doing what you can, same as all of us."

Rina bowed her head. She was doing what she could, all right, but it was not the same. The other magi were able to use their powers to help, but not her. All she could do was run water like a-

She paused, and then finished the thought:

Like a *slave.*

The word hung heavy in Rina's mind. She fussed at her dirty robe, smoothing out the wrinkles in the cloth and scratching at the mud caked on it. Her spark was all that kept her from her past life, and yet she could do nothing with it. Not here. Not even back in Alphard.

Rina bowed to Harlan and hurried away. Since her arrival at the Zelen palace three years earlier he had always been kind, but sometimes that kindness hurt her more than Quentin's cruelty could.

She slowed and came to a halt after a moment, her head turning left and right as she scanned her surroundings. The smoke had blinded her again, and this time confused her bearings. She was now walking away from the Copse, not parallel to it. Rina sighed and turned around, intending to trace her steps back to Harlan.

A series of loud hoots and whistles filled the air, and with it a scream no one on the cordon wanted to hear:

"They're breaking loose!"

The shout came from Rina's left. She spun in that direction and ran. After a moment of slipping and sliding through mud she saw Corrine, a young earth mage who had recently attained her Third Stone Mastery. She was down on her knees, the earthly light gone from her eyes. Her magic was broken, and it would be many minutes before she would get it back.

Not enough time to deal with the dozen saplings that surged toward her. Free from any elemental hold, they flowed around Corrine's kneeling form, hooting and clacking their branches with great excitement. Making enough noise to rouse the dead, they continued their mad run toward Rina, and toward the wildfire that blazed behind her.

"Somebody stop them!" Corrine shouted. She sucked in a lungful of smokey air, then coughed and wheezed. "Someone… help," she managed to gasp out.

It was futile. All of the earth magi on the cordon were busy keeping their own sectors covered. Burdens could be shifted to allow for those magi closest to an incident site to respond, but none of them would make it in time to stop the saplings from completing their suicidal run into the inferno. No one could help them.

Except Rina.

She clenched her jaw. She'd already witnessed so many saplings perish before Master Elis set up the Copse and its earth mage cordon. The sight of their canopies bursting into flames and the sound of their bark splitting as the sap flowing through their trunks exploded had evoked many painful memories in her. She couldn't allow any others to suffer that way, not if she had a choice in the matter.

Rina closed her eyes and was once more in Master Elis's office in Alphard. He held out the douter for her to take, but this time the taper above the brass extinguisher was lit. She accepted it without the usual trepidation she felt at the sight of an open flame. She looked over at the table, where her dormant spark lay in its brass chamberstick. She bit her lip and placed the lit taper against its wick.

Warmth infused her chest and spread through the rest of her body. The burning sensation in her lungs vanished, and when she opened her eyes, her vision was filled with a red-orange hue.

She looked at the saplings shambling toward her. "You mustn't go near those flames!" she cried, though she knew they would not understand her. Before a Shentef tree reached its first century its intellect was that of a mewling babe at worst and a troublesome toddler at best.

Rina brought her hands together, palms pressed and fingers steepled. A hot disc formed in her chest, floating above her spark. When she broke the disc in half, heat rushed into her arms and settled into her hands. She separated her hands and pointed at the ground in front of her.

A three-foot-high wall of flame appeared where she indicated, its colors soft and its crackling muted compared to the merciless blaze behind her. She stretched this wall for several yards in either direction and bowed its ends away from her, creating a semi-circular barrier of dancing light.

The familiar pain returned to her legs, and with it the smell of cooking meat. Unshed tears stung at her eyes. "Forgive me," she whispered.

The first of the saplings touched her fire and felt its kiss on its bark. It let out a startled yelp and backed away, its limbs creaking and groaning in protest to the sudden change in movement. It slammed into two other saplings, and they spent a moment trying to untangle their branches.

The other saplings reacted to her fire in the same way: a scream of fear and pain emanating from the tiny orifices midway up their trunks, and a writhing of retreating roots. Rina struggled to maintain the fire's relatively low temperature. It was hot enough to frighten the saplings, but not enough to hurt them unless they lingered.

Rina considered tying off the spell and letting it run its course, but only three saplings continued moving forward. Once they touched her fire they would back away, and she could extinguish-

Something struck the back of Rina's head, hard. Pain exploded behind her eyes, and she blacked out.

When she roused, she found herself lying in the mud. Dully, she wondered at the purity of the air despite her spark being doused, and after a moment realized it was because the wildfire's smoke would not sink that low to the ground.

Rina's eyes widened. The wildfire! The saplings!

She tried to rise, but her muscles would not work. She looked around and saw several saplings standing in a tight group. She counted nine.

"How many broke through?" a male voice asked. It was Harlan. His green robes were covered in fresh mud, as if he had slipped and slid in his haste to aid Corrine.

Corrine stood nearby, her arms wrapped around herself as she studied the saplings with a weary eye. "There were twelve in all."

Harlan grunted. "Three dead, then. Why do they always run to the flames like this?"

Tears filled Rina's eyes and ran down into the mud. She let three of them go? How had that happened? What struck her?

"Three dead, *and* nine injured!" someone else said. Rina could not see him from her prone position, but based on the purring growl, she could tell he was a Maurian. And an angry one, at that.

Harlan raised a hand. "Calm yourself, Tristal. Their injuries are superficial."

Tristal hissed. "They were deliberately burned! That is hardly superficial!"

"What's going on here?" Rina raised her head and saw it was Quentin. The student was out of breath from running. He looked down at Rina and his eyes narrowed. "What has she done?"

"We don't know yet," Corrine said.

"Look at the saplings!" Tristal retorted. "It seems obvious to me."

Quentin nodded. "And to me. She used her fire magic, even though it was forbidden."

It had been the only way! Rina opened her mouth to say just that, but it felt like something coiled about her jaws and clamped her teeth together. She balled her hands into tiny fists

"I find it surprising, though," Quentin added with a smirk. "One would think a slave would know how to follow orders."

Corrine stepped over to Quentin and glared up at him. "*Former* slave, in case you've forgotten." She smiled. "One would think it'd be easy to remember such details about a *fellow student*, Quentin." She put extra emphasis on the words as if they were a jab.

Quentin's face reddened. "You dare compare us as if we're equals-"

"Enough!" Harlan shouted. "Both of you." He turned to face the saplings. "What *I* find surprising is that she used her magic at all. The two of you have seen her in combat exercises. Even when she's being pummeled, she won't use her power directly against an opponent. So, why would she do it here?"

"She went spark-mad." Quentin shrugged. "All fire magi go through it."

Corrine snorted. "Is that a fact?"

"Corrine, please." Harlan turned his face toward Rina. Gone was his smile from before. "It appears she's awake."

Corrine dropped to her knees and helped Rina into a sitting position. Quentin folded his arms and glared down at them both. "We already know she's guilty," he said. "We should send her back to Alphard."

Tristal came into view then. The Maurian moved with the grace only a feline could manage. Yellow eyes with slits for pupils stared down at Rina as he stalked around on bare paws. Dark fur covered his face and limbs, and his torso was protected by sturdy laminate armor.

"Send her away?" Tristal's lips peeled back to reveal sharp fangs, and his forepaw closed around the knife at his waist. "After her crime?"

Rina trembled beneath Tristal's furious gaze. "What crime?" Corrine demanded. "We don't even know her intent!"

"Should it matter?" Quentin asked. "She broke faith, and therefore she cannot be trusted to stay." He shrugged. "That's all there is to it."

Harlan thought about it a long moment, then sighed. "Unfortunately, he's right."

That cut deep. Rina bit her lip. Quentin and Tristal's minds were made up out of spite, but Harlan was a *teacher*. Couldn't he see she meant no harm? She needed to say something, but how could she with Quentin and Tristal both ready to pounce?

"I think she was trying to help," Corrine offered. "She was the only one nearby who could, and she did what she could."

"You '*think*?'" Quentin shook his head. "That's not good enough, Corrine. What do you know? What did you see?"

"I was on the ground, Quentin, and smoke was everywhere. I couldn't see much of anything at all, and you know that."

"So you didn't see anything, but you're certain you know not only Rina's actions, but her intent."

"And what about *you*?" Corrine stamped her boot in the muddy ground. "You weren't even here, yet you act like you know everything. I wasn't aware prescience was an earth magic skill. Do you learn that in your senior classes?"

"Is that how you speak to seniors?"

Rina stared at the two of them, her eyes wide. Corrine and Quentin argued a fair amount, but she'd never seen anything like this before. Corrine was really going all-in on helping her out, but Rina could tell that Harlan wasn't fully convinced. The teacher had that distant look he got when he was deep in thought, likely mulling her fate. The way things were going, she would be sent back to Alphard, if only to placate the Maurians and get her away from Tristal.

Would that be so bad? She could return to the palace, and to her studies. She could hear the breakers in the harbor again, and she could be away from this gods forsaken forest fire.

Yet if she accepted their summary decision it would be as good as admitting guilt. That was the same as embarrassing Master Elis. She couldn't–no, she *wouldn't* do that.

Nor could she escape the satisfaction she felt at finally doing something useful with her magic after all this time

"I–" Rina's voice failed her the moment that single word left her throat. She stood there, mouth agape, but nothing came out except air.

Corrine looked down at her. "Rina?" She offered a hand and pulled her to her feet. "Have you something to say?"

Rina nodded, then opened her mouth to speak again. "I would–" She hesitated again and cursed herself for it.

"What is it, lass?" Harlan asked. He studied her intently, his eyes seeming to beg her for something he could grasp onto. "What have you to say for yourself?"

"I–I would–like to speak with the Royal Magus!" The words came out in a rush.

Quentin scoffed. "Why should we involve so busy a man with this nonsense–"

"At once!" Rina shouted. She grasped at her robes, her brown knuckles turning white from the strain. "At once," she repeated in a much softer tone.

Quentin started toward her. "You impudent little-"

Rina squeaked in fright. She shut her eyes and waited for the blow.

"Quentin!" Corrine snapped. "It is her right."

Rina's eyes opened in time to see Quentin back away, his upraised hand dropping back to his side. "Corrine, you cannot be serious. Surely you can see–"

"In this smoke and haze? Ha!" Corrine glared up at Quentin, and her arms closed protectively around Rina. "I saw very little of what transpired here, and you even less."

Quentin looked like he wanted to object further, but Harlan grabbed his arm. "Leave it," the teacher said. "Corrine is right. Rina will stand before the Royal Magus, and we will let him decide."

Rina breathed a sigh of relief, but a new apprehension filled her. Now she would have to defend herself in front of the man who was her mentor and savior.

Shortly after returning to the magi's camp, Rina found herself standing before a large, gnarled table fashioned of living roots. It had risen up from the ground at the beckoning of one of the Maurian shamans. Several chairs were formed in similar fashion along one side of the table, their seats cushioned with moss and lily leaves.

Most of those seats were filled with Maurians Rina did not know by name, but she recognized them as those assigned to help the magi, first with the question of the ailing saplings and now with fighting the wildfire. Their clothing was varied: some wore laminate armor similar to Tristal while others wore tunics made of treated bark or short robes fashioned of spider silk. And their fur was just as colorful, ranging from calico to black to orange-and-striped like the tigers of her homeland.

Repat Idris, the Prince Consort of the Maurians, sat next to the table's central chair. His black fur had a glossy sheen to it even in the wan, smoky light on the forest floor. His golden eyes were unreadable as they calmly studied Rina and the three witnesses standing next to her.

Seated to Idris's left was Master Elis, the Royal Magus of Zele. Blue eyes that had seen four centuries of life flitted between Rina and those standing with her. She bit her lip and lowered her head to avoid his stern gaze.

"All right, let us be about this quickly," Elis said, his voice gruff from too much smoke and not enough water. "That fire won't put itself out, and we're wasting manpower being here."

Where Elis was prickly, Idris was calm like a lake's surface on a moonless night. "On that we are agreed, old friend." He nodded to Tristal. "Tristal was the first on the scene. I would have him speak first."

"Granted. Quentin, you will be next. Then you, Corrine."

Tristal's testimony was nothing more than an impassioned tirade against Rina. In his eyes she was a pyromaniac ready to burn down the entire forest, and he all but called for her beheading. Rina was left shaking after he bowed to Idris and stepped back into line.

Quentin testified to catching Rina in the act of channeling her spark earlier in the day, and he still insisted on spark-madness as a possible answer to what occurred. "It is the risk all fire magi face whenever they use their power," he had said with a smug look in her direction.

Only Corrine showed any kind of impartiality in her testimony, stating for all in attendance that the whole situation occurred because her earth magic had not been enough to stop the saplings from breaking the cordon. "I will say this, though. A dozen young trees ran toward the fire, and nine of them made it back to the Copse." She nodded in Rina's direction. "Whatever magic she used must have worked."

Corrine's words brought little comfort to Rina. She had set out to save all twelve saplings and would have had she not been interrupted. Three died needlessly.

A silence descended among the assembled as Master Elis considered their words. Rina tried to keep from shaking as she stared down at her boots.

After a while Elis spoke. "Rina, child."

Rina jumped slightly, but she kept her gaze lowered as she said, "Y-yes, Master?"

Elis cleared his throat.

Rina felt her cheeks flush. She took a breath to steady her nerves and then raised her head. "Yes, Teacher?"

Elis nodded and smiled. "It is your turn to speak, child." He folded one wrinkled hand over the other and rested his chin on his knuckles. "Why did you use your power? You know fire magic is forbidden here."

Rina felt several sets of eyes on her, and she pretended she was back in class and merely answering an academic question. "Yes, Mas- Teacher," she said. "Fire magic is forbidden, but I had to act. The saplings would have perished otherwise."

"Lies!" Tristal shouted. He stepped forward and pointed at Rina. "She sought to burn them!"

"Tristal, calm yourself," Idris said. "You have had your chance to speak."

"Repat, I cannot! For all we know this is not the only fire she has started since coming to the Shentef!"

Quentin looked at Rina as if to say, "Look at the trouble you bring to us."

Tristal continued. "Our home has suffered no fire since our ancestors transplanted saplings from the destroyed First Forest. That was more than three thousand years ago!"

"Tristal," Elis said, "am I to understand that you are accusing one of my magi of starting the wildfire?" His irises turned orange and his sclera red. "Do you not forget that I, too, am a fire mage? Does that make me a suspect, as well?"

"No one is suggesting such a thing," Idris said hastily, raising his forepaws to quell both Tristal and Elis. "Magus, we trust you implicitly." He looked at Tristal. "As well as those you vouchsafe, yes?"

Tristal bowed his head. "Please forgive my outburst, Magus."

Elis waved dismissively as his eyes returned to normal. "While I will admit the timing is suspicious, the truth is we don't yet know what caused the wildfire, nor will we until we can get into its point of origin."

"We are getting away from the present issue," Idris said. He turned to Rina. "Continue with your testimony, human."

"Yes, Repat," Rina said. She clenched her hands to hide their trembling. "The saplings had broken free, and Mage Corrine could not stop them in her condition." She bowed toward Corrine. "My apologies."

"You do not need to apologize for the truth," Corrine said. "No mage can quickly recover when their concentration is shattered like that."

"No one else was nearby, and they were coming right for me. I was in the best position to act."

"Did you fear they would attack you?" Idris asked. "You humans do not know our forest, so it would be understandable if you acted in a misguided sense of self-defense."

Rina shook her head. "No, Repat. I did not fear them. I feared *for* them." She blinked away tears. "I have seen so many beautiful trees perish since coming here. My fire was meant to protect them."

Tristal growled low in his throat, and Quentin shook his head. "How could fire do anything other than harm a tree?" the student asked.

"Be silent, Quentin," Elis said. "That is what we are investigating."

Rina felt Quentin glaring at her as she thought about how to answer the question. She looked at Idris. "Repat, these saplings have no memory of fire, no concept of the pain of being burned, yes?"

Idris nodded. "That is true, not only of the young but also the most ancient of Shentef trees. What Tristal said earlier was no exaggeration: this forest has never been touched by fire." He looked at her curiously. "Why the question?"

"Among humans," Rina said, "it is not uncommon for children to be curious to the point of getting hurt."

Master Elis chuckled. "I get it now." When Idris looked at him, he explained. "A child wants to touch a hot pot that will surely burn his hands, so you verbally chastise him against it. He still wants to do it, so you smack him. The idiot *still* wants to do it, so you finally let him. And after he recovers from the burns, he never does it again."

"Are you saying young Rina here burned the trees to teach them a lesson?" Idris asked. He nodded thoughtfully. "I see where that could be effective."

"How can you be so calm, Repat?" Tristal demanded. He took a step toward Rina. "She mutilated our trees!"

"Those trees suffered no permanent harm!" Corrine shot back. Her robes swirled about her feet as she stepped forward and placed herself between Rina and Tristal. "And last I checked they have stayed away from the cordon, choosing instead to wait deep inside the Copse. I would say the lesson has been learned!"

Tristal pointed at Rina. "And shall we burn *her* to teach her that it is a sin to invoke fire inside the Shentef? Does she not understand the pain my people have suffered? Our first home was lost to inferno, and now our second home is at risk!"

"Tristal, be silent!" Master Elis's voice cracked like a whip. "Be silent, or I will have you removed from this assembly, your rank and title be damned."

Elis turned back to Rina, and she thought she saw sympathy in his eyes. "Child, show them your legs."

Searing pain flared up in Rina's legs, and a flash of panic ran through her chest. Still, she couldn't disobey him, not here. Not after she'd already embarrassed him by putting him in this situation. She bit her lip and grabbed the hem of her red robes. She took in a shuddering breath, and then pulled them up to her thighs.

Several of those in attendance gasped in shock and revulsion, including Tristal and Corrine.

Rina's legs, from her knees down to her toes, were hairless and white rather than brown, their texture like smooth wax.

She felt a gentle hand on her shoulder. "Oh, Rina, I'm so sorry," Corrine murmured. "I never knew."

"This child well knows the touch of fire, my esteemed friends," Master Elis said. "I dare say she knows it better than any of us here."

Idris looked troubled. "What happened to her?"

"It occurred during her… past employment."

Slavery, he meant to say. Rina shut her eyes. She remembered very little of that fateful day. There was the laughter of her previous master, the pain of the oven, the smell of cooking meat, and lastly a burning sensation in her chest. After that she awoke in the royal palace in Alphard.

"You may lower your robe, child," Elis said, and Rina was happy to comply. As she smoothed out the dirty fabric Elis continued. "It was during this incident that her powers manifested. I was to be present at a feast for one of the Zelen nobles on the outskirts of Alphard, but when I arrived his manor house was burnt to a cinder." He nodded to Rina. "I found her in a fountain, its water boiled away from the immense heat of her spark." He smiled sadly. "She tried to douse herself but did not know how."

"To be burned so, and then to become a fire mage?" Idris shook his head. "I wonder if the Seer who rules over all magic is a little obsessed with cruel irony."

"That could be," Elis said, "or it could be that those who suffer the most from a particular element are likely to be the most judicious in its use. I have never seen her use fire with malicious intent."

"Nor should you, I would think." Idris turned back to Rina, and she was shocked to see tears in the Prince Consort's eyes. "You have my condolences, human."

Rina nodded her thanks, too stunned to speak.

Even Tristal appeared mollified. "That puts a new light on the matter," he admitted. "No one who has suffered so would ever use fire with intent to harm another." He lowered his head. "My apologies."

Rina fought to keep a smile from her face. They believed her!

Quentin stepped forward. "A wrong is still wrong, no matter the intent." He looked over his shoulder at Rina. "She cannot be allowed to use such magic in Shentef il Sewet."

The hope blossoming in Rina's chest began to wither and die.

"Is it still wrong if the action saves lives?" Corrine put her hands on her hips and scowled at Quentin. "Nine saplings owe their lives to Rina."

Quentin shook his head. "I'm not disputing that. The fact remains she was under instruction to not use magic, and she did. Her reasons–and the ultimate outcome–matter little. She broke the rules, and she must be punished for it." He turned back to the table. "Teacher, you must see-"

Elis glared at Quentin.

Quentin cleared his throat. "*Master*, you must see I'm right. Rina simply cannot be trusted. Sure, her use of magic this time worked to everyone's benefit." He paused. "Well, not *everyone's* benefit."

The death screams of the three sapling's echoed in Rina's mind, and she tried to block them out.

"This is stupid!" Corrine said. "Quentin, you merely wish to embarrass Rina!"

"What evidence do you have of that?"

"This is how you always-"

"Peace, both of you!" Master Elis cried. His brow furrowed as he looked from Quentin to Corrine to Quentin again. He sighed. "As much as it pains me, you are correct, Quentin. Whatever the reason, commands were broken. And while I feel no punishment should occur, something must be done to make things right.

"Rina cannot stay. She will return to Alphard."

Word of Rina's exile spread swiftly through the camp. Before she made it back to the tent she shared with three other students, she received a bundle of dried provisions. She was also given a pair of waterskins not unlike the ones she had been delivering to those on the cordon.

Rina's tent mates were not present when she lifted the canvas flap and entered the cramped confines. She was grateful to be spared that humiliation, at the least. It did not take much time for her to pack her things. What few possessions she had were secured in her student's cell back in Alphard. All she had brought with her were spare changes of clothes and her bedroll.

The tent flap opened as she finished tying her bedroll to the bottom of her rucksack. She looked, hoping it was not one of her tent mates.

Her stomach dropped. It was Quentin, a smile on his face as he poked his head into the tent.

"I thought I would help you pack," he said, "but I see you have that well in hand." His smile widened into a grin. "Do enjoy the trip back, and try not to burn down the palace while you are there. I need a place to sleep when I return, you know."

Rina heard his laughter as he walked away, and she resisted the urge to throw something. Tears burred her vision. Why did he torment her so?

She ran out of the tent and kept up the pace to the edge of camp. A tall, dark-skinned man waited for her there, leaning against a longbow. Brown eyes studied her from beneath a green hood. "You ready to go, little one?"

Rina bowed. "Yes, Warden Gethin."

"Then let's be off."

Gethin set a quick pace that Rina struggled to keep up with. His legs were long and hers were still growing. Soon she was out of breath, but she didn't complain. She was pleased that the forest warden was to be her escort back to Alphard. He had always treated Rina with kindness whenever they crossed paths in the palace.

After a time Gethin slowed to a more moderate pace. When they were walking side-by-side he glanced her way. "I'm the one who struck you."

Rina gasped. She thought Tristal had been the one who attacked her. She dropped her gaze to the forest floor.

"Tristal and I were together, surveying the cordon," Gethin said. "We came across you, and Tristal got angry. He gets into these blind rages from time to time, especially where this forest is concerned."

Rina could well believe that, judging by the day's experience.

"I knocked you down before he could do something rash." Gethin bowed his head. "I hope you can forgive me for that."

Rina did not know what to say, so she just nodded.

"In truth I was angry with you, as well," Gethin added. "I spoke with the Royal Magus in private about what I saw, but later I had words with Corrine and learned her side of the story." He smiled. "I understand that nine saplings owe their lives to you."

Rina's hands tightened around her rucksack's shoulder straps. It should've been twelve who survived, but she dared not say that to Gethin.

"Aye, it should've been twelve, but you still saved nine."

Rina looked up, her eyes wide. Gethin was no mage, and none but the mythical Soulweavers had the ability to read thoughts!

Gethin smiled. "It is no magic, girl. Your face gives away a lot." His smile vanished as quickly as it had appeared. "Those deaths weigh on my mind, too. Had I known what was happening, had I been able to stay Tristal's paw any other way..." He shook his head. "We would go mad, you and I, were we to pursue that line of thinking.

"So, instead of focusing on how you should've saved twelve, concentrate on the fact that you saved nine. Or, conversely, remember that it should've been twelve that died, if not for your efforts." He smiled at her. "When you look at it that way, isn't it amazing that you spared even one from that terrible fate, let alone nine?"

He was trying to comfort her, even in his own pain. Tears spilled over Rina's eyelids, and she buried her face in her hands as her body was wracked with painful sobs.

"Lass, here," Gethin said after a moment. The warden handed her a handkerchief. She wiped away her tears and rubbed at her nose.

"And don't worry about this exile," Gethin said after she calmed down. "You saved lives. Whatever else comes from doing the right thing matters not."

Rina sniffled and nodded her thanks.

They continued on in companionable silence, stopping once to drink some water and then again when Rina's boots became mired in a muddy hole. Her mood improved, and before long she was giggling at one of Gethin's stories of his younger days. The warden was usually quiet, but he could tell a tale when the opportunity arose.

A hot gust blew Rina's hair into her eyes. She squinted against the sudden heat and tried to straighten her short locks. Gethin stopped, his eyes searching and his nose sniffing. "The wind's shifted. The fire will spread this way now, and it will come quickly." He pointed to the dried grass and shrubbery surrounding them. "The shamans and magi have sucked this area dry. It'll go up like tinder."

The trees surrounding them must have realized the same thing. They started calling to one another, and their branches banged together in a deafening racket. Rina covered her ears. The ground beneath her feet stirred, and she jumped away. The tree nearest her was an old kapok with a wide, thorny trunk and a canopy that disappeared into the leafy darkness above. Its vast root system churned up the earth as it struggled to move its bulk away from the approaching blaze.

Gethin placed a hand on the kapok's trunk. "Easy there, girl," he murmured. To Rina he said, "Some of these are a couple hundred feet tall or more. It'll take hours for them to uproot themselves, and by then it'll be too late."

Rina touched the kapok's thorny bark and felt vibrations running through it, like the feel of a cat's throat as it purred out of fear. She thought of this tree bursting into flames, its trunk orifices wide as it screamed its death wails.

"We should hurry," Gethin said, turning north again. "The Royal Magus needs more earth and water magi, though I doubt they'll arrive in time to handle this. The fire is too out of control." He grunted and shook his head. "If only it could be corralled somehow."

Rina ran to catch up. "Corralled?"

Gethin nodded. "Yes, like horses or cattle, or the saplings in the Copse. If only we could do that to the fire."

"That's it!" Rina came to a halt and turned to face the wildfire. "I know what to do!"

Gethin stared at her a long moment. "What're you talking about, lass?"

"Forgive me, Warden. I'm not being clear." Rina closed her eyes as a memory from childhood came to her. "Before I was sold into slavery, I lived in a farming village in Vishal. Each year before planting certain fields would be set aside as fallow. And each winter the fallow fields would be burned to ready them for the spring planting."

"Burned?" Gethin frowned. "I've never heard of such a thing."

"It helps rejuvenate the soil, according to my mother." Rina's eyes widened. "That might explain why the saplings are acting the way they are! They sense the topsoil's restoration, and they are trying to get to it." She put a hand to her chin. "Although, I wonder how long they'd have to wait to get any benefit from it? It was months after a burn that we would–"

Gethin waved a dismissive hand. "We can worry about that later. What about the fire?"

"My apologies, Warden. When the fields are burned, certain measures are done to prevent the fire from spreading. Brush is cleared away and nearby vegetation is burned off to create a firebreak. The village men will even dig trenches that the fire can't jump. Once the fire consumes all of the fuel in the field it dies out on its own."

Gethin scratched at his face. "It could work," he murmured. "There's a narrow stretch of open land up ahead, one of the many areas reserved for saplings whose upper branches can't reach the forest canopy. It lies empty at the moment." He smiled. "Fallow, if you will."

Rina stroked the nervous kapok and closed her eyes. She reached down for her spark and was surprised at how quickly she ignited it. Not since her power first manifested had she so easily been able to draw on it. Warmth flooded her limbs, and the bitterness of the smoke disappeared from her mouth and throat.

She stepped off the path and started walking west. Gethin grabbed her robe and held her back. "What's your intent, child?"

Rina looked up into Gethin's eyes, her mouth set in a firm line. "To fight fire with fire."

The clearing was as Gethin described. Bright afternoon light shined down on the brown grass that filled the narrow expanse. Rina squinted at the sudden illumination and shielded her eyes with a hand.

Fire had spread almost to the opposite edge of the glade, moving along the ground and licking its way up the trunks and into the lower branches of the trees. Hot wind blasted Rina and Gethin and carried on that current were the moans and screams of a dying section of forest.

"Stand back, Warden," Rina said. She pressed her palms together and pushed the fire into her hands.

"Farmer's Scythe," Gethin muttered. "Some of them are trying to run." He pointed to a pair of small cork oaks that were half-engulfed in flames. Their trunks wobbled right and left as they stumbled toward the clearing.

Rina watched their struggle and saw other trees doing the same. After a moment's hesitation she created a high wall of flame in the grassy clearing, directly in front of the stricken trees. They screamed.

"Forgive me," Rina whispered as she stretched the wall of flames for dozens of yards in either direction. Tears spilled out of her eyes, but she remained firm. Those trees were already dead, but there were so many behind her that could be saved.

The dried grass near her fire smoldered and quickly caught. Soon all of the undergrowth in this section of the glade was on fire. Once it burned away the wildfire would be unable to advance.

But the wildfire's front was huge, spanning hundreds of yards. The dry glade stretched as far, and all of it needed to be burned if a proper firebreak was to be made.

Rina looked at the strands of power running from her fingertips to the magical fire she had created. She imagined taking those strands and tying them together. Once she pulled the knot closed, she felt the spell's burden ease off her consciousness. The wall of fire would continue on for several more minutes before dissipating on its own.

Rina ran to the edge of her barrier and created another wall of fire. She held onto the spell until most of the vegetation there was burned away. She then tied it off and ran to the next area.

She stumbled on a writhing tree root, and Gethin caught her. "Are you all right?" he demanded.

"Just tired," Rina said with a shake of the head. She had never drawn so heavily on her spark before today. Fear gnawed at her gut as she straightened. Was she strong enough to make this work?

Rina ran a short distance and formed another wall of fire. As she did this, she heard voices behind her. She risked a glance over her shoulder. Several earth and water magi were clustered together deeper in the tree line. Corrine was with them, and she was pointing in Rina's direction.

"We need their help," Rina said. The wildfire was almost to the clearing, and not all of the grass had been burned away.

Gethin nodded. "I'll go speak with them."

"Stop her!" someone shouted. Rina's heart skipped a beat, and the fire she was trying to construct flickered and almost went out. She poured more magic into it and then turned her head. Tristal was bounding toward them both, a look of rage on his feline face.

"Change of plans," Gethin said. "I'll handle *him.*" He ran toward his friend, his arms waving. "Tristal, wait!"

Rina hastily tied off her spell and started running in the opposite direction. She wanted as much distance between her and the angered Maurian as possible. She hoped Gethin would be able to convince him of what they were doing.

She did not get far before her feet sank into mud. She looked down and saw the earth had swallowed her boots whole, and the thick muck was climbing up her legs.

Quentin stepped out from behind a thick mahogany, his eyes glowing with power. Rina tried to back away from him, but the mud tightened around her legs. Quentin shook his head. "First you stir up trouble earlier today with your paltry magic, and now this? Douse your spark."

Rina wilted under Quentin's fierce glare, and she almost complied out of habit. Instead she shook her head. "I can't do that, Quentin."

"You dare use my name like we are equals?" Quentin's eyes narrowed. "You're spark-mad, and for that reason alone I'll forgive your transgression. If you cease your magic at once, that is."

Inwardly Rina cringed, but she stood her ground. "I can't do that. I need your help, or this forest is lost."

The glow in Quentin's eyes brightened, and clumps of earth rose around him and formed into hardened spheres. "Don't make me use force." He grinned. "Your precious Master Elis isn't here to help, and you've never beaten me in a duel."

Rina concentrated on the earthen balls floating around Quentin, and at once they burst into flames and burned to ash. Quentin jumped back, a look of shock on his face. "Please, Quentin, don't make me do this!"

"You dare assault me?" Quentin demanded, his eyes shining bright. "Ex-slave or no, you need to learn your place."

A clump of dirt struck Rina on the side of the head, and another between her shoulder blades. She cried out in pain.

"I can't believe Master Elis thinks you're more powerful than me," Quentin said. "What use is power if you're afraid to use it?"

Rocks and blocks of mud struck Rina from different angles, and she staggered under the impacts. Her vision blurred and darkened at the edges, and her spark fluttered in her chest. Panic welled up inside her. If she lost consciousness, her plan would fail and more of this precious forest would burn unnecessarily.

No. That won't happen.

She reached for the weak, fluttering spark and latched onto it with her mind. Power surged through her body, and she used that energy to create a ring of fire above her head. She pulled at it until it was several feet in diameter. With a grunt she flipped the ring through the air and brought it down around Quentin.

Quentin laughed. "That won't help you." He called back the clumps of earth and set them to smothering the fire ring wrapped about him.

Rina stared at Quentin's gleeful expression. "Forgive me," she whispered before she clapped her hands together.

Fire and light exploded in front of Quentin's face, and the earth mage screamed. He fell back onto the ground, his hands scrubbing at his eyes. The smell of burnt hair filled Rina's nostrils, and she fought back the urge to vomit.

The mud holding her legs loosened and sank back into the ground. She extinguished the ring of fire surrounding Quentin and stumbled backward.

"Rina, are you all right?"

Rina turned and saw Corrine running toward her along with Harlan and the rest of the water and earth magi in this area. Corrine stumbled to a halt in front of Rina. "Are you all right?" she asked, repeating her earlier question. She looked down at Quentin, who still writhed on the ground. Her lips turned upward. "I guess I should be asking *him* that."

Harlan dropped down next to Quentin and examined his face. "He's only stunned." He looked up at Rina, a smirk on his lips. "You must've really surprised him, or else he has a jaw made of glass."

Corrine laughed aloud, but Rina could not share in their amusement. She had tried to keep from hurting Quentin, but the idea of using fire against another was still appalling to her. "I did what I had to do," she murmured.

Harlan did not seem to hear. He helped Quentin to his feet. "I'll get him someplace safe, then rejoin you. Worry not, either of you."

"Worried, about him? Please," Corrine muttered. She frowned at Rina. "What's going on? We came when we heard that the fire had changed direction, and then we saw you here."

The other magi called out similar questions before Corrine quieted them. They silently waited for an answer. The sudden attention made Rina nervous, but time was essential. "Everyone, I need your help. We need to cordon off this new fire, and I cannot do it alone." She quickly explained what she had been doing, and what she needed the water and earth magi to do.

"That sounds like it could work," Corrine said with a grin.

The others agreed and moved to their positions. Corrine nodded to Rina before running to join the other magi. Rina watched for a moment as the earth magi carved wide trenches through parts of the clearing. The water magi called rain to wet the trees on their side of the glade and to douse any loose embers carried by the wind.

Rina set fire to more of the clearing, tying off the spells as she went. She moved at a shambling trot, and her breath came in hot, ragged gasps. She needed more energy

She reached deeper into her spark for that energy. The glow spread from her eyes and moved into her head, neck, and shoulders. Soon she was wreathed in flames, and even her robes began to scorch.

"Rina!" Corrine appeared at her side. The earth mage was covered in mud and breathless, but her glowing eyes were full of concern. "Rina, you have to stop. You're burning out!"

Rina's brain felt like it was going to boil from the intense heat inside her skull. "I'm fine," she said through gritted teeth. Fire shot out of her hands and engulfed a wide swath of grass, burning the blades to ash in an instant.

"No, you're not." Corrine grabbed Rina's wrist and then drew back with a startled curse. She held up her burned fingers. "Do you see what I mean?"

"I'm fine!" Rina repeated and was surprised by the growl in her voice.

"She's going spark-mad," one of the earth magi nearby said to a companion.

The companion chuckled. "That has to be the calmest display of spark-madness I've ever seen, then."

"Calm or no, she'll kill herself at this rate!" Corrine shouted. She raised her hands in front of her, and the green light in her eyes grew brighter. "Rina, stop or I will force you to!"

Rina's eyes wept steam. "Please don't. I have to protect this forest."

She turned her attention back to creating yet another wall of flames. Her vision was almost completely red now, a result of the sheer amount of elemental power coursing through her body. She had heard some older magi refer to it as "redout." It was the first warning sign that a fire mage was becoming consumed by her own magic. A loss of control would soon follow, and then loss of consciousness if she was fortunate.

If she was unfortunate, she would self-immolate and die.

Hoots and yips rose up behind Rina and almost broke her concentration. "The saplings!" someone yelled. "They've broken the cordon again!"

Rina spun around and through the red haze she saw the saplings bounding through the dry earth. There were dozens of them this time. She reached down into her core and drew up more fire. Pain shot through her chest and stomach, but she pressed her hands together and focused on the young trees. She was going to save them, even if it killed her.

Bright balls of light appeared in front of each of the charging saplings. The balls hovered there for an instant before exploding. The saplings shrieked and crashed into one another as they came to a halt, their canopies singed, and their bark blackened from the flash. As one they started shuffling back toward the Copse.

"Good work!" Corrine said with an excited laugh. "Just like what you did to Quentin!"

Rina blinked in confusion. "That wasn't me."

A loud whoosh filled Rina's ears, and a wave of heat washed over her back. She turned and saw the entire glade was on fire, its dried vegetation quickly turning to ash and smoke.

A hand touched the top of her head, and when she looked up, she saw Master Elis. His eyes glowed red and orange, and a slight smile was on his lips. "Gethin mentioned trouble, but it seems things are well in hand here, child."

Gethin and Tristal stood behind the Royal Magus, along with Repat Idris and several Maurian shamans. The warden smiled at Rina.

"We will take it from here, Rina," Elis said. "You gave us the opportunity we needed."

Rina felt the power she had held onto draining out of her. The forest turned brown and green again, and she coughed from a lungful of smoke. "Master, I'm glad you're here."

Elis gave her a look.

Blackness filled her periphery. "T-Teacher," she corrected herself before she shut her eyes and collapsed against him.

By the time the wildfire was completely extinguished, several hundred acres of Shentef il Sewet's northwestern section had burned. The ash-covered soil smoldered for days after, even with the rain called by both the Maurian shamans and the Zelen water magi. Once cooled, what was left was a bare expanse of chalky mud.

It was on the border of this bare expanse of chalky mud that Rina sat, unmindful of the dampness soaking into the backside of her filthy robes. Her hands were outstretched to hold the wiggling branch of a teak sapling. The young tree had worked its roots into the ashen soil and a contented vibration ran through its fragrant-scented body. Like a cat, it was purring in pleasure.

Thousands of saplings did the same all through the area burned by the wildfire. At first the Maurians had been afraid to let them near, but Master Elis convinced them to allow first a few in, and then the rest when they saw the results. The saplings had been emaciated and sickly only a few days ago, but now their canopies were a vibrant green and their bark had hardened up again.

She heard footfalls behind her and turned her head to see Master Elis working his way through the mud. She started to rise but settled back at a gesture from the Royal Magus.

Elis stood next to her for a moment, his ancient eyes surveying the now healthy saplings. "Who would have thought a forest needed a good burning every once in a while to be rejuvenated?" he asked in a soft tone.

Rina said nothing. She had been Elis's student long enough to know when he was talking to himself.

"And to think one of my students figured it out," he said with a chuckle. He patted her on top of her head. "Excellent work, child. You not only helped bring an end to the fire, but you solved our original purpose for coming here."

Rina allowed herself a small smile. Though generous beyond measure in other ways, it was rare for the Royal Magus to pay compliments.

With a grunt Elis sank to his knees next to Rina. "This was a mistake," he muttered. "Now I'll never be able to get up."

Rina giggled, and then clamped a hand over her mouth. She looked away.

Elis laughed. "Child, I may be old and ornery, but I won't bite. It was said as a joke." He grimaced and rubbed at his back. "Well, mostly."

Rina smiled. "I can help you to your feet, should you need it."

"I have no doubt of that," Elis said. He sighed. "I'm sorry we did not have much chance to talk these last few days."

Rina nodded. It had taken her a couple of days to recover from her ordeal, and during that time she had briefly answered questions from Elis and Repat Idris. She had also had one awkward encounter with Tristal, who had dropped to his knees to beg forgiveness, both for his treatment of her and for his earlier accusation. A search of the burnt zone had revealed a sizable meteor as the instigator for the wildfire, and likely of the earthshaking boom they'd all heard

"How did your visit with our esteemed Quentin go?" Elis asked suddenly. "I believe I told you to apologize to each other for dueling outside of class?"

Rina bit her lip. She had tried to apologize to Quentin, but the student would hear none of it. *"This is not over between us,"* he had said with a threatening glare.

"Out with it, child," Master Elis said. "What happened?"

She repeated Quentin's words. Master Elis snorted and laughed. "Well, to Drahnah's Pit with him, then! I'm sorry you didn't burn off more than his eyebrows. His pride could use a good scorching, as well. Did you know his name means 'fifth?'"

"Fifth?"

"Aye, as in *fifth son*. He is noble, yes, but a fat lot of good that will do him. He's fortunate he has magical talent, or I daresay he'd be off fighting the Ketrites or plying the demigod-infested waters near Fargo Deep." He shook his head. "Do not worry yourself over him, child."

She bowed her head. "Yes, Mas- Teacher."

Elis smiled. "Do you know why I have you call me 'Teacher' instead of 'Master' as the others do?"

Rina thought about it a moment. "Is it my habit of referring to those above my station by that title?"

"Above your station? Ha!" Elis slapped his thigh. "You say it to anyone who gives you a stern gaze, be they king or shopkeep. At least with 'teacher' I only have to share that with a handful of others."

"Yes, Teacher."

Elis looked at Rina. "You know, for a long time I feared your meekness would hinder your growth, not in power but in the application of that power. The time here in the Shentef has proven those fears unfounded." Elis nodded in satisfaction. "You will stand up when you need to and do what is right, even if it means defying my orders." He grinned at her. "I like that in my protege."

Rina felt her face flush and her pulse quicken. She stuttered a reply, but Elis just laughed. He jumped to his feet in spite of his earlier claims of difficulty and offered a hand to her. "Come on, child," he said. "Let us be back to Zele before I take a chill and die in all this muck."

Rina took his hand, a bright smile on her face. "Yes, Teacher!"

END

The Tomb of Ro'Erd

By William Joseph Roberts

"What do superstitions and legends teach you, my child? That is what Rae'lan, Goddess-Queen of the Suarathan people once asked my master as he stood before her." The old bard glanced about the campfire at each of the muddy, soot-stained faces that stared fixedly back at him. "Bound by both clasp and chain, but yet he stood tall and proud. Unwavering, even in the face of the slow and torturous death that was sure to follow."

"Then! Do you know what my master did?" The bard scanned the crowd with a serious glare, then smiled wide. "He laughed! He laughed such a haughty and spiteful laugh that it echoed throughout the Dark Queen's hall. I know this to be fact, mind you, because I was there with him. I witnessed this firsthand along with many more of my master's adventures."

The old man tipped back and drained the wooden flagon in his grasp, then held it out to be refilled before he continued. "Can any of you guess what my master did next?" He glanced about with a questioning look at his captive audience, surprised that not one of the grimy tinkers had answered his question. He glanced about and waited for a breath longer, then continued.

"He spat!" The old man laughed. "My master spat on the ground at the dark witch's feet. You could see the rage rise up in her as it seethed beneath the surface and boiled up from the dark depths of the queen's black soul. And do you know what my master's reply to the Dark Queen was? No? Not even a guess? Not from any of you?" His gaze quickly darted from one onlooker to another.

The bard sucked in a long breath and stared at the group with a wild eye. "His answer," he growled, then pointed to the largest man among those gathered. He stood and poked the large tinker in the chest with a boney finger. "That any man, be he sane or be he possessed, may ascend and be worshipped by both sheep and slaves alike. But should he keep his wits about him, a man may climb to the highest summits of Heaven and Earth. Destiny be damned, and sit atop a throne of bone and steel, cleaved from the face of the world by his own two hands."

The old bard turned, looking about the group that surrounded the campfire, then let out a great roar that echoed through the dark forest. The large tinker jumped, taking a step back from the bard.

"Then, with a mighty stretch, he tore loose from the chains that bound him and leapt upon the Dark Queen. His iron grip constricted about her thin pale throat. The entranced masses of the Suarathan watched, unmoving with their dull-eyed stares, as the last flicker of life ebbed away from the Queen's limp form. Helpless as a babe without her powers of speech, her dark charms had become her very own undoing," the old poet growled. His eyes wild with fury, he began to pace about the fire and took a cup from the hand of a young lass that sat near where he had been seated. He supped, then returned to his seat with a satisfied gasp.

"That night," the old bard continued. "Once the followers of the Goddess-Queen Rae'lan, broken free from her spell, saw what had transpired whilst she kept them in their enchanted stupor, they wept and cried out for forgiveness. Though they could do naught but as commanded, they could see and remember all that had transpired. Since that night the Suarathan people have spat curses and whispered silent prayers in my master's name. Srón na Caillí, the Witch's Noose is what they have called him since that night. A man to be feared and revered whenever he might tread foot upon the dusty lands of their people."

The old bard stared off into the depths of the roaring campfire, momentarily entranced by the flickering orange glow of its flames.

"But what was his name?" A squeaky young voice said, breaking the silence.

The bard shook free of the memories that flooded his mind and looked in the direction of the voice. "I beg your pardon? What was that you said?"

"I asked, what was his name?" A young, soot-covered girl with hair the color of butter spoke up from the edge of the crowd.

The old bard laughed. "He goes by many names, my child. Seems to me that he has a new name for nearly every new land he has visited."

"But what do you call him?" the young girl asked.

The old bard smiled and thought for a moment, then looked back at the young girl. "Above all other names, I will always call him my friend." He smiled wide and patted the ground next to where he sat. "Now come, child. Sit with me, while I regale you with another tale of my master and my dear friend. Draven!"

The old bard laughed then snapped his fingers. "I have forgotten my introduction!"

"Of who?" asked the young girl.

"Of my master, Draven." The old bard smiled then relaxed. Closing his eyes as if in meditation. He hummed a rhythmic beat as he tapped at his knee then began to chant and keen in time. Others joined in, eager to set his pace and hear the next tale. From memory, he began his recitation in a sing-song camber that accentuated and complimented the chanted beat.

Between the time when the great dynasties of Angara battled for control, and the third coming of Breniniara the Wise, the world was a wild and unfettered place where lawless abandon thrived. Driven by the corrupt whim of gods and kings alike, dark magicks slithered across the lands as deadly as a serpent silently stalking its prey.

In time, even those who dwelt beyond the ragged edges of the civilized world would come to know my master's name. With his soul afire and his countenance aflame, he marched forth from the north and west, out of the mountain Valleys of the Mauga. From the putrid swamps of the Atlantean plains to far beyond the rocky crags of Ashadame, he tread forth across the world. To leave his mark and have his name rest upon the tongues of men for ages to come. To be sung of in both saga and song as all of the great heroes of old before him.

The Red Wolf of Morrag, The Witches Hound, The Bladed Devil, The Nightwind, and the many other countless names that he more than earned by his skill of craft and razor-sharp wit. But among all of his titles and names, was neither that of the warrior, nor poet, nor king. It was something else entirely. Something known only to the gods themselves. With reckless abandon he ventured forth, to travel the width and breadth of this world. From the Serpent kingdoms of Azkateri in the east to the untamed jungles of Mezora to the south where the Pictish tribesmen, skilled and trained from the time they could crawl in the art of moving between realms like shadows in the night.

Neither mire nor waste nor civilized lands could break or tame this mountain man. He conquered the jungle peaks of Tuathakan. He crossed the great plains of Angara to seek the dusty temples of Surath-Durgra. He trampled the bejeweled western coasts of Angeraine beneath his sodden feet and forever left his mark upon the Laurasian lands in the north, where to this day, the devil gods of Del and Corimaen, who dwell beneath an ice blue sky, will forever curse his name.

And so it was, in the days of old, when I was but a young man. I, Callum, a humble bard, and poet, sat bound by chains, deep within the temple of Mashkergruela where it was that I first crossed paths with this restless soul. Nude, unarmed, and bare of feet as he was, it was by his own hand we were freed. And since that time, many moons gone, I have served as his voice and the teller of his tales. By my own charge of burden, I recite his adventures to spread forth his epic deeds. Through both rhyme and verse, unfettered by time itself, even the gods sing his praise!

The great, wide-bladed axe dove deep into the skull of the Azkateri soldier with little resistance. Placing his foot upon the soldier's chest, Draven pried the axe blade free. The dying soldier reflexively reached for his blood-splattered face, where little of his hawk nose and dark features remained.

"Fall back!" Draven rounded on another of the Azkateri soldiers. He sidestepped the large man who stood nearly twice his own height and held a massive tower shield before him. Draven dodged, rolling to the right as the giant of a man thrust a spear in his direction. "Follow the waters upstream and let us regroup!"

"Move and let a real man show you how to handle a beast such as this," Blacktuth roared as he charged at the striking giant. The metal boss of his large wooden shield buckled from the impact with the Azkateri's tower shield. The giant of an Atlantean pushed with all of his might, digging his feet into the softened earth of the forest hollow.

"Fall back you witless fool! They have greater numbers as well as that giant."

"Then you have much to learn, young Maugan," Blacktuth said with a laugh. "Watch closely and I will demonstrate it for you."

Draven wiped the sweat away from his eyes with the back of his hand. He glanced about quickly. Besides himself and Blacktuth, the massive Atlantean, five others had decided to band together and joined them in reverie after their escape from the Temple of Surath-Durgra.

After days of wandering along goat paths and forest trails, they found themselves at the great walled city of Istel`dar. Its colorful spires of reds and orange stood out as a beacon among the dark greens of the mountain forests and towered high above the city. Chanted prayers in song echoed out from the great towers across the forested valley as they had approached. Most who looked upon the ragged and mixed group watched with a wary eye as they had approached the city gates. As distrustful of outsiders as the Azkateri people were, the guards ignored all but one of the ragtag group.

An Azkateri man by the name of Jaltor who had escaped the temple and journeyed with the rest of the motley mob that Draven had freed, explained what had occurred in the dark depths of the Temple of Surath-Durgra. Suspicious of the others, the guards agreed to their entrance into the city upon Jaltor's sworn oath of obedience and loyalty to the city and the Azkateri people. The group was to be in his direct charge, and none were to wander the city alone. Should they be found doing so without an escort they were to be cut down on sight.

Jaltor, being a merchant and traveler by trade, had visited Istel`dar many times and directed the group to the best alehouses in the city. After making their way through the meandering streets of the ancient city, they found themselves deep within the confines of the Panther's Palace. According to Jaltor, it was an alehouse of ill repute, avoided by the pious and sanctimonious denizens of the city. The black cat's head adorned with a golden crown was known to all within the city walls as a symbol of excess. Its proprietors were known to supply their customers with their every need, be it legal or not, for the right price of course.

It was there that the drink flowed, and the wenches danced into the small hours of the night for those with enough coin to secure their attentions. Until cries of murder and injustice rose up from outside the alehouses walls, hanging on the thick night air like a smothering blanket.

The city residents rallied and called for blood, blaming the foreigners and their treacherous ways for the murder of a man discovered in the alley behind the tavern. Cries against the vulgarity and corruption that the establishment represented were shouted for all to hear as the fault. The dead man was supposedly a father and hard-working stonecutter of the Order, but the townsfolk affirmed to their ancestors that the outsiders had coerced him with drink and sin and then murdered him for his last piece of copper.

As the citizenry ignited all sides of the alehouse, the small, ragtag band of men whom Draven had rescued, charged forth from the rear of the building and fled the city.

Three long days of hard travel afterward, through the rugged lands of the Azkateri, a detachment of the city guards had tracked the band to the craggy hollow where they had settled in for the night and set upon them in the waning hours of daylight.

Blood rushed through Draven's veins and pounded in his ears, but he watched on in frustrated admiration as his newfound friend, Blacktuth ignored his call. The large man backed away from the towering giant and deflected a spear thrust meant for his head downward where the giant buried it into the ground. He pinned the spearpoint in the soft earth with the edge of his shield and brought down the heavy mace across the shaft, splintering it.

A spear, thrown by another of the guards, soared by Blacktuth's head, severing a lock of the Atlantean's dark hair.

"Stay if you wish, but we cannot hold this ground! The rest of you, fall back if you want to live," Draven called as he turned and ran deeper into the hollow. The hollow split, widening to the south and narrowing to the west. Draven leapt across damp, moss covered stones through the small stream and sprinted for the opening of the narrow passage to the west. Toppled columns of an ancient entrance littered the area, restricting movement further.

"To me!" Draven shouted. "Callum, Blacktuth, Jaltor, the rest of you, TO ME! Form up and stand your ground or we will all be dining in the great hall with our brothers by morning!"

As the sun fell behind the hillside to the west, casting the hollow into shadow, one by one the ragtag band struck at the enemy and retreated to the rocky opening; gathering, then forming up to either side of Draven.

Draven let out a long whooping roar, which was duplicated on counterpoint by the others. Their battle cries reverberated throughout the hollow.

The remaining Azkateri soldiers rallied to the giant's call. Holding the massive tower shield close, he battered its edge with what remained of his spear shaft. The giant cried out a bellowing shout that the other soldiers reiterated as they formed up, shoulder to shoulder, shield to shield. The Azkateri line marched forward, stepping in time to their chanted grunts.

"This will not end well. We are too few to stand off a shield wall. Their line will encircle us," Blacktuth shouted.

"I fear you may be right, my friend," Draven said as he looked around, taking in their surroundings.

"While ale or a pretty lass would have been very much welcome this evening, dying was not one of the things I had wished for," Callum said, flexing his wrist and testing the weight of his sword.

"Neither was it mine," Draven growled. "Back! Retreat into the hollow. Form up two by two and we hold!" He nodded rearward and began backing away, never taking his eyes off of the Azkateri line. They fell back the span of a dozen paces, squeezing into the rocky crag where two men had barely enough room to swing. Blacktuth and Draven blocked the path, shields abutted against one another.

"How can we hold against their number?" Callum asked.

"When one man tires, another steps forward to take his place. We hold until the devils are dead, or they tire of this game. If you find opportunity to strike from behind, then by Morrag's beard, do so!"

The Azkateri line continued forward by the pace of the ever faster chant.

"Prepare yourselves!" Draven rocked, checking his footing on the soft soil.

The shield wall advanced and the massive tower shield slammed into both Blacktuth and Draven. They held their ground from the fierce blow, but only just. Both warriors braced themselves for the next push but found spear and sword tips thrust at them around their shields. The broken shaft of the giant's spear crashed into the top of Draven's shield, nearly knocking it free of his grip. He dodged right, just as a sword tip penetrated the air where his skull had resided. Knocking the sword upward with his shield he brought his axe down on the swordsman's arm, severing it from his body.

"Ro`Erd!" Someone cried out from behind. "We must flee before our transgression is punished by things of this wicked place!"

Draven glanced back quickly, spotting Jaltor pushing his way forward. "Jaltor! Stand down before I punish you myself!"

Blacktuth let out a bellowing gout of laughter as his mace crashed down upon the helmeted head of another Azkateri soldier. "The fight has only begun, and the merchant wants to flee." He laughed and deflected another of the giant's blows. "Where is the fun in that? There are so many more Azkateri my mace wishes to meet!" The large Atlantean let out another haughty and mirthful laugh.

"We cannot flee," Draven shouted, swinging his axe in a wide overhead arc that just missed its mark.

"If we do not, then the demons that protect the Tomb of Ro`Erd will undoubtedly consume our souls or press us into service of their dark master!"

Mumbled gasps of Ro`Erd danced on the tongues of the Azkateri soldiers. Their line loosened as some broke and ran from the hollow while others' resolve waivered. Fear washed over a great many of the men that remained in the shield wall, unsure if they should stay or flee.

Draven looked to Blacktuth and gave the man a wide toothy smile. "Perhaps today is not the day that we will visit the great hall?"

"Such a pity," Blacktuth said with a laugh. "I was looking forward to the pretty lasses and a warm meal."

The giant Azkateri soldier pressed forward, bashing his shield into both of theirs followed by the crashing of the broken spear shaft. Each of the massive soldier's blows struck with what felt like the force of a charging bull.

"The fight is not yet over my friend," Draven said. "You may just yet get that chance."

They both laughed and broke free of the craggy opening.

"Charge!" Draven cried. "Cut them down before they can rally!"

Blacktuth stepped left, swinging his mace downward in a backhanded arc to find its mark at the back of the giant's knee before bringing the edge of his shield across the man's lower back into where his right kidney should be.

Draven charged forward, striking the outside of the giant's left knee with his own shield before bringing his axe upward, knocking another soldier's helmet free from his head. Turning, he planted his axe into the giant's back, then wrenched it free with a sickening twist. The giant's knees buckled. Blacktuth crashed into the monstrous man once again, shoving him backward. He fell with a roaring groan as the large Atlantean clambered atop his chest and brought his flanged mace down upon the Azkateri's hawk nosed face.

Diving below the whistling blade of a brave Azkateri fool, Draven rolled to a stop then heaved his great blade at the unfortunate soldier, embedding it deep into the man's back.

The others charged into the fray with renewed vigor. What remained of the Azkateri soldiers who were not immediately engaged, fled for their lives from the darkening hollow and into the surrounding woods.

Blacktuth roared with each ferocious blow dealt to the giant. Draven gathered his axe, wiping the blade free of blood on the soldier's tunic, he approached the bloody Atlantean.

"Blacktuth! My friend, the beast is dead, and you were the one to kill him!" No sooner had Draven touched the Atlantean's shoulder that the man rounded on him, bloody mace in hand. Bracing the heft of his ax with both hands above his head, Draven blocked the powerful downward swing of the mace.

"Stand down!" Draven wrestled against the Atlantean, a hopeless battle in the end. He rolled left, pushing the mace to the ground, throwing off the man's balance. Draven had seen this happen many times while defending his own village from raiders and thieves. Blacktuth had succumbed to the bloodlust brought about by a berserker rage. He knew that little could be done if his friend had been fully embraced by the demented compulsion. Draven backed away while he had the chance. "Do not force me to send you to the next world as well!"

The massive Atlantean let out a bestial roar that was suddenly cut short and replaced by a gurgled cough. Unseen by neither Blacktuth nor Draven, Callum had scooped a helmet full of water from the stream and doused the raging beast of a man. He shook off the water as would a dog, then turned to Callum, a predatory glare burning within his eyes.

"Blacktuth!" Draven shouted, but he did not respond. "Blacktuth! Leave the lad be! We've bodies to loot and mead to celebrate our victory!"

"And a wee dainty lass if we were to dress Jaltor for the part," Callum said with a laugh as he continued to back away.

The Atlantean's chest heaved with a great breath then slowly he let out a long-appeased sigh.

"I'll dress you as a wee lass and put you up for sale at the next market we come to," Jaltor said as he appeared at his companions' side. The others of their group, Baatar, Jochi, Kaahti, and Lotan, returned from giving chase to the Azkateri soldiers and gathered about Draven.

"We should leave at once," Jaltor said. His voice quavered as he continued. "By the blessed mercy of Aapep, I swear that as surely as I still draw breath, we are standing upon cursed ground. We must flee this place immediately," he said in a hushed tone, then looked about as if he feared someone would hear him.

"Curses of a snake god do not bother me in the slightest," Baatar said, sheathing his sword. The wiry Angaran stretched, popping his own neck with a loud crack. "As with any other serpent that has crossed my path, I'll cut off its head and roast it over a flame."

"That does sound good," Blacktuth added.

"It isn't a curse of Aapep, but that of Ro`Erd, an ancient sorcerer, said to have dabbled in the dark arts and cursed the necropolis that I am sure lies just beyond that craggy mouth." He thumbed over his shoulder at the narrow hollow behind himself.

"You babble like a mad man," Kaahti said, shoving Jaltor aside as he scrutinized the opening.

"Necropolis means tomb," Callum said.

"And a tomb means treasure," Lotan finished. "But before we test the curse of a madman, we should see what these fine Azkateri soldiers were kind enough to leave for us." He knelt and began unbuckling the straps that secured the dead soldiers banded leather armor in place.

"I have to agree. Search the bodies and take anything of use. Then we can pay our respects to the mad magician," Draven said as he stepped toward the giant soldier he and Blacktuth had taken down. "Do you suppose this one's armor would fit you, my massive friend?" he said, turning back to Blacktuth.

The large Atlantean stepped over, examining the body. "Perhaps with some adjustments, but what good is armor if it is full of holes?"

"After a bit of mending, it would be as good as new," Baatar added as he approached. "To make that suit fit your frame, there would be enough material left over to repair the damage that the two of you have done."

Callum laughed. "Would you listen to him? He fancies himself an armorer now."

The rest of the group laughed at Callum's jesting provocation.

"I am actually the son of a Master Armorer, who for more than twenty years has created works of art for the high court of Grumaer. Not only did he create master works for the royal guard, but for the king himself, as well as the previous three kings."

Draven laughed. "It doesn't sound like he's that great of an armorer if your king has been replaced four times in twenty years."

"The armor did its job well enough when the need arose," Baatar said seriously. "But even the best of armor cannot protect a man from poison and treachery."

"That is as true a statement as I've ever heard," Blacktuth said, clasping Baatar on the shoulder. "If you would, son of a master, help me to rid this giant of his protection before he begins to stink."

They laughed and immediately went to work removing the giant's armor.

Against Jaltor's protestations, Draven led the group deeper into the narrow hollow, which was barely wide enough for a horse to pass in some places. Time had taken its toll on the passage. Crumbled stone and trees as thick as a man's leg littered the path. Near the end, the path sloped upward and opened into a secluded lake, surrounded on all sides by shear moss covered cliffs. Stairs carved into the stone wall lead down from the opening along the water's edge and around to the ruined remains of a temple. Draven admired the ancient spectacle before him. Even now in its crumbled and decayed state, the sheer enormity and splendor of the necropolis boggled the mind. Eight pillars stood spaced evenly along the water's edge in front of the temple entrance, each topped with a statue that must have towered another twenty feet if not more. Carved reliefs stood out along the cliffs to either side of the complex. They made their way to the portico along a flagstone path.

"Whoever it was that built this place, they were no doubt master stonemasons," Kaahti said. He gently caressed the fine lines of the statue of a woman in repose who was joined by two other napping figures that corralled a number of small children.

Draven reached out as well, running his fingers across the fine lines of the carved granite as they continued toward the entrance of the necropolis. The statues were of such fine quality one would expect the women to wake and stand at any moment. He could almost feel the warmth of the skin under his touch.

They continued up the path to the entrance. The primary structure stood three stories high with a number of overhangs and balconies that jutted out from odd locations across the structure. Dozens of life-sized statues of Azkateri soldiers stood at eternal attention along either side of the entrance, as if they guarded the occupant of the tomb within.

"We should not be here,' Jaltor warned. "We should leave here and never return!" The Azkateri merchant looked as frightened as if he were a hare fleeing a wolf.

"The dead are dead, nothing more," Lotan said.

"But this place is cursed," Jaltor argued.

"Bah!" Blacktuth chuckled. "Curses are made to keep the frightened sheep at bay."

"Or to deter those thieves brave or foolish enough to challenge the cunning traps left behind to protect the grave goods," Lotan added.

"Darkness is nearly upon us," Draven said loud enough for all to hear. "Let us set up camp beneath the portico. Callum, Lotan, Kaahti, go and find what you can to build a fire. The rest of us will examine the entrance."

Without a word, they did just as ordered.

"You are all mad, you know that, don't you?" Jaltor huffed. "But I do not know who is madder: The lot of you or I, for staying here with you. I fear that I would not survive alone in these woods with soldiers in search of us, should I leave your company."

"What do you know about this place?" Draven asked. "You said it was the tomb of Ro`Erd? How did you know that?"

"There were carvings in the stone at the entrance to the hollow. They were the arcane sigil of the necromancer himself."

"Necromancer?" Those around the Azkateri merchant stopped and turned their attention to him.

"Yes, did I not say that before? That is why we must leave this place."

"No, you did not mention it before. You said that he was a sorcerer, nothing more."

Jaltor blurted out a nervous laugh. "Oh, he was much much more than a simple sorcerer. He was a commander and general as well as sorcerer for most of his career in service to my people. The legends say that after a great battle with a powerful wizard of Ashadame, Ro`Erd discovered a collection of tomes and works dedicated to the dark arts of necromancy within the wizard's lair. Sometime afterward, my people began to fear him and the unchecked power that he wielded. It is said that from this stronghold, built by the fetid hands of the undead, that he commanded his armies to prey upon the lands of my people and those along our borders for generations. From those ancient tomes he had learned the secret of immortality, but in doing so he had lost his humanity, becoming a soulless shell of the great general that he once was."

"A once great king, from the coastal city of Jenstan, rallied the people and gathered a great army against the Ro`Erd. The necromancer rallied his armies of undead servants, gathered from a multitude of battle fields across the land. At his command, the legions of the undead cut a swath of death and destruction across the realm, swarming over even the strongest of city walls as if they did not even exist. Their numbers continued to grow, leaving behind cities of the undead in their wake."

"That was until a priest of Aapep, then nothing more than a cult, wielded the power of the god himself and retaliated for the people against the undead hordes of Ro`Erd. Ot`Seg gathered many volunteers to the cause in his march across the world. In the final battle, on a field not far from where we ourselves stand; Ot`Seg and Ro`Erd, who were more than evenly matched in both magic and might, fought with a ferocity not otherwise seen since, as their armies clashed all around them. In dealing the death blow to Ro`Erd, Ot`Seg freed my people and defeated the dark armies, who collapsed on the field of battle as the necromancer's last breath escaped from between his cold dead lips.

In that last fatal breath, it is said that Ro`Erd uttered the words of an ancient spell to ensure that his soul would be forever immortal. Ot`Seg himself was dealt a mortal wound as well during that same conflict. And before his soul could slip between the bonds of this world and the next, he cast a spell, binding himself and Ro`Erd to prevent the Necromancer's return. Then he charged those in his direct and closest counsel to return the body of Ro`Erd as well as his own to the dead necromancer's stronghold. There they were to be buried, with the full rights of an Azkateri General as they both were. Once completed, they were to secure the ancient tome and the knowledge it contained within the tomb. To ensure that neither could return to the land of the living, Ot`Seg's followers were to secure the area by placing protections and wards throughout the stronghold."

Cautious, Jaltor continued up the wide steps leading up to the portico and the entrance. "See here," he said, pointing to the door as he hurried toward it. "The writing is in ancient Azkateri but is still readable.

"What is that?" Jochi asked as he hurried past Draven and Blacktuth, pushing himself between the two warriors. He fondled the fiery dark orange gemstone that was set into the granite door.

Jaltor smacked Jochi's hand away from the stone.

"What does it say?" Draven asked as he followed the merchant to the doorway.

Jaltor hummed between whispered syllables. "It roughly translates to, the dead shall rise no more."

"Roughly?" Blacktuth laughed. "I thought you said it was in Azkateri?"

"It is in ancient Azkateri," Jaltor said. "This language hasn't been spoken in nearly two millennia. It is similar to the modern tongue, but only just."

Blacktuth looked to Draven with a sideways sneer. "What do you suppose of this place? Leave the dead to their eternal slumber, or shall we have a look about?" The large Atlantean stepped forward, examining the doorway. "With the right leverage we should have little trouble opening this doorway."

"Please, let us leave this place," Jaltor said pleadingly to Draven.

"Leave? We only just arrived," Callum said as he returned, dropping an armload of sticks at the top of the steps. Lotan and Kaathi followed close behind the bard.

Draven stepped forward to examine the door more closely. Dust crumbled away as he traced the seam with a finger. "It does not look to have been opened in recent time, nor marred as if it has been opened by force before." He turned back to the others and smiled. "What say you, men? We work well enough together in a fight. I'm sure this opening will be no match for our combined skills, nor the dead within."

"Perhaps there is enough treasure within to outfit each of us properly as a free company for hire," Blacktuth suggested.

"Wouldn't that be something?" Callum said with a laugh. "From prisoners to soldiers of fortune. Oh the songs I could write about that."

Nods and unanimous ayes from the others sealed the decision.

"Mad men, the lot of you!" Jaltor shouted as he stormed away toward the water's edge.

"Then so be it." Draven chuckled. "Let this be our first act as a free company."

"The free company of Draven the Red," Blacktuth shouted, then slapped Draven across the back.

Together they toiled into the night, prying and bracing each marked finger length as the massive stone door rose, opening with great strained shouts. Once inside, they set the locking mechanism, then lit the torches and braziers found within. The orange flames flickered, casting shadows that danced about the great wide space. It was divided by columns that rose up to support a domed ceiling high overhead. They wasted no time exploring the corridors and chambers that branched off, leading deeper into the forgotten stronghold. At the entrance to each new room a beautiful fire opal blazed in the light cast by the torches. Purples, greens, and bright blood reds shimmered within the glowing orange of the large acorn sized stones. Each man hurried to the next opening, making short work of the embedded stones with daggers and blades pressed into service to quickly separate them from their settings.

They discovered that all passages within the complex lead back to a single alcove, deep within fortress's walls. Dust covered scenes, carved in relief, and adorned in deep blues, reds, and golds decorated the curved wall of the alcove.

"Of all the rooms and corridors throughout this place, we find nothing, not even so much as a copper but for this carving?" Baatar stepped closer, holding his torch high.

"Perhaps it is a message," Callum said. "That figure, surrounded by skulls must be the necromancer. And that one," he said pointing to the opposite side of the image, "Must represent the priest, Ot`Seg. One is dark, the other is light."

"And in the center, the blazing orange of a fire opal," Draven said. "Just like the ones we have collected elsewhere in this place."

"Could be that the entrance to the tomb is behind this wall," Lotan said as he stepped closer to the wall, examining it.

"Could be, or it was nothing more than a story in the first place," said Jochi, dejectedly.

Blacktuth stepped forward and began tapping at the surface of the carving. He rapped his knuckles softly on the hard stone wall, beginning on the darker left. He tapped at random points, making his way across the wall to the right. Upon rapping the surface of the fire opal at the center of the image, the sound of a hollow thunk returned to his ears.

"That sounded more than promising," Draven said.

"I'd say so, as well. Here," he said, handing off his torch, "Stand back." Drawing forth his mace from the loop of his belt he drew back then struck at the wall with a mighty swing. The center of the wall crumbled with the first strike, giving way to another chamber.

"You are all daft or mad," Jaltor growled.

"Then perhaps you should return to Istel`dar," Draven said. Stepping forward he thrust a torch through the opening. "They may go easy on you if you explain to them that you were being held under duress." He laughed, then turned his attention back to the opening. "The wall is thin in this space alone," he said, looking about inside the hole. Kicking at the lower section of the wall, the plaster and stone easily crumbled from the strike.

"May the hands of Del and Corimaen guide and protect us." Kaahti whispered to himself in silent prayer. From the corner of his eye, Draven saw the Laurasian kiss the tip of his thumb and forefinger before pressing them to his forehead. He looked back to the others and smiled. "Shall we meet the devil of this place and free him of the burden of his riches?"

The men cheered in agreement as Draven disappeared through the opening. The chamber opened then turned, leading upward a few hundred paces before leveling out. Draven stepped carefully as the narrow corridor widened to suddenly form a great vaulted sepulcher. Stacks of bones and skulls filled the round cavities that honeycombed the walls. In the center of the chamber lay a stone sarcophagus, the figure and likeness of an old man in robes decorated the cover. In the center, above where the figure's heart would be, and held in the figure's hands, rested a fire opal larger than a goose's egg. It glimmered and showed bright in the flickering torch light. Racks of weapons, shields and armor sat at the far side of the room, flanking the life sized statue of an armored priest. The figure held its helmet under its left arm, its right hand resting over a flanged mace, holstered in the figure's belt. Golden boxes and silver trinkets decorated the space between cavities where the lines of arched stones merged. A chest of wood and iron rested below at the base of the armored priest, its contents expelled from the dry and rotten wood. Golden chains and silver coins lay piled from the opening as if they had melted their way through the container.

"Have you ever seen so much gold?" Callum said with a shuddering breath.

"Never in my life have I ever seen as much in one place," another said.

Callum pressed past the onlookers, inspecting the sarcophagus. Lotan and Jochi dove toward the spilled chest, stuffing pockets and pouches alike.

"You fools doom us all," Jaltor cried. "You'll bring the curse down upon us for certain."

"You worry yourself too much, merchant," Draven said. "If the dead can harm the living, then why have they not stirred? Collect only what you can easily carry. We do not want to leave here encumbered on the chance the guards are waiting for us. We will return for what we cannot carry out in the morning." Draven continued forward, examining the weapons in the racks. Rusted blades of many shapes rested in the ancient racks. Draven reached for the haft of a spear which crumbled like dried leaves in his grasp. The corroded copper tip clattered to the stone floor of the chamber.

"Why do you suppose this is the only weapon not rotted in the entire place?" Blacktuth asked as he examined the mace in the belt of the statue.

"Perhaps it is magical," Callum joked.

"Or perhaps it is cursed," Jaltor said.

Blacktuth gripped the head of the mace and drew it from the statue. He rolled the weapon in his palm, swinging it to test its balance. "If I could not feel the shaft in my hand, I would never know it was there. It weighs almost nothing." He held up the weapon, examining it in the torchlight. "Merchant. What does this inscription say?" He stepped over to where Jaltor stood and held the torch above the merchants head.

Jaltor examined the weapon, moving his head to focus his gaze. "S..s...Svinski Čekan," he said.

Blacktuth shook his head, not understanding the words.

"It is ancient Azkateri for…," Jaltor said then drifted off in thought. He mumbled to himself for a moment more before a look of realization struck him. "It roughly translates to Pig Hammer."

Blacktuth smiled wide. "Svinski Čekan," he said with a nod. "I like it very much." He tucked the mace beneath his belt then gathered treasure from along the alcoves.

"Do not touch that stone!" Jaltor begged.

Draven turned to find Kaahti reaching for the opal held within the hands of the figure atop the sarcophagus.

"And why not, Merchant?" Kaahti laughed. "With this treasure alone, I could buy my own palace and more. Do not be jealous. There is still treasure to be had here." The Laurasian snickered, then took the stone from its resting place. He tossed it in his palm, checking its weight then held it up in the nearest torchlight. "See?" he growled. "What did you expect would happen, merchant?"

Most of the men laughed at that and continued to stuff precious stones and coins of gold into anything they could.

"Leave him be, Kaahti," Draven ordered. "We have all had our superstitions at one time or another." He turned his attention from the ruined weapons to a gilded box full of precious stones. Sliding the box into a pouch of his own, he stood upon the base of the statue to reach another such box, just out of his reach.

The fetid stench of putrefied earth assaulted Draven's nose just as the clatter of bones falling to the stone floor drew his attention.

"Iiyee!" Jaltor screamed. "Blessed Aapep protect us. We must flee this place!"

Draven spun about, his axe at the ready. He watched with shocked horror. Three skeletons, reassembled by some mystical force from the scores of bones within the honeycombed cavities blocked the only exit from the room. Jaltor spun on his heels and dashed for the exit, stopping abruptly as one of the skeletons impaled him through the eye with the pointed shaft of a broken bone.

"By Morrag's beard! To arms you lazy dogs! The enemy has drawn first blood!" Draven charged at the three skeletons blocking the doorway only to be knocked aside like a child by another who leapt from one of the cavities.

The clatter of bones and the rumble of stone upon stone resounded in the domed chamber. Draven felt the auditory hum coming from the stone sarcophagus. "Cróm! Flee! We will make our stand below!"

Before he could stand, Draven was thrown into the far wall by a force so powerful, the lid of the sarcophagus launched into the air, shattering against the chamber's ceiling.

Jaltor let out a gurgled scream as his arms were wrenched from his shoulders and his flesh torn away. More skeletons formed, climbing down from the alcoves. The sounds of steel against bone echoed in the chamber. Draven fought to stand against two of the fleshless demons that clung to his back. He planted the butt of his axe haft against the stone and pushed with all his might. Once up to his knees he wrenched his own arm free from the skeletal hands and gripped it by the skull, smashing it into the second one. Drawing up his axe he chopped and hacked his way through a dozen more such creatures, only to find them reforming behind him as fast as he had dismembered them.

Wind rose and rumbled about the chamber. Draven looked up at the source of the sound as he fought back three more skeletal foes. A figure in a tattered black robe rose from within the sarcophagus, floating above the open vessel. Held in one fleshless hand was an ancient looking leather bound tome, while the other made motions in the air that left traces of spark and flame in their path.

"By Cróm and Dagda and Danu! The wizard lives!" Draven shrugged off another skeletal assailant as he twisted, bringing his axe blade down through the toothless skull of another then arching overhead brought the blade crashing down through the ribcage of yet another. "Kill the wizard, and we stop this scourge!" Daring to glance about the room he found Callum and Kaahti holding the entrance against a wave of the ceaseless demons.

Blacktuth roared from beneath a pile of skeletal forms. Rising up like a great bull that bucked a predator from its back he flung bones and skulls across the room. He fell backward, crashing against the rotted armor stands, crushing bones against the stone wall. The beast of a man clamored and crashed through the reanimated demons with nothing more than his fists, then headbutted another, shattering its skull to dust, a number of its ancient teeth embedding themselves in his forehead.

Draven spun, swinging his blade in a wide arc of devastation that carved its way through a half dozen more of the creatures as they formed in front of him. Gurgled and raspy cries of pain escaped a pile of bones on the far side of the room near to the door. Draven could see a dark pool of blood oozing across the flagstone lined floor of the chamber from beneath the jumbled mass of awakened bone. Baatar erupted in a maniacal bout of laughter. He bashed the pommel of his sword through the skull of another animated skeleton, then charged headlong through a number of others that shattered from the full force thrust of his shield.

Draven hacked and bashed at the unending onslaught as he made his way toward the resurrected wizard. Blacktuth roared, once more drawing Draven's attention. The massive Atlantean held a skeletal creature in the grip of either hand, using them as weapons against their boney brethren. The shimmer of a blue ethereal glow caught Draven's eye. Trying to focus on more than the threat in front of him, he spotted the ancient flanged mace, once held in the carved belt loop of the armored priest's statue, glowing at Blacktuth's side.

Draven fell back as a surge of assailants formed and pressed forward, all but swarming over him. He swung and chopped at the overwhelming horde of reanimated corpses.

"Blacktuth!" Draven shouted. "Use the mace! Destroy the necromancer!" Draven shifted and swung, crashing his blade through three more of the demons. He spun in a whirlwind of motion, axe held tight as he did so to free himself of the onslaught. Charging forward, Draven brought the blade of his axe around in an overhead back handed swing that dove low, glancing momentarily from the stone floor before arcing upright with all of his might as he leapt into the air toward the resurrected necromancer.

The hand of the dead wizard which held the leather bound tome flew free from the cloaked figure. The hand and ancient book tumbled as the wizard roared with an ethereal scream.

Twisting in mid leap, Draven pushed off from the top edge of the sarcophagus, rounding on the floating apparition. He straddled the opening on the stone coffin and swung with all of his might, bringing the blade of his axe down squarely into the wizard's chest.

Fiery lightning leapt from the wizard's other hand, striking Draven across his ribs. The stench of seared flesh bit at his nostrils as he focused his consciousness against the staggering pain of the strike. A fiery tendril that extended from the wizard's finger snaked its way up Draven's chest, across his shoulder and down his right arm. His strength failing, Draven's knees buckled as his grip released from the haft of his axe. He collapsed, falling into the stone coffin beneath him. The wizard's spell continued to burn and sear his flesh.

A rumbling growl emanated from beneath the ragged black hood. "Meso do meso i koska do koska, život što go davate za da me napravite cel."

"By the Great Mother's blessed embrace," Draven gasped as he watched muscle and sinew suddenly manifest upon the wizard's remaining skeletal hand.

The wizard bellowed a triumphant, ethereal laugh that sounded like the screams of a thousand souls reaching out from the turbulent tornadic winds of the nethers.

Draven's sight clouded then narrowed slowly as darkness encroached from the edges of his vision. The wizard's laughter faded away as if Draven had suddenly been thrown into the distance. The shabby black robes fluttered about in the mystical wind that buffeted the room, giving the visage of creatures crawling about beneath the rotted cloth.

The wizard suddenly lurched forward, falling atop Draven within the sarcophagus.

"Die you unholy devil!" Blacktuth roared. Pulling himself up onto the lip of the crypt he reached down, drawing the undead wizard in a vice like embrace, forcing the shaft of the blue glowing mace about the wizard's skeletal throat.

Draven shook the blinding fuzz of the wizard's spell from his head and pushed himself upright. As he reached for the wizard's robes, Blacktuth suddenly convulsed and began to foam at the mouth. Draven strained with every ounce of strength left in his fatigued muscles, wrestling both the wizard along with the ancient mace away from the Atlantean. He planted the fighting corpse in the bottom of the sarcophagus, forcing all of his weight down upon the undead wizard. He tore the mace away from the wizard's grip, biting at the grasping hand like a dog with a bone, then brought the weapon's flanged head down upon the skull of the ancient Azkateri wizard. The skull crumbled beneath the impact of each strike, reforming to its previous condition before Draven could even draw back his arm for the next swing.

Ethereal laughter escaped from the chattering visage of the shivering skull. The wizard flicked its remaining wrist, tracing a circular motion in the air with its boney forefinger. Fiery sparks hovered in the air behind the boney appendage as it moved and swayed.

A fiery orange glow from beneath the wizard's ragged black robes drew Draven's attention. He ripped open the robes to reveal a large, egg sized pendant that hung from a heavy gold chain. A same warm glowing orange as the large opal pulsed with the wizards raspy laugh.

"Not today, wizard!" Draven brough the head of the mace down upon the face of the glowing orange stone. A deafening clap of thunder resounded in the chamber as the strike split the stone asunder, shattering the gold setting. Draven flew upward and out of the sarcophagus. Mortally striking the statue of the armored priest, Draven crumpled and fell limply, his fall arrested by the unconscious body of Blacktuth at the statue's feet.

The world erupted in a sudden cacophony of raging winds and the thunderous cries of souls. The winds of Niflheim broke forth across the great void and unleashed its chaos upon the mortal plane. A host of voices screamed, begging for release from the depths of the nether beyond. The winds reversed, drawn back into the chamber by a vortex that formed within the confines of the stone sarcophagus with colossal force. Draven gripped both Blacktuth and the statue of the armored priest for fear of being drawn across the ethereal plane into the darkness of the demon realm.

The winds raged for moments that passed like months. Debris, bones and trinkets of gold danced and swirled in the ghastly glow of the nether realm. Before Draven could catch a breath to curse, the winds died, relinquishing their hold they retreated back across the opening of planes, taking the light of flame with them.

"By the blessed mother!" Draven let out a roaring cheer. "Who still lives? Call out and state your names!"

Baatar and Kaahti each called out, weary from their ordeal.

"Is that all that remains?"

"The devils dismembered the merchant," Kaahti said. "I saw that well enough with my own eyes.

"Blacktuth is here with me," Draven said. He rested a hand on the Atlantean's back. "And by the Dagda's blessing, the great bear still breaths." He laughed. "What of Callum, Jochi, and Lotan?"

"If either of those thieving Mezoran bastards survived, it would be a miracle," Kaahti said. "They must have been overrun by a half score if not more of those hell spawn."

"It is beyond me how any of us survived," Baatar said. "Maybe the gods took pity on us and our foul luck?"

"More like they want us alive for a bit longer so they may watch us suffer for their enjoyment," Blacktuth said then spit. He grunts painfully as he shifted his position.

"And what of Callum?" Draven asked.

As if commanded, light appeared from the sloping corridor, growing brighter with the footfall of booted feet upon stone. Callum burst through the opening with a burning torch in hand, gasping as if he'd sprinted the full distance uphill while returning to the chamber.

"Where did they go?" Callum thrust the torch ahead of himself, looking into each of the compartments within the wall.

"Where did who go?"

"Them! The undead! Where are the bones?"

Draven grabbed for one of the snuffed torches and relit the taper from Callum's flame. He held the light high as he took in the barren and empty chamber. "By Cróm," Draven growled. "Callum speaks true. Look about you. Not a bone or coin nor body remains in the room."

"By all the gods, he's right, the room is empty," Kaahti gasped, then fumbled in his jerkin. Coins clanked and clattered as he bounced them in his hand. "Those demon spawn may have made off with the rest of the treasure, but I at least still have what I had gathered before the dead returned to life.

Each man quickly checked their own pockets and pouches. The fire opals collected throughout the stronghold had crumbled into sulfurous smelling dust. Draven handed the ancient mace back to Blacktuth, then the torch. He reached into his tunic and produced a bejeweled box. The golden clad case still contained the gemstones it had previously held. Picking out a single stone from the dozens of similar stones, he held it up in the torchlight. The flickering light flashed through the deep blue crux of the star sapphire as if a heart beat deep within the stone.

"I'd say our fortunes are not so foul as such," Draven laughed. "Besides our wits, neither gods nor devils thought to check our pockets before departing this place. In a few days' time, I promise, you will have full bellies, ale all around and a warm bed with a wench besides."

The men cried out with a cheering roar. "Hail to Draven the Red!"

Delano

by Jon Michael Kelley

At the age of seventeen, before I'd been irrevocably polluted with doubt about such things, I managed to hunt down a myth named Delano. Had I been just a few years older I might have dismissed this legend outright and kept on searching for a more traditional, affordable, and closer tradesman to fix the toy; the toy my strange Uncle Kaspin bequeathed me, and the very reason for my journey to find Delano, the renowned puppet-maker. And find him I did, growing old upon the fringes of this province; marinating there in his own undeserving deification.

I also discovered this man to be quite off-center. Whether this was a result from his decades of seclusion or the very thing that had driven him to seek such privacy, I can't be sure.

I eventually came to know that *Delano* was not his given name at birth, and to also learn that it means 'the dark'. However, I eventually found that to be most inconsistent with the truth, for in the end I recognized him to be the keeper of light. Or, perhaps more aptly, its incarcerator.

And, from here on out, I shall no longer refer to the item my dead Uncle Kaspin left me as a "toy", even though it is in accordance with all the defining criteria for such a thing, as neither its intent nor manufacture was meant for any child. It is in shape a perfect box, so that is what I will call it.

The box my Uncle Kaspin had left me upon his final withdrawal was most certainly a jack-in-the-box, as it had the necessary dimensions and accoutrements to sell that idea; the real giveaway being the whimsical artistry, though in a bad state of wear, depicting a jester on all four sides, each one springing from its box and wearing, in varying colors and designs, his own frill bodice with a double-ruffled collar, a checkered cockscomb hat with silver bells, and that absurdly wide and impish grin, all screwed tightly at their corners. Although not depicted, one could easily imagine the polka-dotted pantaloons. And on one side was a tarnished silver crank that, when turned, would produce a discord of metallic jingles before ejecting its tenant in unabashed flamboyance. At least that was the universally shared expectation, yet one I was unable to make happen, as the lid refused to open. Was quite broken, it seemed. And its successful dislodgement eluded more than just my own capable hands, as I'd had more than a few craftsmen tinker with it. Instead, it produced in its aged and neglected state not a full-throated jingle but rather a sound more like the distant dribbling of rain upon a tin awning.

Despite many best efforts, the lid remained tightly – if not supernaturally – shut. And it was near the end of my ever-growing discouragement at finding a competent repairman when I'd been told the legend of Delano, long rumored to be the inheritor of great and miraculous secrets once held by this province's most esteemed toymaker. Or something to that effect. And since I'd grown quite intrigued with the damnable recalcitrance of Uncle Kaspin's box, it was of obvious consequence that I sought out this myth Delano and his inherited skills.

As a younger boy, my fascination with all things paranormal was a consuming one, particularly with those noisy and mischievous spirits. And it was during the height of one of my ambitious periods of ghost-hunting when my father pointed me in the direction of town; specifically, to its historic district. There, he promised a good number of spooks could be found frequenting the same vintage buildings patronized by those giddy summer tourists. He went on to claim that ghosts were quite often found in the seasonal employ of crafty store proprietors and shrewd inn keepers, and that a sort of celebrity had even been achieved by a few of the more 'disreputable' phantoms. And I sincerely believe it was this mocking, albeit good-natured, that had ignited the slow burn of my eventual and total disbelief in all things occult. That, and a perennial reluctance by anything paranormal to leave any traceable spoor.

He'd followed through with a hearty slap on my back, and a chortling of a kind normally avoided by my father, his humor all but lost in those days; hard, desperate times afflicted with an economic mange that eventually left most of the town exposed to the immoralities that breed opportunistically under such conditions. And this procreating continued with hearty abandon, as does the depravity, as evidenced by the town's crumbling edifice, the rampant crime and startling poverty, and its overall slow submersion into the black, bitter ground.

It is without much doubt a place endeavoring to become a ghost itself, as are so many other towns seeming to do within this province. There is an abundance of peat here, and I just pray that nature eventually preserves enough history, leaves enough skin intact on bone, that future generations can glean the necessary lessons from it.

But, back to my father: a clever if not haunted man. And his point – although not until his death many years later had he *truly* finish making it – was well taken. That point being: Ghosts existed only in the imagination – but live there they did, and to chase and tame such things should always be an *internal* endeavor. He implied that very thing to me, though more succinctly in a rhyme, when I was too young to care. Funny how, in our later years especially, we find upon recollection that it is the tone that most often chaperones the more significant truisms. But then, the important proverbs always seem to be melodically woven.

Following those ghost-less boyhood years a cold, intractable skepticism settled deep within me, along with the conclusion that when we die only a cruelly naive fib issues from our lifeless bodies, and ventures nowhere far except to the gullibly hopeful standing next in line.

And had I known Delano would share those same feelings, I would have stayed home.

But I stuffed my broken box and a few days' provisions into a gunny sack and headed off to locate this legend. And it had taken me a course of three days searching through the province's lower backwaters, meandering hills, and decaying vestiges of stone settlements that I had no idea even existed. Asking a cottager here, then a tinker there, to be eventually led at one point by at least four attendants through vast fields of ashen brush and unmerciful thistle, only to enjoy the occasional shallow interlude of stagnant, hatching water – all the while trying to understand the sullen drivel coming from my darkly cloaked entourage; one comprised of gypsy ancestry. There came toward the end a few others of less evident stock, unless you were kind enough to assign the state of slobbering privation a tolerable pedigree. And despite such shameless idiocy, and profound reticence in some of their cases, the romantic idea had occurred to me more than once that most, if not all, of my escorts had already been expecting me, given the seemingly effortless task of procuring their assistance.

Not expecting *me* specifically, but the *idea* of someone like me.

Late in my search, I distinctly recall a particularly somber route, one that had set upon me a feeling of such utter hopelessness that I had literally felt its suffocating weight as it bore down.

Trudging beneath a low and drizzling ceiling of sky, I remember thinking: This is what the land of broken promises must look like. All the falsely sworn oaths and fallacious guarantees ever made, now sloughing off their skins and laying bare the gray calcified disillusionment beneath. Not those trifling promises adults swap one another, but of the pretty and shiny kind they make to their children.

And meandering through this horrid area was an oily-skinned, slow-moving river that lapped a sickly yellow froth upon its shores, flanked on either side by a single skeletal row of dead birch trees, each one of those incredibly tall and seemingly pollarded to the next, bending toward its opposite twin to affect a stark, emaciated archway that proceeded endlessly into the bleak and twisting distance.

The land itself stunk vaguely of a once-piquant chemical used in extracting silver from the mines not far from there, just to the east, and the very reason for their permanent closures as it was believed (though never proven) that this chemical was responsible for the slow deaths of thousands of children well over a century ago. And the evidentiary plague that continues to drape gray these adjacent lands tends to support that hypothesis.

Finally, I was ushered from that dying wasteland into one that was already dead and bloating, presenting graphic evidence of having been recently scavenged, and so convincingly that I glanced into the dense canopy above me – a tight and chaotic weave of gnarled phalanges – wholly expecting the carrion eaters to be there, waiting in tempered anticipation.

That was when I knew I was getting close, as one of my more colloquial escorts had earlier assured me that when one searches for a slippery and most antisocial worm, it is the lightless, loamy reaches where they are eventually and most often found.

Why she chose to make Delano's comparison to such a loathsome creature would soon become evident.

When the last of my escorts skulked quickly away, a withering cottage debuted upon a barren crest of hill. Then, she told me the Puppet Maker had finally been found. "Delano!" she cried. "The Dark One!"

His complexion, however, suggested nothing of the sort. Delano was a tall and lanky man, silvery-haired, unkempt in an unruly sort of way, and his deep, angular features intimated a mischievous countenance I might have instead expected upon the denizen of the box I'd brought for repair.

Stooping below the listing overhang of a gabled porch, he was watching my approach and nodding slowly, like a man who was coming to terms with something regretfully unavoidable. There was no railing to lean against; so, he just stood there, his thumbs hooked at the shoulders of his wide and garishly plumed suspenders – a plethora of loosely affixed and moderately-sized feathers of all kinds and colors running their full lengths – set against his tea-stained pullover shirt, and blue dungarees whose hems were crying to be lowered. And being shoeless only accentuated his eccentric pose.

No, nothing in my view remotely suggested even the residue of a toy maker, or even fixer of such things. Except for those gaudy suspenders, I would have thought no one of that skill and ebullient character resided within a hundred miles; just this old and bitter and defeated chameleon who'd managed to mimic his solitary existence to these forbidding surroundings.

"I'm hoping there is some potted meat in that bag of yours," he said, thumbing his suspenders up tightly, then – in synchronized fashion – releasing them to slap loudly against his shoulders, dislodging a few of the less tenacious feathers. They floated down to an unstable deck with envied indifference.

Food? That stopped me cold. It never occurred to me that I should bring a gift, or humble offering of some kind. After all, I wasn't truly expecting to find a deity, so naturally I wasn't expecting him to act like one. "No," I said finally. "I'm afraid I do not."

"Perhaps a confection? A red piece of fruit? A winning lottery ticket – something that might quell my mounting ambition to kick your sorry ass off my land?" – *slap* –

"I brought you a toy," I said, not yet having realized it was nothing of the sort. "It's my understanding that you used to build such things, and that you might know how to go about repairing this one." I was beginning to feel quite awkward under his intense gaze. "Its primary function," I explained, "is arrested in place, as if by… magic."

"Magic?" – *slap* – 'Magic left here on the five o'clock and hasn't been seen since."

"Yes, magic," I insisted. "As crazy as that sounds."

He thought for a moment, then said, "You appear too old to be playing with toys, and too young to be so enamored with an heirloom. Is this for a beloved younger sibling? A neighbor's terminally ill child? I mean, it's just that you've come a long and uncomfortable way to be wanting your marionette re-strung. I'm assuming it's a puppet, or something of that clan. Am I right?" – *slap* –

"Well, a kind of acquaintance of those," I said, growing a bit perturbed. "My uncle left it to me upon his death, so your misgivings about my capacity for fond attachments are incorrect." I placed the sack gently on the ground in front of me. "It's a jack-in-the-box."

A perceptible glint rose in his eyes, and he brought his thumbs out from beneath those feathered straps and slowly lowered them to his sides. "A jack, you say? From a *dead* uncle?"

"I have yet to see the box's resident, the very reason for my being here, but yes…"

An uncanny stillness had seized him, and his voice was suddenly without its glibness.

"The lid is frozen shut?" he finally managed. "That's the 'magic' you referenced?"

I nodded that it was.

With apparent difficulty he raised his right hand toward me, pointed and said, "Pick up that bag and come closer."

I obeyed and strode toward his porch, and as I did a granite headstone came into view, just off to my left about forty or so yards, too far away to read the epitaph. Nonetheless, I was struck with the notion that Delano had become a widower in some distant past, as the only burst of vibrant color I'd seen in three days, aside those feathered suspenders, was the small memorial of flowers bunched around that marker. So, I naturally assumed it was his beloved wife. To have imagined it being a small son or daughter was just too grim, so I chose not to.

I stopped at the porch's short run of rickety stairs, then reached out and offered him the bag.

He tilted his head to an acute angle and stared quizzically. "I don't want your muddy socks, boy. Just reach in and give us a peek at that jack."

I backed up, just a step. "Before I get too generous, perhaps you should invite me in?"

Still with that same quizzical look, he straightened his head, let it slant the opposite direction, then began moving it slowly back and forth between the two points, as if he were cautiously committed to some form of spinal exercise. "Maybe. I. Should." Then his neck froze midway between bends, and there he remained, just that way, staring; and long enough for me to reconsider my proposal, if not the entire reason for my visit.

Then suddenly chipper, he snapped straight and said, "Tea?" But there was never going to be any tea.

As we entered, I was warned to keep my hands at my sides; that, to touch a single item, either liquid or solid, static or in frenzied motion, would result in something quite painful that would, he promised, leave a nasty and permanent mark. Only two types of toys were apparent, and both were in boggling abundance. On either side of a narrow pathway leading from the foyer to the living area was a cluster of exceptionally small pinwheels and their toothpick-size shafts – each one no more than six inches high – sprouting from the wood floor like chrome-colored hibiscus, and so closely bunched that if a pattern had been intended it was not immediately discerned. Then upon entering the next larger room, a combining of the living and dining areas, one was besieged by a surplus of wooden puppets sagging from the walls, most of their smiles bearing false witness against their slack and painfully disjointed postures; though a few other marionettes, those with dark costumes and even darker eyebrows, smiled in less obvious contradiction, appearing to be truly enjoying the torture. There was a disorienting lack of furniture (though I wasn't given a full tour of the abode) that upset me quite more than it probably should have, as I remember thinking that this man was even more mentally unwell than he first appeared, thereby inciting a sympathetic response that I was prone to having back then, when confronted so intimately with the sick and impoverished. I would soon learn, however, that Delano was neither.

As we approached the cellar stairway, Delano handed me a sweater he'd snatched from a wood peg. "You'll need this, so put it on." After I slipped on the garment, he stepped aside and motioned me to go first.

The descent was unnaturally long and steep, and changed direction twice, each instance intervened by a short landing before taking a right-angled turn. At the bottom I was assaulted by a stagnant, briny odor, and a draft borne of some crevice just this side of an arctic plain.

Of tundras and tide pools, I was reminded.

There was enough light to read by; a most peculiar glow, and one whose source I could not readily locate.

"To your left," he instructed, his breath pushing visibly past my face. "See the stools under that mahogany workbench? Pull one out and make your acquaintance."

I did as he instructed, then finally reached in and rescued the box from the bag. As I placed it upon the workbench he immediately gasped and drew back a few steps. Then, with bridling hesitance, he leaned forward and focused determinedly upon the thing, as if he were trying to verify the species of a potentially venomous snake.

Without looking up, he reached into the shadows above me and pulled a chain that set about the chamber a bluish tint, inciting the present chill to deepen. Then he took a long breath and instructed me to gently lift the box and search the bottom for a set of initials.

I had grown to know its exterior well and, without looking, assured him that no letters were engraved anywhere upon the box.

"Until now, you didn't have the resources to see them," he said. "Look again, under this new light."

I did – and to my amazement clearly found, after tilting the box to a certain angle, three large letters embossed along one edge. "T.W.W.," I said; clearly, the initials of its creator.

"Oh, my, my," he finally whispered. After a moment of awe, caution surrendered to a kind of reverence profound enough to continue keeping him at bay. It was now plainly evident that Delano had determined an immediate kinship to the box. And it was no wonder, I'd thought, as both shared an almost identical lust for inaccessibility, and an unusually odd if not flattering antiquity.

There was another, deeper drawing of breath, then he exhaled the words "an original", as if he'd been presented for years with nothing but compelling counterfeits. And by the way his face then contorted I thought he just might cry. Instead, he put both hands together and pushed them to me, palms up, as if he were expecting communion.

I gingerly placed the box into his outstretched hands. Then, debasing the poignancy of the moment, I had to finally inquire about the origins of that foul brackish odor, as neither my nose nor stomach was acclimating well, if at all.

Just for an instant, his eyes pivoted to a distant, shadowy corner before springing back to join an unapologetic scowl. "Nothing that can be helped, I'm afraid."

But when his attention was lured back to the box, I stole a moment and traced his prior glance back to that dusky recess and observed, after my eyes adjusted to the viscous gloom, what appeared to be small metal cages stacked atop one another; traps one might use, say, for the humane capture of baseboard-dwelling rodents. But before I could be certain about what those cages were for, or that they were in fact cages at all, his voice reclaimed my attention, and may have very well drowned out the sounds I'd just begun suspecting were the stirrings of waking things; things perhaps inside those very enclosures.

"I'd given up hope of ever seeing the last one," he announced, then finally pulled up a stool and sat down opposite me at the table. “Now this lid, you see, has been locked not from the outside,” he began in a secretive tone, “but from within. Upon its imminent demise – when it senses its own death drawing near – the tenant of the box will lock itself in to assure that its remains are safely secured until a person of a certain … accreditation, let’s say, can retrieve and properly dispose of them.”

When I was finally able to speak, I said, “You’re not really suggesting that the puppet in this box was once a living thing?”

In a kind of drunken indignation, he half-backed, half-slanted away from me. “I most certainly am,” he assured, “—as were once the tenants of twelve more just like it!” Then he cocked his head again in that same obtuse way he had done outside. “Certainly, you’ve heard of the ‘Baker’s Dozen’?”

“Only those of crumpets and bagels,” I confessed.

He appeared genuinely surprised. “You mean to say, you really don’t know the lore of the Thirteen Jacks?”

“It's not ringing any bells,” I admitted. “But then, I was a sheltered child.”

So, he told me the legend of two inventor brothers who, after the Eastern mines had been shut down for good, had constructed a handful of these items (thirteen, I was to believe) that marveled above all others in their construction, magical inspiration, and asking price. And with the eventual sale of just the first few, and the promise of more to come, our province and its many satellite communities were brought back from the brink of financial and moral ruin. That was it in a nutshell.

And the inventor brothers did all this, he added, *and* managed to build at the same time a most successful line of travelling ovens.

"Hence the 'Bakers' Dozen'?" I guessed.

He nodded. "The Brothers Whittington," he winked. "Thad and Bill." He regarded the lingering vacancy in my eyes with growing concern, then said finally, "You know, *Thaddeus and William* Whittington?"

"Oh, of course," I said, finally understanding. "T.W.W." I'd been thrown off as I was anticipating those initials upon the box to belong to just *one* toy maker. At least that was my excuse.

He then directed his concentration back to the box; specifically, to a rather small hole near the lid that, once again when tilted keenly, only existed in the presence of that queer blue light. "To your right is a long tray," he said. "In it, you'll find a pair of metal devices whose thin and elongated purpose is to affect surgical precision, though either one can – without fear of losing its revered identity – double as an ice pick. Hand me the smaller of the two."

As my fingers fumbled about the tray's contents, he said, "How strong then is your remembered history of the Eastern mines?"

I admitted that I knew some of that history, primarily about why they were shut down well over a century ago, having been deemed responsible for the deaths of thousands of children. I handed him the instrument.

"Lies," he said, aiming the tool at the box, then delicately inserting its pointed tip into that small and most ephemeral hole. He stopped at that moment and remained carefully still as he continued: "It wasn't the chemical leaching that killed all those children and sickened so many others. See, one day in the fall – and a damned miserable day that was, too, rain as cold and thick as mud and every bit as transparent! – these two veteran miners of solid repute found something ensconced – more like hibernating, I should amend – inside a wall of igneous rock."

Just then, as if having been alerted by some internal timer, he gave the tool a quick twist, then immediately retracted the tip. There was a faint hissing, as if air were being released, followed by a brief but cloying stench; one that rushed past the more obstinate one, leaving it momentarily inoffensive.

It was prudent to assume that the veteran miners of whom he spoke were none other than the Brothers/Bakers Whittington, Thad and Bill. However, that he thought it necessary to describe the weather conditions of that particularly nasty fall day nearly one-hundred-twenty years ago, and with such vivid detail, did more than suggest his actual but most impossible presence. An insinuation that became an annoying splinter that I just couldn't seem to pull. So, I asked him about it.

Yet again, he cocked his head in that imbecilic way and glared at me for a disturbingly long moment. "You might want to leash that inquisitive imagination," he finally offered. "You don't want to know the half of it, boy."

"Half of what?" I asked.

"Why, the meaning of constrained life," he smiled, "and of course the vastly more important ramifications of eternal death." On that, he grabbed the box with one hand, then reached around the side with the other and gave the crank two rapid clockwise turns, then back half a turn, then forward again three more times in quick fashion. I immediately recognized a significant improvement in the quality and weightiness of the jingle, now sounding more like a belled cat in a rolling drum.

He leaned in, as if the walls had ears. "Before I open this box and introduce you to its tenant, you're obliged a warning that what pops out may be the desiccated remains of what was once an entity quite evolved beyond the traditional wire and papier-mâché and may seriously dislodge the snug fit of your beliefs as they pertain to established reality."

I told him it would take more than the chewed leftovers of time and silverfish to convince me that life on a spring once existed in that box; that, like sylphs and forest nymphs, such things didn't exist no matter how badly one wished otherwise.

"But before you open that lid," I reminded, "there's still the matter of those miners and what they found in that wall of stone."

His smile grew ever wider, to a length that exposed stained molars not seen otherwise.

"Afterwards," he promised, then pushed the crank in until it made a clicking sound, then lastly gave it one slow clockwise turn.

The lid opened but not compellingly, as I'd expected it to famously do upon spring hinges, but rather in a leisurely way, as if being pushed up by miniature hydraulics.

I leaned across the table and stared into the opening, and my very first impression was that a butterfly had gotten inside, died there, and the only evidence of its unfortunate interment were the delicately thin fragments of its red and black wings suspended in the staggered latticework of cobwebs. Searching farther, I then realized that those remains were not of any lepidoptera but rather the colored remnants of a chimney hat, as I'd found, searching past the gossamer, that wire framework of adjoined rectangles upon which that red and black checkered rice paper had once been fashioned.

In that heightened silence, I once again heard those restless papery sounds, like something small pushing across a stone floor littered with fall leaves.

With my finger, I brushed aside more cobwebs and searched ever deeper into the box. I found that the accordion spring, loose now in its cradle and naturally oxidized, still maintained an impressive resistance for its age, but I doubted enough to ever again dispatch a jack with that glee-inducing will.

Then I found the jack's vestigial remains at the bottom, having been displaced from their springy perch, and they appeared even smaller than I'd imagined they would. Its upper body was still intact for the most part, covered by once garish clothing now long ravished, with visible sections of its emaciated and mummified trunk showing dully through the frayed gaps, allowing one the occasional glimpse at the imprint of diminutive ribs. Both arms still dangled from their sockets, and I could only imagine the brittle sinew that kept them attached, wondering how they could remain so after three days of being jostled about a most rutted and asymmetric wilderness.

I found no legs because, as Delano had advised me just then, it never had any.

The most alarming thing though was its petite skull. The top was round enough, but as I continued my inspection downward a most disconcerting image began to form, as the normal inclination to picture it as human, given its personage, was diverted from a less anthropomorphic track and onto a more avian one, as the bones' distinctive thinness and fragility became suddenly apparent, as did an especially wide deviation between the orbital sockets, as if the eyes had been placed on either side of the head rather than together up front. And the lower mandible and maxilla were fused together, and appeared to have grown prominently outward, as if having metastasized into the lower pointed chin, all combining to form a predominate protrusion and thereby leaving one with the numbing realization that the traditional ingestion of food had never been necessary to maintain its survival. If it once had a mouth, it had been an immovable grin in the form of one long and thin convex line, slanting upward on either side, and tightly screwed at the corners.

And all about the floor of the box were tiny vertebrae, strewn about like so many teeth; teeth it never had, and enough of them to suggest that the neck had been unusually long.

I finally looked up at Delano, who was still smiling that incredibly wide smile.

"I realize that you've just been rendered temporarily speechless," he said, "but when that ability returns may I have some assurance that your earlier tone of condescension will have been tucked away for later arguments?"

Wide-eyed, I nodded that it would. Then I said, "Was ... was it of sufficient flesh and blood to have had a spirit?" I asked this because I had an instant and unshakable concern that those swishing noises I kept hearing were the restless continuations of the dead jack; that, upon opening the lid, its ghost was freed and was now shuffling around, finding its bearings, perhaps dazed and confused by the combinations of strange light. Until remembering, that was, that I'd begun hearing those noises *before* the lid had been sprung.

Delano seemed to truly consider my question, and upon his ruminations became quite reflective over something. After many moments, he said somberly, "At my age, when you dream of a long-lost friend, you see his visage as it had been when you last saw him, and not as it should be those many years later. Why do you think that is?"

I admitted that I had not a clue.

He looked distraught. "I'm afraid that it is just one slip of evidence that the soul, or spirit, does not exist, at least not after death. When the mind attempts to put a face upon a memory, in its limited capacity it can only reflect a countenance as it was last remembered. Simply, in an unconscious or dream state, the mind has not the proper inclination to advance the theory of age. You see, the mind is caught sleeping, so to speak, when the dreamer is sleeping. If there existed a soul, however, or shepherd of the mind, one would suspect that those kinds of oversights would never occur, as the mind and spirit are to work in tandem and would share a truer responsibility to the self until death do them part, or so mythology would have us believe."

He sighed; shook his head. "Their creators didn't have souls, so why should the jacks be so privileged?"

If not downright absurd, his reasoning was at the very least flawed and untenable. But then I'd asked myself if it was really any less believable than the more popular dogmas people engaged. And, in fact, the longer I considered his proposals the more I recognized a kind of skewed logic. I had not yet been fully acclimated to the agnostic side then, and still wanted to believe in the existence of a soul and an afterlife, but my countless meditations about such possibilities these many years later always bring me back to that cold and damp and malodorous cellar, and into Delano's profound cynicism. And to consider other things not yet mentioned.

But I'm the most convinced that his little allegory was inspired by his own imaginative efforts of trying to put a matured face on that jack – or recall a younger one, as I frankly suspected by then that he had once known that puppet in its animated and most aberrant form, but so long ago that he'd since forgotten the authentic image. Given the circumstances, that was perhaps defensible.

There again, the reason might have been solely attributable to a true and recurring and most terrifying haunting: That every time he closed his eyes, *he did remember* that jack's face *as it had once been.*

Delano's eyes widened upon a sudden thought, and he began tapping the box with a finger – but he was only feigning a surprise notion. "*However*, there can be injected a sort of …continuation, or perhaps even a revivification, of life, if you're lucky enough to have the proper syringe and elixir."

"Do you mean a resurrection?" I asked, though not believing for an instant that he had such talents.

"That's exactly what I mean." He rose from the table. "Very well. I'll need two weeks."

I just sat there, gaping. That was it? That was where we were going to leave it, this …miracle? This great artifact of potential wealth? It might have been old hat to him, but I was beside myself with unbearable wonder.

"C'mon, boy, up the stairs and back to your cozy environs."

I protested, telling him that my part of the province wasn't so cozy either, and that he'd promised to tell me about those miners and of the mysterious things they'd found in rock – and then it struck me that he never had the intention of elaborating upon those details but only used them to extract my reaction, to see just how much I did know and what I believed to be true and what I believed to be myth. And most importantly what, if anything, my Uncle Kaspin had told me before his death. Yes, I was by then convinced that he had known my uncle, intimately so, and accused him of such.

He wheeled on me with an anger that was both bitter and repressed. "I should tell you, boy, that your cherished uncle, one Jerome Bishop Kaspin, was a thief and a blackmailer! He was a miner on the Whittington crew and being a cunning man watched furtively from the tunnels' shadows as brothers Thaddeus and William chiseled out their incredible find and stowed it away in trolleys, hiding it in plain sight amongst the ore. Chunks of what appeared at first to be regular rock, but when examined closely turned out to be something – but then again not so entirely – different. These creatures were later extracted from their natural silicate vessels by brothers Thaddeus and William in private seclusion, and their magic was subsequently identified quickly thereafter. And a plan hatched.

"And it was by no coincidence when directly after the removal of these fantastic creatures the land became sick and quickly passed its disease on to the people, the most susceptible being the very youngest of their children. Thousands died before the poison subsided and a kind of raw, gray equilibrium caught hold. The mines were blamed. Then, months later, after witnessing the hugely prosperous sale of the brothers' first jack and their charitable donations with the proceeds dispensed amongst the province's most appreciative populace, your uncle threatened to go public with what he knew unless they, brothers Thaddeus and William, built the next jack for him, free of charge – and to certain specifications that deviated from the original drafts. And what deviation might that have been, you think?"

"To not give it a mouth," I said.

"That was the biggest one, yes," he affirmed. "When each of those jacks was fitted with a mouth, the tendency to use it was not a reluctant one. The jacks had no digestive system, so they didn't eat – but talk and filibuster they did, and quickly ingratiated themselves to the masses with their sermonizing and encouraging propagandas. And each of these jacks was most amenable to its owner and displayed a subservience that would make a dog jealous. So naturally your uncle got to desiring a jack for his own amusement and, given their loquacious nature, decided that he wanted his jack to possess that same obedient trait – just with less chatter; you know, the way some men like their women to be inclined. But it wasn't for the love of quiet that Jerome wanted a mute jack, but rather to all but eliminate the possibility of any future testimony against him by the jack regarding his devious ways, and of course the wretched mistreatment – or dare I say torture – he would ritually bring upon it."

"You make him out to be an evil monster," I said in defense of my uncle, "but I can assure you he was no such thing–"

"First off, let's put this uncle business to rest," he said. "How could he be your true uncle when I knew him well over a century ago? Somehow, someway, he years ago slithered into the graces of your family and rooted in and did so for purely selfish reasons; reasons neither you or I can properly imagine at this point, and perhaps never will, and during his chicanery developed a fondness for you, thus his leaving you this jack, though I admit that this ability at such selfless affection seems quite a capricious jaunt for dear Jerome." He moved in closer.

"Don't underestimate the prowess of Jerome Bishop Kaspin. He was a con man and trickster of the first order."

"Which begs the question," I said, "of how you – either of you – could have possibly been alive well over a century ago?"

"Everyone who had a close and extended association with any one of the Thirteen Jacks went on to demonstrate an ability to live beyond his or her expected years, as long as said associations remained tethered. Once the bond was broken, as all but one eventually was, that one being Jerome's, the normal aging process resumed, and death could prevail in the end, when it wasn't hastened by other means."

"You were an owner of one of the original jacks?"

"I was, yes," he admitted, then looked away, downtrodden. "But I dispensed with its enclosure and remains the same way I eventually got around to doing the other eleven: I buried it, and deeply, back into the damp cold of ground."

"So then, you're back to aging naturally?" I said, confused. "But ... my unc – or, rather, Mr. Kaspin – was still able to ward off death, even though the jack had long since died within, because...?"

"Because those remains still produced a wattage of magic, though naturally quite diluted. But just enough for one man, if he kept it incessantly close. And Jerome apparently did."

"But Mr. Kaspin is now dead. So, what happened to the magic?"

Delano put on a griefless smile. "Why, I hear dear old Jerome died at the hands of a knife-wielding mugger." Then he regarded me with sudden realization. "But... You didn't know that, did you?"

I was shocked and told him pneumonia was the cause given.

"My, but you really are sheltered. Anyway, a befitting end for dear Jerome, I should think, as the *honor* among thieves, it would seem, is not a discriminatory one. You see, the jacks' magic doesn't annul death and therefore couldn't render invalid the steel blade that killed Jerome. It just keeps the *natural* process of death at bay. And while we're there, you should know that all the jacks ultimately took their own lives. They didn't sleep, and I fear it was the soaking black quiet of the early hours that ultimately bogged them down. That time during which their owners slept. When all in the province slept unwittingly, thus allowing the jacks to contemplate without interruption their lonely incarcerations and struggle to interpret some meaningful sense of what each one must have finally been convinced was a redundant, superfluous existence that was in direct contradiction to what they so passionately sermonized. Just as another species of alleged high intelligence is so often prone to realizing. It caught up with them, in the end, that isolating speculation. Yes, their strict confinement was their undoing. Imagine being stuck in quicksand but never sinking beyond your sternum, your eyes and thoughts forever open.

"And more than a few of those owners took the same grim route following the suicides of their jacks. The bond – or love, if you want to call it that, and I can assure you that we can – that developed between the jack and its owner was as steadfast as any between great friends. I believe even more so. Just try and imagine the fierce emotions such life-prolonging magic would inspire between giver and receiver."

"And a reversal of roles, to be sure," I reminded. "The puppet now the master."

I glanced back at the box on the table, thinking just how terribly disappointed the jacks must have been, in the end, with their creators – then I selfishly wondered if, in just my short time as owner of that box and its dead tenant, I might have been exposed long enough to that replenishing force to have eked out just a few more hours. Days. Maybe even years?

"That's why the land went dark, as you stated," I said. "When the brothers removed those creatures from their natural placement, they didn't realize they were taking the very things that pulsed life itself."

He nodded, saying, "But they quickly found out. And instead of just a miniscule few, imagine if they had found a better majority. What kind of pestilence might have befallen us then?" He took my shoulder and, with a warmer approach, escorted me to the bottom of the stairs. "Two weeks," he reminded. "Just two weeks. Then I shall have for you a working jack-in-the-box."

"Just one more thing," I said. "You said the creatures were 'hibernating'; a rather *specific* description, yes?"

He nodded. "I've long come to believe that they are in a kind of pupa or chrysalis state and aren't through maturing. That they may, in fact, be the very crux of such progression for all of us.

Perhaps once they metamorphose, or evolve, then so will we in kind. So will everything that has a biological right."

"Two weeks, then?" I said earnestly. "You promise?"

"You have my word," he assured. "After all, it is all of but two things I have left to give." He then handed me my bag, and its diminished weight was a candid reminder that I was leaving without the box, and that I was low on provisions.

He seemed to sense both concerns, and said, "Just go back the way you came, and I'll have someone meet you at the river with some goods and fresh water. And, please, dispel your worries that I'll be absconding with your property. Let me assure you that I am no thief – but I'm no saint, that's for certain," he confessed. "Those remaining jacks that I couldn't legitimately buy back, and there were only but a couple that I could, had to be finally obtained through other, less honest means."

"You hired Mr. Kaspin, in other words."

"That I did. And the only payment he would accept was my promise to never employ another like him to go after his own jack, as he had also refused long ago to sell it back to me for any price. Therefore, I am a man of my word, and you can be assured that I'll be here when you return in two weeks, as will a repaired jack."

I told him that I found it hard to believe that my ex-uncle would have turned down any substantial amount of money.

He laughed, and it was the only time I heard him do so. "You see, when you are of the proclivity of not believing in an afterlife, as was Jerome, then when you discover something that may in fact be this mortal life's answer to the everlasting, you will have then also found an attachment that no amount of money could ever buy. Now, off you go."

I was not completely satisfied with his assurances, and in a pall of regret I managed to make my way up the stairs, step by grueling step, with a very tiny part of me grateful to be free of that stench and clinging cold, but a vastly greater one afraid that I was abandoning my salvation from a crippling naiveté about what life and death truly were to one another and was instead leaving it to a stranger whose own innocently optimistic interpretations had long ago turned into the bleakest of conclusions.

At the top of the stairs I removed the sweater, and it wasn't until doing so that I recognized its fabric as being of the most exclusive kind. I suspected it was old simply by the feel, but it was difficult to estimate as it had been kept extremely well. No, this was not something one would find in a pauper's hamper. I chanced a look at the inseam, and to my good fortune found within it a sewn tag. On it were the initials T.W. printed in a black and stylish calligraphy, the manufacturer's name stenciled below.

T.W. I mused. *Thaddeus Whittington.* So, had I just been confronted with a rather remarkable coincidence, or had Thaddeus Whittington truly been the original owner, and Delano a thief? What was I to make of this?

After a moment's consideration, I returned the sweater to its rightful peg, took a very deep breath, and left through the same doorway from which I had entered, the puppets appearing not the least bit saddened as I did. And a vigorous breeze must have pushed through some lower gap between door and threshold, as every one of those pinwheels had been set spinning. Wildly so.

As I left the porch, my attention was once again drawn to that granite grave stone and the vibrant trusses of flowers at its base.

My first disappointment upon reaching the grave was finding the flowers to be convincing imitations of the silk variety. I was saddened somewhat but not truly surprised, as it would have required a greater imagination had I found so many of them to be real. My second disappointment was the engraving upon the granite headstone; not just of who it was, but how he had died. The epitaph read: "In loving memory, Dearest Brother William, gone by his own hand, this day, __."

Upon this, I quietly returned to the cottage with a cunningness my faux Uncle Kaspin would have envied. I descended the stairs, careful to mimic my timorous steps to the ambient noise rising from that cold cellar; whispered words, unintelligible. Delano was either talking to himself, I decided, or the dearly departed in that box.

I stopped just a few advances from the bottom and found the old toymaker hunched over that table. To his left was one of those metal containers I'd glimpsed earlier, and just to the left of that was what I'd initially suspected to be a slab of formless paraffin roughly the size and shape of a plump rat. Then it moved, and I realized I might have very well been witnessing the same kind of creature – perhaps even one of the original bounties – found by the Brothers Whittington, Thad and Bill.

And Delano was talking to it, and upon a more intellectual verve than one would normally expect to hear lavished upon a glob of jelly.

I also noticed a small piece of shredded newspaper still clinging to its side. Obviously, its cage was papered.

I ascertained its front, or head, to be the tapering translucent end where two black dots gleamed on either side, just beneath the surface; its eyes, I presumed. This end also seemed to be leading the bulk, and as I watched its elastic, undulant locomotion I was reminded of a leech, though that is not to suggest I was repulsed, as I find the fluid movements of certain annelids to be quite entrancing, as their gracefulness can achieve a pronounced calming effect upon the observer. As it approached the table's edge, the pupa's curiosity was tentative, this time reminding me of a rodent the way its "snout" twitchily examined the drop-off.

Delano nudged it back a few times with his free hand while his other worked leisurely over the box, though exactly in what way I could not be sure; only that an oddly shaped and lustrous instrument was being used.

And then another realization: The origins of that mystery glow that I could never track down before became suddenly and quite eerily apparent, as it was coming from this creature. It radiated light – but that wasn't *quite* true. To be more accurate, it projected that light, or energy, the way a ventriloquist does his voice. And this light was of a whisper, and no discernable beams radiated outward from the creature that could be followed and proven as the source; only that the glow had just enough of a corresponding rhythm to the pupa's fluid movements that a relationship could be made, reminiscent of the way water projects the rippling lattices of moonlight upon a ship's hull.

Then the creature froze and stared at my position. It appeared – as much as a tapering roll of amber jelly can appear – just as curious of me as I was of it. Delano sensed my presence then (or, perhaps he'd known all along of my return), and said, quite calmly and without looking back, "My, how time flies. Has it already been two weeks?"

I apologized for my intrusive return, then fumbled for a reason (though not the coercing one just yet), finally saying, "I ... I forgot a most important detail. What will be the cost of repair?"

Silence for a long moment; then he said, "A pair of leather suspenders. It's about time I replaced the present ones. And take note that I have buttons sewn on to hold the straps, so don't bring me those cheap clip-ons."

"Shall I have your initials stenciled in, as well?" I asked. "T.W. for Thaddeus Whittington?"

His head dropped, and for a moment I was convinced that he'd fallen directly asleep while standing up. Then he slowly opened his eyes, and said, "Thaddeus died along with his most cherished twin brother William. Now it's just me; Delano."

"And your little friend there," I reminded. "Is that number fourteen, or were the numbers originally taken quite beyond that total, and still captive in those cages?"

"When you stumble upon stray coins, you fill your pockets. When you stumble upon diamonds, you find orifices you thought you never had. But after so many years the seats of thrones, like self-delusion and aspired glory, settle into a hardness that assumes the true shapes of who we really are. Once achieving that, Brother William and I finally returned the remaining few, those we hadn't already transformed, to the ground; all but one, of course, and only because William insisted that I keep it to remain alive long enough that I might eventually find a way to reintroduce to the collective something that could unite them once again and bring them hope, while in the process performing my own self-reformation, if you will. You see, William believed in the soul, an afterlife, and he always hounded me about my dogged resistances to such possibilities. A characteristic he especially found even more baffling after we'd discovered these remarkable creatures." He placed a gentle hand on the thing, still at the table's edge and unmoving, regarding me with a kind of guarded wonderment. "I believe that time of which William spoke has finally come, thanks to you."

"Did your brother believe in hell, as well?"

Delano nodded, ashamed for his brother. "William took his own life, this is true, but he did so in the clutches of unbearable grief after the loss of his jack." He smiled. "But, no, William did *not* believe in the existence of hell, but only and exclusively in the most forgiving of eventualities."

I nodded. "Suspenders, then?" I said.

"Yes, and of leather. Nothing fancy, just … durable."

I told him that I understood, and promised him my prompt return in two weeks, and not a second later.

As I once again exited Delano's cottage, I was witness to what I initially believed to be a harbinger of things to come, as it appeared that some great un-imagining was taking place, as a white shroud of mist was descending upon the land, as if on cue, slowly infusing the defoliated claws of its reaching forests, then consuming below the austere swatches and the pallid hills that lumbered miserably into a forlorn future, as if whatever universal mind was imagining these lurid realms was now gently waking from this nightmare, and the clichéd mist that surrounded the edges of those nocturnal realms now slowly imploding. Then everything evaporated into frosty whiteness.

I looked back toward the cottage and was not sufficiently convinced that its disappearance was just a temporary one.

Upon my agreed return, Delano welcomed me back with an invigoration and ambitious jubilance that was non-existent in his demeanor two weeks earlier. He made promises of the great things he and I would accomplish, and the shine we would eventually restore upon the province's dulled and pitted surface.

Then he finally asked: "Did you bring the payment I asked?"

I reached into the breast pocket of my shirt and handed him the tiny leather suspenders. "I had a hunch," I said. "The seamstress came highly recommended, and I believe she made accurate the scaled-down dimensions I gave her. If the fit is improper, I can always–"

"Nonsense!" he said. "Now, heft me and my permanent residence up, and let's be off to bring back wonderful and miraculous things."

It has now been three years since Delano's reformation, and he remains committed to the explanation that his desire to continue his existence as a jack was to simply carry on the tradition he and his beloved brother William had started and tweak it. But there was nothing simple about that explanation; not when you knew the tragedies that befell every one of your thirteen predecessors.

But then, those other jacks had not been *self*-engineered. At least that's what he reminds me every time I inquire about his ever-lengthening bouts of melancholy.

And the machine that Delano just recently invented – the one he guarantees will produce, once and for all, irrefutable proof of the soul's existence – requires only one volunteer to step inside its confines and sacrifice his or her life. The only drawback, he openly and truthfully admits, is that the extraction may be of a lengthy and most excruciating kind.

Thus far, we've had no volunteers. But just as is his invention, the concept is a new one, and may take some time for the collective to absorb.

I just hope we find someone soon, as the daily resignation that flitters across Delano's eyes grows longer each time. And it scares me, as we have become such great, great friends.

Delano

End

The Dying Book

By N. V. Haskell

The babe's high-pitched screams ensured that no one slept, and I had given up any hope that the wagon's rocking would soothe her. After three solid hours of wailing discontentedness, it was clear that she would not be settled. Not by me at least. I was becoming convinced that she hated me, and her hate would be justified.

I took her cries personally despite knowing how irrational that was. There was no way she could have known or understood the events of the evening that led us here. Still, it was rare for me to encounter a problem that could not be overcome, and I huddled in the wagon holding the angry babe, refusing to meet the eyes of the other passengers. Tears of frustration brimmed my eyes. It was unfortunate that magic couldn't be worked on children.

The older woman across from us pursed her lips and edged closer, offering to take her. Without hesitation, I thrust the ruddy-faced child at her. The woman sang a song like memory, soft and gentle, and soothing all around. The babe fussed a few moments more, her face still squalling-red, but slowly she quieted and stared up at the singer. There was a collective sigh amongst the group, dirty glares vanished behind heavy eyelids as the wagon rolled on.

"What's her name?" The woman asked.

"Oerina," I said. A lie, but to tell the girl's real name would only invite death to all who heard. The girl did not know her name anyway or, if she did, she should best forget it soon enough.

The old woman smiled warmly as the girl reached one clumsy hand toward her face. I half wondered if I could hire the old woman for the remainder of our journey since she had a magic I could not replicate, and it would be worth all the money I had to keep the girl placated.

"Is she your first?" She asked between hums.

I nodded, spinning lies with truth. "I never even held a babe before this one."

She smiled. "Hm. Where's her mum?"

"Gone, I'm afraid." There was no need to elaborate, people always filled in their own stories.

The woman nodded, understanding. "I guess she's about ten months. A year, maybe?"

"You have an eye, madam. She'll be one turn next month." I studied her. "Do you have many children?"

Her gentle smile did not change, but her eyes dulled enough to let me know the rest.

"Aye. I had five. Though the gov took three of 'em before their thirteenth birthdays. They left me two to grow." She sighed. "Suppose I should be thankful they left me them."

I was quiet. They had also taken me during one of the collection times. I was sold from one noble house to the next until Master Ripiel recognized some small magic in me. I counted my stars lucky for that fateful intervention, his claiming of me saved my life. It had taken the slaughter of four noble houses during an uprising for child slavery to fall out of favor. But the king had never made it illegal, and now he never would. The old ways died hard.

I cleared my throat. "I haven't seen my parents since before my fourth birthday. Don't even know which region I hale from."

She shifted the babe to one arm and patted my knee. "But look how well you've turned out. With one of your own, and both of you looking so fine."

I swallowed uncomfortably while looking at the girl in her bejeweled slippers and satin gown. The garb would have been ridiculous even for a minor noble but especially on this wagon where any noble would not dare show face. Master Ripiel used to say that managing details whilst under stress was one of my biggest failings, and I had been under a considerable stress when I had taken the girl.

The woman coddled the babe for the rest of the night, even seeming to enjoy it. She cleaned her bottom and fed her a bit of the food from my bag and by the time the sun painted the sky in blues and oranges, the girl was deep asleep.

The roosters announced the morn as we drove into an old village where the structures leaned uniformly away from the mountains in the distance. The woman showed me a way to swath the baby around my chest and over one shoulder so I could bundle her whilst having use of both arms. Her eyes narrowed as she tsked at my ineptness.

"You need the help of an experienced person, son," she stated flatly. "For your sake and hers."

"I am heading to my sister's house just west of the border." I said, "She has agreed to take us in until we can make other arrangements."

"I thought you were collected. How is it you know your sister?" Suspicion ebbed behind her eyes.

"Sister from one of my former houses, not sister by blood, ma'am." I said too quickly.

"You're travelling very light, aren't you?" She asked.

The other travelers had already grabbed their bags as they departed the wagon, leaving it empty. I wore only a large satchel that held a book, parchment, some fair amount of coin, and some food scraps.

I coughed, hoping for her sake that she would let it go. "It's a fresh start, ma'am."

"Left in a hurry too, didn't you?" She asked.

I shifted from foot to foot as my jaw tightened. She was turning out to be more observant than was beneficial. I hated imparting folks when their names were not written in the book. The effects of death, even singular, always rippled toward more than intended. And this woman had already done us a great service.

Noticing the tension in my posture, she patted my arm. "It's all right, love. I won't tell anyone about you. But I suggest you both dress lower, just in case one of them irritated passengers noticed." She motioned toward a small storefront where gowns and frock coats were suspended in the single window. "Selia won't open until she's got the cows fed, maybe a couple more hours, but when she gets here, buy the plainest stuff you can. Get some better walking boots, too."

She motioned toward a tavern that leaned heavily to one side. "You can get decent food there and," she pointed toward a livery, "find further transportation there." She sniffed as her eyes grazed the length of me. "They sell horses, but don't let old Han's son swindle you. He has no fondness for strangers."

She stared another minute, chewing her words in her mouth before spitting them out. "As much as you might want to, renting a carriage will draw too much attention. And wagons going further west than here only come through once every two weeks. I'm sure that you are in a hurry to be off?"

I nodded, silently considering multiple ways to deal with this woman while listening to her talk and making a mental checklist. I couldn't afford the fatigue that would follow the heavier spells and wondered if we made too much of an impression to wipe the memory of us away.

She leaned closer and whispered conspiratorially, "The gov didn't leave me my last two children, I took them and ran. I once wore the same look that I see in your eyes." Her wrinkles deepened with empathy. "It took me a long time to lose it."

I breathed relief and reconsidered my options. "Thank you, ma'am. I don't know how to repay your kindness."

She shook her head. "Nothing to repay, lad. Someday you can help someone else when they need it."

My gaze slid down to the sleeping girl bundled against my chest.

"Best of luck to you both," the woman said and turned to leave.

My hand snaked out and lightly clasped her shoulder, holding her in place. I whispered only a few words in her ear before I let go and stepped back. When she turned around with wide, confused eyes, we were lost to her. Her gaze swept through the area twice before she shook her head and turned away, shuffling down the street. Even if they tracked us this far, I hoped the old woman wouldn't remember much about us. It was better this way.

My desperate belly overruled any fear of dysentery as we ate a hearty breakfast at the leaning inn. The girl fussed upon waking but took a few bites of the soft oats they served. I didn't know what babies ate so decided to stick with the simpler fare to avoid accidentally killing her. We traded our fine clothing for drab, homespun clothes in the small shop. In exchange for the satin shoes, Selia gave us a simple blanket and a large amount of cloth diapers. The babe had experienced nothing less than the finest fabrics against her privileged buttocks but when I changed her, she did not fuss at the lesser garments.

Han's son attempted to swindle me when I purchased a bay gelding, but he didn't know that my kind cannot be swindled. In the end, he gave us the horse, saddle, saddlebags, blanket, bridle, and feed for a third of what they were worth. I thought of making him give it to us for free, but that would evoke too strong a memory to cover, and every spell took more energy than I could afford.

Each interaction drained me a bit, having to alter each memory was always tiring. They would remember an overweight man travelling alone, the outline of the swathed baby aided in contributing to the image, and it would be difficult for them to recall anything else if they were questioned. By mid-morning we were riding west with the bright sun upon our backs and the map in my hand.

Chaos would be descending upon the country, the likes of which couldn't be remembered, and I held the only heir to the throne against my chest.

The bodies would have been discovered by now. Three fresh names collected for the book in my bag, never mind the casualties of association--bringing my total to thirty-four. Three names a month had been Master Ripeil's price for living in luxury. He was one of the few people who had managed to maintain full possession of his powers without much oversight. Most folks found to have a bit of magic were used for entertainment, their lives ending when their magic ran out.

Three names a month hadn't seemed like much when I agreed to follow in Ripeil's footsteps. But as my score met double digits, I felt the weight of it upon my soul.

Ripiel had warned me that our magic was finite. It came with an unknown expiration and would cease working without warning. There was a day when we would be as powerless as everyone else, he said. But while I had it, I should use it to make a better life. Without hesitation, I added my name in service to the book and had been completing contracts ever since.

When a familiar name appeared in Master Ripeil's book he sighed heavily and shook his head. "This is why you should avoid making friends in high places. We are not allowed to put emotional investments before business. Remember that."

We planned everything out, as we usually did, and drove the carriage near to the man's manor, hiding deep in the woods to avoid notice. Assessing the rhythms and routines of visitors and servants, we tried to determine when our target would be alone. Unfortunately, he was a popular man prone to regular evening feasts and had at least one mistress, a common woman who sold goods to the manor. His wife was informed every time that lady stepped onto the premises. But the way he leered at the servants made me think that his interests were varied.

Ripiel clucked his tongue and sighed. "This fool married too far above his station. His wife is one of the queen's elder sisters and probably our contractor." He peered at me with arched eyebrows. "It would be a simple thing to have the queen add his name to the book. Honestly, with the lecherous behavior we've witnessed over these last few days, who could blame her?"

The following evening, we waited until the stars were clear before creeping into the house. Conveniently, the lady of the house had gone to visit her sister that morning, providing us with a rare opportunity. The manor had few guards, the lord believing that his popularity worked better than armed protections. I sent two of the guards into a deep slumber while Ripiel handled the others in a grislier way.

The candles still cast soft shadows when we entered the lord's antechamber. We froze upon hearing the distinct rhythmic grind of bed frame and floor as a low groan issued from the bedroom. Ripiel shook his head and motioned me into a shadowy corner until our intended target was alone. After half an hour, we finally heard a soft snore.

The floor creaked as tip-toeing steps moved toward the door. A thin girl, too young and too pale, opened the door just enough to ease herself through. She wore only a thin shift and carried the rest of her clothes bundled in her arms. She hurried out the chamber doors without noticing the forms in the shadows.

Ripiel entered the bedroom alone, as he had done a hundred times before. I had offered to do it myself, to spare him the murder of his former friend, but he had insisted.

It never took long. Just a hand placement and a couple of words. Once it is completed, you run before anyone discovers you. But after five minutes without the stir of magic, I knew Ripiel was spent.

An angry voice rose in the air, followed by a desperate whisper and a sickening, soft sound of metal entering flesh.

Master Ripeil's voice ordered me to run but I stayed and waited. Both our lives were forfeit if we failed to fulfil the contract. I slid deeper into the shadows as a large, naked man barreled through the doors. Ripiel was crumpled on the floor behind him, a pool of darkness spread from his chest as he moaned and writhed. But I could not help him.

The lord turned around, clutching a dagger in front of him. His belly jiggled low over his manhood as he spun and stepped with surprising agility.

"Where are you?" He hissed. "I know you're in here." He shuffled the dagger to his other hand nervously as he studied the room. With one hand he tore the curtains from the windows. Then he wildly thrust the blade beneath his desk, stabbing at nothing while simultaneously spilling a pitcher of water onto the floor.

Sipping in a slow breath of whispers I encouraged the water to spread across the floor and into his wandering path. His panic prevented him from noticing when the water morphed to oil and coated the boards with slickness. One foot slipped from beneath him, sending his large frame crashing. The man's leg bent at an unnatural position, pale bone jutting through ruddy flesh. He howled with a twisted face as blood swirled into the oil and the dagger skittered across the floor toward me.

Stepping into the dim light, I eased closer to him as the lord howled so viciously that spittle flew across the room. He threatened and cursed, thrashing against his pain as he attempted to reach me. His cheeks were ruddy and blotched, and he watched with bulging eyes as I placed my toe upon the dagger and slid it back to him. It was too dangerous to get close to him.

As his fingers tightened on the dagger, he jabbed at me, but I was safely out of reach. I raised a hand and mimicked holding the dagger speaking a few words so that his arm followed my movement. Slowly, I drew my hand across my throat while the dagger in his hand did the same. Blood spilled onto the floor; his voice trapped beneath gurgles as his eyes widened in disbelief.

I waited until he'd ceased twitching before retrieving Ripeil's body. It had only taken a short dagger between his ribs to end him. Gently closing his eyes, I bent to lift the elder man but a soft cry from the antechamber stopped me.

The girl stood in shock inside the doorway. Having hastily donned the rest of her clothing, she carried a tray of biscuits and wine that threatened to topple from her trembling arms. She tried to scream, but the sound did not escape her lips. I felt the weight in my stomach then, the sigh of my soul, as I considered my options.

Usually, Ripiel would have handled these unfortunate events but now it was left to me. Memories could only be altered around seemingly unimportant things, but it was exceedingly difficult to erase trauma, and what she witnessed was traumatic. With a word, I caught the cry in her mouth and froze her where she stood, the tray stilled.

"I am so sorry, dear girl."

I brought Ripeil's body home with me. Although a barrel of coin awaited me, the payment seemed a pittance compared to what I'd lost. I buried him between those two old sycamores he always favored, not too near the river. I mourned him deeply for as long as I dared, until another name appeared in the receiving book. Followed a week later by another. There were always contracts to be completed, and that is how I became King Frenhk's weapon.

I'd been fulfilling the book's obligations for close to a year, with none the wiser that I now acted as my Master. All was happening just the way Ripiel had prepared me for. When the names appeared in the book, I had four weeks to complete the tasks. After receiving the names, I studied the intended, created a plan, and executed them as quickly as I could. There was always plenty of coin waiting for me when I returned. Enough to pay for servants, wine, and sex.

Things were good until the wrong name appeared on those pages, followed in quick succession by two more wrong names. I was at a loss. The drying ink smeared on the pages of the dying book somewhere within the king's chambers before transferring its command onto my receiving book a county away. I stared at the script for a long while before putting it down and walking away, hoping that it would change. But the names remained fixed in messy black ink. Someone had stood before the dying book and written the names of the royal family, with one exception.

King Frenhk was hated for more than his consigning of children. He had a vicious temperament and had doled out quick punishments and unreasonable taxes for over forty years. Everyone waited for him to die, though those words were only whispered over a few pints in trusted company and isolated conversations. There was much doubt that his son, Alver, would prove any better a ruler. I had it from a reliable source that

Alver's mother had died after the king had tired of her and written her name in the book.

The new queen was thirty years the king's junior and a quiet woman who avoided politics. They had a baby girl who was nearing her first turn.

I stared at the book for days not knowing who could have accessed the book. The thought that I was being drawn into a coup, or that the book had fallen into the hands of a disgruntled servant made me equally uneasy. But the real issue that plagued me was not the killing of a tyrant and his family, it was trying to design how I was going to murder one--let alone three--members of the well-guarded royal family.

I did not know if the names were visible in the dying book until the contract was fulfilled, or if they vanished as soon as they transferred to my book, the receiving one. If they remained visible, then the king would know to expect me and the odds of completing this task were negligible.

According to my contract, I had four weeks to complete the assignments, and each day following that expiration extracted a price. At least that is what Ripiel had said, and I had no desire to discover what that price was. Using all Ripeil's old journals and texts as guides, I formed a desperate and foolish plan. If I failed in any of the three contracts, it was likely that I would die either way.

It took a week to secure a room in the village outside the castle walls. I dedicated the next week to studying the prince who, in all his arrogance and privilege, was easy to track. His day-to-day routine was predictably filled with hunting, fucking, and thwarting the efforts of anyone who tried to reign him in. He was better suited to studying sex and food, than commerce and politics. It was useful that our preferences aligned.

On certain nights the young prince would sneak into the village searching for new exploits of either sex. It took three nights of lingering in his favorite pub for him to notice me. I flirted just enough to get his attention and disappeared before he could reach me. Offering the spoiled boy a toy before removing the offer only served to increase the value. It was an enjoyable dance and if he had been some minor noble, I might have made good on my offer. We were near the same age and the mutual attraction between us almost gave me pause.

While that dance continued in the evenings, I spent my days in stolen servants' clothes and slipped into the castle. The guards' memories were easy to obscure and by the average amount of them, I concluded the king was unaware that his name had been listed for execution. I studied Frenhk from a safe distance. The man was large and solidly built with a perpetual scowl etched on his features, but he proved to be just as predictable as his son in his interests.

The queen's movements hardly fluctuated from one day to the next as she was routinely encumbered with the babe and nanny. By all observation, she was a doting mother. Every day she ate lunch with other noble ladies then took long walks in the maze-like gardens. She sat at her desk, wrote letters, and retired early each evening though often the lanterns in her chambers stayed lit until early in the morning. One of the greatest challenges would be that the nursery was adjacent to her own, and it was difficult to determine when the nanny was there or gone.

A simple poisoning would have been nice, do the lot of them and be done with it. But everyone knew the most dangerous job in the country was that of the king's taster and since the royal family were rarely in the same room together, they would have to be dealt with individually. The timing would be tricky since it would all have to be done in one night and I would have to be far away by the time the alarms were raised in the morning.

Three weeks after the royal names first appeared in the book, I was sitting in the pub, eyeing every lad who entered. Alver slipped through the doors wearing an elaborately beaded frock coat, which I assumed was the dullest thing he owned. In this environment, so close to the castle, seeing a young lord or lady trying to blend in and have some fun with the regulars was not unusual. It wasn't long before his gaze discovered me, the toy who had taken itself away, and sauntered over. He leaned against my table and made awkward small talk for which he had a lack of talent. But I suppose one didn't need too much skill at flirting when one had money and title. With his dark curls and wickedly boyish grin, he was appealing. I simpered to him and gave a bit of sauce back, which only furthered his advances.

He pressed to escape together to my rooms, but I just shook my head and told him that my bride was sleeping there. He raised his eyebrows, and I continued my lie, "We didn't have much choice in the arrangement, believe me."

"I have a similar fate awaiting me," Alver said before hinting at other places we could go. I claimed that there were too much family around and could not risk being seen.

"I suppose that it wasn't meant to be," I said, dropping a hint of longing as I cupped his cheek in my hand.

His eyes brightened with a look I'd seen him give right before he was going to do something troublesome. He smiled.

"How about an adventure?" He asked. "I know a secret way into the castle."

I chuckled as I tenderly tucked a dark curl behind his ear. "What if they catch us? The guards would kill us right away."

He flashed a broad grin. "Trust me."

We stumbled into the night; my arm wrapped around him for more than balance. He led me down a small footpath that wound through groves and brush toward the castle's back wall where the gardens were rimmed with thick, thorny hedges that were grown intentionally too dense to allow much in. However, there was just enough space between two offset hedges to squeeze through. Gripping my hand, he tugged me through, ducking down when the guards passed. Alver pulled me in for a swift kiss beneath the dark sky before we darted across the gardens and up a narrow staircase.

Rushing down winding halls and hiding in corners until more guards passed, we eventually entered his quarters through an unguarded small door. My unguarded awe at the ridiculous splendor on display in the prince's rooms was genuine. Rubies and emeralds glittered from the tapestries that adorned the walls, scattering fractals of light across the carpet as the lantern sconces flickered.

"Whose rooms are these?" I feigned caution and nervousness until he kissed my palm and insisted there was nothing to fear.

His kisses were filled with longing and desperation. When our lips parted there was a deep loneliness in his eyes, that weakened my knees. It was best to be quick before I lost my resolve.

When Alver retrieved a jug and began to pour wine into two cups, I placed a hand on his wrist to stop him. Pulling him in for another kiss and stoking the fire between us, I took the wine from him and finished the pour. He did not notice the extra moment that my hand lingered over his cup while I plied him with questions and fawned over his taste.

I toasted to his health. It was cruel, I know.

When he tried to kiss me, I led him into the bedroom and made him recline. He was a handsome boy, and he might not have made a terrible king, but it was not his fate to ever find out. I smiled sadly as a sudden cough startled him. He made to rise, but I pushed him back onto the plush blankets. Confusion flashed across his face as he struggled, but I whispered words that cemented him to the bed. He would not be able to cough up the poison that was already swimming through his blood.

I curled a lock of his hair between my fingers. "I've tried to make this easy on you."

His eyes widened as denial shifted to understanding.

"I am truly sorry, you don't seem like a bad sort. But once your name is in the book…" I sighed and kissed his brow. "If we were not who we are, we would have had a lovely time."

Death was swift, thankfully, and I hadn't used enough magic to tire me. Locking the small door that we'd entered through, I slipped down the quiet halls and headed toward the next name on the list.

The king's chambers sat in the highest corner of the castle and were well guarded, until I arrived. Those poor souls were left slumbering against each other. Come morning they would be labeled conspirators and executed without trial. I tried not to think of their families or the wide rippling waves of my actions.

Opening the door a fraction, I slid inside. Frenhk's rooms were surprisingly musty and more practically decorated than his son's had been. The king lay alone in his bed, a large form even from two rooms away. His tossing and grunting diminished any sound that might have reached him as I wriggled into a corner and waited for him to settle. But sleep would not take him.

Frenhk grunted and rose, dragging a robe around his shoulders. Muttering as he walked, he headed to a smaller door I had initially overlooked behind his desk. He stopped briefly to strike a match and light a lantern. His shoulders brushed the doorway as he disappeared through it, then returned a moment later carrying a familiar book. He placed it on a large desk and stood with his back to me, flipping through the pages and spitting curses.

What lay before the king was a forgery of the Dying book. It's mate, the Receiving book was well hidden beneath the flooring of Ripeil's quarters. The books were identical including the small, star shaped emblem at the top outer corner of each odd page. One could only see the star if they had a bit of magic in them. The book Frenhk stood over did not have that emblem. It was a gross oversight by the forger who didn't know of it. As I peered around him, I could see the names most recently written on the page, though they were not the names I had received.

I whispered, sealing him as tightly as the words would let me. There was no point in risking him bashing my head in with his fists. With a quick hiss, his lips fastened shut, his hands rooted to the desk, while the skin of his bare feet merged to the floor in fleshy tendrils.

"You lost it." I said lowly while moving to the other side of the desk. I pulled the book toward me and rifled through the pages of familiar names. Thousands of names littered across the pages, spanning decades and predating Frenhk's reign. The forger had done a good job after all.

Frenhk's face grew mottled and ruddy as he struggled to speak and move. But his words were muffled by the seal of his lips. His straining slid the desk a few inches, serving as a reminder that he was fully capable of snapping me like a twig if he'd been able to move.

Killing a king is an odd opportunity, it gives one pause to consider how that legacy will be written. What should I say to the man who tore apart families and condemned children to a lifetime of slavery?

I wanted to say, "I was a child stolen and sold. Lucky enough to be picked out by a broken man with bloody hands and a guilty conscience who trained me to follow in his footsteps. Unlike the other children who were worked to death, raped, or murdered. You thought nothing of using them and discarding them." But instead, I did not speak. He deserved no explanation even though I wanted to tell him that this job was personal, that I was glad to be the one to destroy him.

We stared at each other, while a vein bulged down the side of his temple.

I sighed. "I just want you to know that this situation-- me in your rooms about to kill you--is an exact result of your own actions."

I closed the book and pushed it closer to him.

"I received three names in my book a month ago. Alver was the first. Your name, of course. And the queen's name." I said, leaning slightly closer to him. "I was surprised, but not displeased, to see your name written there. Though I wonder who is to thank for allowing me to provide a much-needed service to my country." I sighed, wondering why I was rambling and delaying. Perhaps I was enjoying it too much. But wasted time would only get me killed. "I am not sorry for what I am about to do."

His eyes bulged as my magic settled on his skin. His mouth sealed completely as his nostrils pinched tightly together, stealing his breath. He attempted to flail in his panic, moving enough to slide the heavy desk forward but still unable to move his feet or remove his hands from the desk. His skin ripped with his force scattering drops of blood across the wood. His bones cracked beneath his force as he squealed. Brown eyes bulged out as his face morphed to purple, then blue.

I counted the minutes that it took and, even though I tried not to enjoy my work, I found that I did not entirely hate it in that moment. As death took him, I released his feet and hands, his large form falling over his desk, on top of his false book. His muscles jerked as his bowels and bladder released.

The fatigue hit me like a punch to the stomach. I doubled over, grasping my dizzying head and attempting to fortify my will. There was only one name left.

Nausea unsettled me as I stood outside Queen Jormal's doors, not wanting to enter. The guards were curiously absent, and I toyed with the idea of leaving. If left alive, she would be queen regent, her daughter someday to be queen. She might even be a good queen, she had a grace and a kindness to her. If I killed Jormal, it would leave the princess alone in the world with only a nefarious aunt and too many advisors to raise her. A lamb alone in a house run by wolves. I would do to her what they had been done to me. I thought a hundred different ways but, in the end, the contract must be completed. It was the promise I made when I entered my name in the book. It was the queen's life or my own.

I entered the room slowly to find the queen sitting in a window seat, staring out into the dark gardens. Long dark hair cascaded around her shoulders. She did not turn when I entered.

"Is it done?" She asked quietly.

I froze before the closed door.

She turned to look at me and her youth startled me. She was younger than was rumored, closer to my age, maybe younger, closer to Alver's age. Tears stained her cheeks.

"Are they dead?" She asked, her tone elevating.

I nodded.

She looked down. "Only one name left. I hoped you might save me for last. Given the placement of the rooms and the easy exit from here. It is what I would have done, had I been fortunate enough to be in your position."

I licked my lips, the urge to leave sliding over me again. "May I ask you a question?"

"You want to know why." She said and grew still and silent for a long minute before continuing. "I heard him talking about my daughter, our daughter, and what bargaining he could use her for when she was older. He spoke of how much money he could make from her. Of which country would be best to secure her to for his own interests. He did not even pretend it was for the good of the country or our people. Just wanted to use her for his own gains." She sighed. "She's not a year old yet and he joked about making her a child bride if he had to, and his advisors laughed with him."

She stood and poured herself a glass of wine, the liquid danced through the glass.

"I never wanted to be queen." She glanced up. "Not if it meant being married to that horror parading as a man. I have a friend, a servant who was bought by my house from this one when she was but ten years old. She has been my companion and...

more." She took another sip and gazed out the window. "She spoke of the things that happened here, about what the king had done to her and other children. I began to wonder what would happen to Rosalee if something were to happen to me?

"How far should a mother go to protect her child?" She dared me to answer, her eyes flashing. "He bragged about the book on our wedding night, a veiled threat if I should displease him. I know what happened to Alver's mother. It took some time and a lot of help, but we made a good replica of the book. Did we miss anything?"

My mouth was dry as I whispered, "The star." I stepped closer but she did not retreat. "Why your name? Why the prince's name?"

Her expression hardened briefly. "I saw enough of Alver to see his father in him. His arrogance and refusal to be corrected, even when he knew he was in the wrong. Once, when he was drunk, he told me that once Frenhk died no one would ever hear from us again. It was the sincerest he had ever been with me."

"But why put your own name in the book?"

She pursed her lips. "Before I answer that I need you to make me a promise."

"What is it?" I asked.

"I need you to take Rosalee across the western border. I have a cousin, Oerina, who will take her and raise her in hiding. She will be safe there, which is all I want for her, to be safe and loved. I have a map to guide you." She retrieved a rolled piece of parchment and a large book from an armoire. "In exchange for your agreement, I offer you the Dying book." She placed it on the table, the roll of parchment with it. "Perhaps, you might find a bit of freedom for yourself."

The book's magic pulled at me.

"If Rosalee stays here, she will never be safe. If I leave with her, we will be hunted, and they will kill me, leaving her vulnerable. If we stay, there will be rumors of a conspiracy to murder the king and they will execute me, leaving my child to be raised at the mercy of those who only seek to use her." She sighed, tapped the book with her fingers. "It is the best way to protect her."

The nanny lingered in the doorway of the nursery. She was older than Jormal, her clothing plain and demure. She held a squirming bundle in her arms, one hand reaching out as the babe struggled to see beyond the confines of the blanket.

I looked back to the queen. "There can be no witnesses."

"I know what needs to happen." The woman said with a clipped tone. "They'll kill me for surviving no matter where I go or what I say."

I sighed, knowing the truth of her words before returning to the queen. "I know nothing of children. Why me? There must be someone else you could trust with this?"

She smiled sadly. "You and Ripiel have been true to your word in the past. If you give it, then I might hope that my daughter may grow to a healthy age and, someday, become a benevolent queen. There is no one else I can trust, and no one more capable to complete this task than you."

I debated telling her that our words were bound only to the book. I had no obligation to the child or her wellbeing. But the weight on my soul grew heavier as I watched the women and the squirming babe.

"I will take her." I held one hand to my chest. "I swear that I will do all that I can to deliver her safely."

Tears brimmed the queen's eyes, pride holding them in her lashes before she gave a curt nod. "Thank you."

Jormal carried the girl into the nursery. The two women stood over the crib, their fingers intertwined, while speaking words of love. She sang a soft song over her daughter and while the women leaned against each other, I stood witness to what no one else had been allowed to see.

When they said their goodbyes and closed the nursery door softly behind them, I asked them to lie upon the bed. They held each other and, for all their controlled manners, I could taste fear in the air.

"I hope to make this as painless as possible." My eyes burned, my voice breaking upon the words. "May death be kinder to you than this life has been."

I steadied myself with a deep breath and said the words that dropped them to sleep, slowing their heartbeats and breath in increments. I watched them still before placing my hands on their foreheads. I whispered a small blessing and paused, stumbling for a moment as the words turned to ash in my mouth. While my whisper still clung to the air, they were gone, and I was left to wipe wetness from my cheeks.

Time was pressing down as I swept into the nursery and filled a simple leather bag with the book, the map, two spare cloths, a large bag of coins that had been left out, and a few biscuits that remained on the queen's tray. I picked up the girl as gently as I could. She was heavier than she looked.

I slipped down those back stairs that Alver had introduced me to and rushed back to the village. If the girl cried, they would catch me since I would be unable to silence her. It was against the rules of magic to work a spell on children under twelve. Teenagers, as everyone knows, have their own rules.

There was a wagon passing through the village heading west. The driver agreed to let us on if I paid double, which I did.

It is likely someone will realize the true Dying book is missing. It is also likely that the Receiving book will be discovered at Ripeil's house, which is useless if no one writes in its sister book. The queen was right--so long as I held the book, I had my freedom.

Following the queen's map, Rosalee and I rode past the western border on a bay gelding, stopping only to eat and rest. I accomplished the heinous task of diaper changing and managed it better than I thought I could. The girl became a good traveler, as the simple magic of the swaying trees and flitting birds fascinated her. Her laugh was infectious.

I do not know what will happen once we reach Oerina's estate, but perhaps she will consider keeping a former stolen child with a few spells left, to watch over the girl.

The Hunter and the Cave

By Wayland Smith

Donabal gripped the cold, rough stone so tightly his fingers turned white and threatened to bleed. He was here. After all the risks, the chaos, the endless tracking down of rumors that were always "My friend at the tavern said…" or "My cousin saw…" This was it. The cold wind gusted again, and he shivered. It was the cold, of course. A mighty warrior engaged in a great quest didn't allow himself the luxury of fear. Or so he kept telling himself.

Carefully, he climbed over the lip of the cave. The opening was enormous. It would have to be, really, if he was in the right place, but it was still impressively large, the roof far out of his reach above. Carefully, he checked his weapons one more time. His sword was in its sheath, loose enough to draw, but not about to tumble out at the worst possible moment. Donabal moved his shield to his arm, from where it had rested on his back for the final climb. It was heavy, the metal rim and center boss holding the wooden shape together. The iron-wood, from rare trees far to the north, was reportedly proof against almost any kind of attack after it set in place. The painted symbols pulsed faintly with their own light, wards against magic, against fire, against beguilement and glamour. Or that's what he'd paid for, at least. Donabal never quite trusted magicians, and reflected grimly that if they failed, he wasn't going to be able to go ask for his gold back.

In his hands rested the great spear, a work of fine metalsmithing and wood-crafting. It was lighter than it should have been for its size, almost as long as he was tall. A lock of fine blonde hair moved in the wind, woven into a specially worked notch just below the head of the spear. Some said a maiden's hair, freely given and blessed by her, gave the weapon added potency. It wasn't likely to hurt, that much was certain, and Healla had wished him success with a kiss that was chaste yet promised more if he returned. He pushed the thought of her aside. This was no time for daydreams, no matter how pleasant.

A long knife hung at his belt, but if it came down to that, he was as good as dead anyway. His bow and quiver were on Faser's saddle, down below. They'd helped him stay fed on the way here but wouldn't be of any use for what was to come. He'd eaten the last of his fresh meat and drunk deeply from the waterskin before climbing to the cave. There was time enough to worry about food and drink afterward, if there was to be an afterward.

Donabal knelt and offered up one last prayer. "I do not ask for glory, or for reward. Let me prevail against this dread beast to protect those it preys on, and end this threat." His hand made the gestures for the Invocation of Protection, asking aid from Kensai, the Warrior Above. Standing, he gripped his spear tightly and moved in, his chain mail and weapons belt making their usual slight rattle and squeaks, which suddenly sounded so much louder than ever before.

The sunlight, not that it had been particularly warming, faded behind him as he advanced, and he shivered again. Curiously, the cavern grew no darker. Another sign, according to lore, that he was in the right place. He nodded grimly. All the signs and portents seemed to say he was on track. Donabal followed the slope down, noting the rock walls were not showing any signs of moving in closer. How big was this cavern? How big did it need to be for what lay within?

Something lay ahead on the floor. He approached cautiously, spear at the ready. Finally reaching the heap, his eyes and brain struggled for a moment to make sense of what he was seeing. It was the skeleton of what had to be the largest cave bear he'd ever seen. Some of the massive ribs and two claws had broken off. They lay on the stone floor. Without really thinking about it, Donabal dropped to one knee and picked them up. He ran the ball of his thumb over the wicked curve, marveling at the keenness of the edge. He dropped the claws into a pouch on his belt. They might be useful at some point.

Standing, he surveyed the skeleton once more. It had been an enormous beast. And it was now a pile of bones. Was he truly going to move forward towards what had done this? He took in a deep breath and let it back out.

He was.

He had to. He had sworn a vow, received the blessings. It had to be done. His honor was at stake, his reputation as a warrior, a defender of the helpless. Not to mention a sizable reward.

Walking forward, he glanced around. The light was less than a sunny day, but more than a moonlit night. Where it came from, he wasn't sure. The rocks themselves didn't seem to glow, but there was no other source he could see. "Magic," he spat the word dismissively, with years of frustration behind it. He'd pit his blade against any other man's, or woman's, and had.

But magic… it wasn't right.

It was cheating, upsetting the natural order. Realizing he was letting his mind drift, he refocused his thoughts on what lay ahead.

The dead cave bear behind, he carefully moved deeper into the cave. He walked past rock and stone, slight gouges in the floor or walls, but nothing to really capture his attention. It was becoming monotonous, a strange mix of almost boredom warring with growing tension. How deep was this gods-forsaken cave?

When the attack came, it almost caught him by surprise despite his wariness. He barely heard the rasp of claws on stone, the hiss of breath. Donabal brought up his shield, putting the warded barrier between his flesh and gleaming, ripping claws. The warrior grunted at the force of the attack and braced his legs. He was pushed back across the cavern floor, mailed boots screeching and throwing off sparks. He jabbed desperately with his spear, but the damned creature was too close.

With a muttered curse, Donabal dropped the spear, hearing the impact on the floor echo through the cavern. It was too close for him to draw his sword. The knife… shaking fingers wrapped around the hilt and pulled the shorter blade as claws raked across his shield, one paw sliding past to let it slice at his arm. The mail held, for now, although Donabal winced at the pressure. The fetid odor of rotting meat and something else puffed at his face and he nearly gagged.

Trying to focus past the stench and the fear, he shifted his stance and drove the blade into the creature. It snarled, and he stabbed again and again. Finally, sinking the weapon in deep enough, he dragged it upward. The creature's hissing and bellowing became a fading snarl as dark blue ichor ran from its wounds. It snapped at his face again, and Donabal pulled his head back as best he could, again choking on the smell. Finally, it fell, and he nearly lost his grip on the knife.

He let the creature hit the floor and then pulled his blade out of its body. He flicked it to one side and then wiped it as best he could, first on the creature's skin, and then on a scrap of cloth he pulled from another belt pouch. While not as bad as its breath, the ichor was far from pleasant smelling. He examined the beast he'd just slain. It was seven feet tall, and very slender, bordering on emaciated. Its scaled skin reflected some of the light, the armored plates a dull orange. Each long, slender finger ended in a barbed talon. "Servitor," he murmured, looking at the reptilian face, the elongated snout, and the serrated teeth. Did its master know it was dead? Was any chance of surprise gone now? Donabal racked his brain for any hint of rumor or story about the connection between a servitor and its master and couldn't remember anything for certain.

"Damn," he muttered, finally stretching up to his full height and checking himself carefully. He wasn't wounded, although his arm ached where the claws had scored his armor. He hadn't heard the telltale sound of metal rings falling to the stone, but he examined the arm carefully. Nothing had broken, although he'd be a great deal happier if he could bring it to a blacksmith to be sure. But there wasn't time for such a thing, even if he felt like climbing back down the rock face, mounting up, and riding the three days back to the nearest village that had such an artisan. And even then, he'd be more familiar with horseshoes and plows than armor and blades.

Donabal had no choice but to push on, picking up his spear and following the slope downward, deeper into the mountain. The cave was unnervingly straight, which struck him as unnatural. The warrior wondered if magic played a part in the creation of this place, and his lips curled in disdain at the thought. He walked on, and finally, there was a change in the passage. The slope was flattening out, and something in the faint echo of his footsteps changed. Instinctively, he moved to the wall, crouching lower, shield raised. Edging ahead, he felt the slope change, growing shallower, flattening out as he walked.

He could see the passage widening into something much bigger ahead and slowed even more. Finally, he came to the end of the entryway he'd been in. The cave widened out into something much, much larger, and his mind boggled trying to take in what he was seeing. And what he wasn't seeing.

The chamber in front of him was vast. The strange light, that he still hadn't been able to determine the source of, was augmented by a few floating spheres of glowing pale blue. There was a vast pile of bones off to one side, and, peeking out from among the pale white, the glint of metal. Donabal was fairly certain he could see shields, swords, and other weapons among the litter of skulls and scattered bones. He could hear running water, and dimly saw the suggestion of some kind of spring or stream on the far wall.

In another section was a collection of shapes that it took him a moment to sort out. Not because they were unfamiliar, but because they didn't belong in a remote cave that was lair to a dread beast. In spite of his caution, Donabal took a few steps forward, puzzling as to how a desk, chair, and several bookshelves would come to be in their own niche in the wall, an opening that approximated the size of a study like he'd seen in the homes of rich men and scholars. The furniture showed good workmanship. The chair looked comfortable, the shelves well-made and filled with large tomes of bound leather.

He blinked and shook his head. This was a mystery for another time. There were more important matters at hand. The warrior looked around again, puzzled by the lack… "Where's the hoard?" he wondered aloud. Shouldn't there be a vast pile of gold, jewels, and other valuables in a vast heap?

"Really? Is that what you're looking for? How disappointing." The voice sounded bored and condescending. Donabal whirled, bringing his shield up to protect him as he felt a massive rush of air, a powerful wind where there had been still air a moment ago. Then everything went brilliant orange as a massive blast of flame and incredible, searing heat washed over him.

The magician had been worth every bit of gold he'd charged. The shield pulsed with power and the fire parted around him. The blast went on for what seemed like hours, but it couldn't have been more than a few moments. When it ended, Donabal raised his head, peering past the shield's edge. And saw something few living beings ever had.

The dragon was massive, taking up most of the space in the chamber. It must have used some kind of spell to hide itself from him before, that was the only explanation. He didn't have anything to compare it to. Maybe some of the sailing vessels he'd seen in ports in his travels. The huge beast had scales of a deep red, with more reddish gold along its underside. Immense wings spread wide, thickly muscled legs like marble columns or great trees from the depth of the forest held its weight. Each leg ended in wide feet with toes nearly the size of Donabal's legs, claws like swords tipping each one. Intelligent eyes of a vivid purple rested above a mouth of teeth that were more like spears. Spines or some kind of gigantic plates ran from the back of its head to the tip of the enormous tail. It was beautiful, and deadly, and an amused expression on its face as it said, "Well, that was unexpected." It blinked. "Are you a wizard, then?"

Donabal felt anger flare and words came instead of the attack he should have been attempting. "I'm no magician!" he protested, then added, "and I'm not risking my life for gold," in a quieter voice.

It tapped a massive claw on the cave floor and peered at the warrior dubiously. "I'm not sure I believe you. It was the first thing you said, after all." It appeared to be considering the matter. "I suppose you must have had your weapons enchanted if you're not a spell-caster yourself. Nice work on the shield. I'll have to look at that later."

The casual tone spoke of confidence. Overconfidence, perhaps. The beast's assumption it would have the leisure to look over his gear after the fight filled him with rage and he leapt forward, driving the spear ahead of him, point gleaming in the strange light.

The dragon's wings flared, and it moved backward, sending gusts of wind throughout the cavern. Donabal pressed forward, jabbing again. The spear struck the beast's right front leg. Green sparks flared and rained down to the floor as the metal met scales and the dragon's expression shifted to surprise and, he thought, pain.

Donabal pushed forward, driving the spear against the scales. There was a horrific sound, like metal on metal but much worse, and the beast bellowed, rising up out of the warrior's reach. "Where did you get that?" it asked in wounded curiosity. Two brilliant red drops fell to the floor of the cave, and it shook its leg, flexing the toes experimentally. "That actually hurt. Well done, mortal." It regarded him with a more serious expression. "Oh, I see. Maiden hair. I didn't know anyone remembered that old tale."

"It's enough for you," Donabal roared. He hefted the spear in his hand and considered throwing it. But great spears weren't made for throwing, and the winds the creature could create simply by moving made him reconsider the idea.

"Don't get ahead of yourself, mortal," the creature drawled. "A nick on the leg isn't fatal," it said, its voice growing colder, far less amused.

Donabal wasn't sure what to do now. In all the ways he had envisioned this fight happening, the beast hovering out of range wasn't one of them. Then again, he hadn't thought it would be talking to him, either. How was it that no one had ever told him dragons could talk? His eyes flicked around the cavern again, and he was struck by inspiration. He feinted upward with the spear and then ran. Not for the entrance. There was no point trying to flee, it could definitely fly faster than he could move. Probably faster than Faser could run, if it came to that. The horse was lucky he wasn't here.

Instead, Donabal ran for the strange set of furniture. It must have some value to the beast. There was no reason for it to be here, and no way it was just some random collection of objects. They were placed far too carefully and meaningfully. Donabal sprinted as fast as he could move, wishing he had a torch handy. Instead, he lunged with the spear, aiming for the bookshelf.

"You will NOT," the voice came like thunder, and he felt an incredible impact along his entire right side. Then he was sailing through the air until his flight was halted by the stone wall. Dazed, he shook his head and tried to remember how to make his legs work.

Just in time, he lurched to his feet and rolled to the right as the dragon's left forepaw swiped through the space he'd been in. Claws raked across rock with an ear-splitting screech, and Donabal winced. When the leg was at the end of its arc, he lunged again, driving the spear tip into its paw. The animal gave a gratifying bellow and reared back, shaking its paw. More brilliant blood fell to the floor.

"You are actually growing annoying," the beast said, examining its paw.

Donabal used the moment of its distraction to take stock of himself. Somehow, nothing was broken, but he could tell that, if he lived through this encounter, his right side would be a livid bruise for days. Still, a small price to pay for fighting a dragon in its own lair. Granting that he survived. He wished he'd thought to buy some kind of concealment charm. Would that have let him sneak up on the beast?

He dodged to the left as it regarded him, and then ran to the right as fast and hard as he could. It let out a bellow as he managed to jab the spear into its tail, something like a third of the way along its length. "I've had about enough of you," the creature snarled and reared its head back. Knowing what was coming, Donabal once again put his shield between himself and near-certain death. Once again, the flames parted and splashed all around him, but didn't touch him. This time, however, the shield began to vibrate and grew warm to the touch. For a panicked moment, he thought the wards were failing and then remembered what the magician had told him. Donabal decided using magic was better than dying, and he thrust the shield forward, concentrating on the runes painted on the metal. The shield shook and then a geyser of fire erupted from it, straight back at the dragon. The warrior hoped it hurt the beast but was more immediately grateful when the metal cooled and felt less like it was about to either burst into flame or melt into a puddle of slag at his feet.

When he could see through the firestorm again, he got another surprise. The dragon was reared back on its hind legs, swiping at its snout, looking for all the world like a dog that had gotten too close to a porcupine. It snorted, and made a strange sound (did dragons sneeze? Donabal wondered) and refocused its attention on him. "I'm simply going to have to get the name of the wizard who worked on your shield. That's some truly impressive work."

Donabal rushed forward, spear extended, pressing the slight advantage of the beast's position and distraction. He bore down, concentrating on the tip of the spear and the beast's lower belly, which made the best target. It turned slightly, and there was a whistling noise, and the last thing the warrior saw was a massive tail moving so incredibly swiftly towards him. Then there was impact and pain and darkness.

He woke slowly, groggily. Pain pulsed through his body. Then, when the pain really registered, confusion filled his sluggish brain. Why was he alive? What was happening, that the monster would spare him? He finally managed to get his eyes open and blinked them several times, trying to get the swaying world to stay in focus. He'd had head wounds before and knew the dizziness would pass eventually.

Donabal was shackled to the cavern wall, in one of the niches he hadn't had time to explore. He could see his arms and armor stacked on a small table, just a few feet away, but they might as well be across the ocean for all the good they'd do him now. He was wearing the thin cloth that kept his mail from cutting into his skin when it was struck. The padding was useful beneath armor, but not what he'd chose to wear as an outer, or only, layer. He had an impressive collection of bruises, aches, and a small cut on the side of his face. At least, it felt small. He couldn't actually see it. Mostly uninjured, alive, and captive. He couldn't begin to fathom the creature's motives in not simply finishing him off, or even just eating him.

As his brain began to function again, his forehead creased, which then brought another wave of pain and dizziness, and he hissed at the sensation. He'd been treated with some care, and his weapons hadn't joined the heap of bones and random objects he'd seen before. But how had a creature of that size managed to shackle him? Donabal glanced up at the metal that encircled his wrists. It was far too small for those massive claws and toes he'd seen on the beast. And why had such care been taken for his possessions? The armor looked intact, the weapons undamaged.

He caught sight of some movement beyond the walls of his recess in the rock and struggled to refocus his eyes. Maybe he'd been hit harder in the head than he had realized. Donabal wondered if the dragon was pacing its lair, waiting for him to wake up. There must be some reason he was still alive, after all. Instead, he saw a thin woman, with brown hair that ran in a braid down her back. She wore a long, pale gray tunic, dark hose along her legs, and short boots that ended just above her ankle. The woman had a vial in her hand, and was slowly walking across the floor, head down, apparently examining the cavern. As he watched, she suddenly fell to her knees and moved the vial to the stone. What was she doing? He saw a dim pulse of light, and then the vial pulsed with a brilliant red he'd seen before. She was taking up the dragon's blood? Was she some kind of magician? A servant? He cleared his throat, realizing how thirsty he was, and her head whipped around, although she couldn't possibly have heard him from that distance.

"Oh, you're awake," she said, springing up to her feet. The tunic flowed loosely around her body, but he had a quick glimpse and faint impression of a nice figure. She walked over to him, placed the vial on the table with his equipment, and regarded him. "I was beginning to wonder."

Her voice was pleasant, but something about it was making his head throb more. Maybe it was just the sound? Donabal tried to speak, managed a croak, cleared his throat, and tried again. His tongue felt rough and dry against his mouth. "Do you have any water?"

"Easy enough," she said. She walked away with an energetic step and returned a few moments later with a waterskin. "Open up," she said, bringing the container to his lips. He guzzled gratefully, relief spreading through his body. How long had he been here, that he was that thirsty? "Not too much at once," she said, taking it away. "Don't want you getting sick all over yourself." She wrinkled her nose. "Not that you couldn't use a bath."

Up close, she had a pretty face, with light brown eyes, a nose that tilted up slightly at the end, and a friendly set to her features. "My apologies for… not being as clean as either of us might prefer," he said, his voice working much better now. "I've been in the wilds a while now, and baths are few and far between." He swallowed again, rotating his head on his neck, back and forth, trying to ease the ache and stiffness. "Are you a prisoner here?"

Annoyance moved across her features, mouth thinning to a narrow line. "That's your assumption? You see a woman on her own in a situation you know nothing about and just presume she's being held against her will?" Her voice took on a sharp edge, which did nothing to ease the pain in his head.

"I see a human in a dragon's lair," he answered, leaning his head back. The touch of the cool stone on his head eased the pain slightly.

"Hmmph," she frowned at him. "I suppose from that point of view, the question makes a certain amount of sense."

"I take it then, that you are not a prisoner. Do you have some kind of arrangement with the beast?" He leaned forward as much as he could, trying to see into the cave beyond her. He couldn't see any sign of the dragon, but then, he hadn't seen it when he first arrived. Maybe it had hidden itself by whatever means it had used before?

She sighed, shaking her head at him. "You really are kind of dense, aren't you? Or maybe you just can't think straight while you're after the dragon for whatever reason." She paused. "Why are you after it, anyway?" She offered up the waterskin again, and he drank deeply.

After she moved it away, he swallowed deeply, savoring the relief to his mouth and throat. "I was told it had been raiding the lands of Lord Golland, killing cattle, and carrying off some of his people." Donabal eyed her again. "I thought you might be one of them."

She snorted. "Lord Golland is a fool and small, petty man with no honor and less sense. I am eternally grateful that, whatever else I may be or might have been, I was never under his dominion, and I never will be." She pushed her hair back with one hand, closing her eyes. "Where to even start… Golland and the dragon made a deal. Don't look so shocked, humans make all manner of bargains when they are desperate and seek to get out of them as soon as the cost comes due. You've never heard a soldier offer up all manner of prayers as a battle begins, only to forget whatever was promised as soon as the fighting ends?"

"I have heard of such," he agreed. "Are you saying Lord Golland reneged on an agreement?"

"There you are. You catch up eventually." She patted his cheek with a surprisingly warm hand. "The dragon, who has a name, by the way, sent messengers and warnings. Fool that he was, Golland believed himself safe. When the dragon began showing him the error of his ways, Golland started spreading lies and sending would-be heroes here in hopes one of them would kill the dragon and relieve him of his obligations."

Pain throbbed in time with his pulse in his temple. "And where do you figure in this tale?" Donabal asked.

"Well, maybe not catch all the way up," she sighed. She straightened and fixed her gaze on him. Her brown eyes found his and then flickered, a purple light filling them.

He jerked back in surprise and managed to hit his head on the wall behind him, sending new waves of pain through him. "How…" he managed, trying to not vomit at the new waves of suffering moving through his head.

"You really don't know much about dragons, do you?" She asked. "Oh, here," she added in a frustrated tone, reaching her hands up to his temples. "We're not going to get anywhere if you get sick all over yourself. Or me." Her warm fingers touched his skin and he let out an involuntary sigh as the pain vanished. Not just in his head, but all throughout his body.

"You're telling me that Lord Golland made some manner of agreement with… you," he had trouble believing this woman was the beast he had fought, even with the eyes now regarding him, "failed to live up to his word, and has been trying to have you killed ever since?"

"That's the short and simple version, yes," she agreed.

"Why should I believe you?" he asked, with no heat or anger, simple curiosity in his tone.

"Why would I bother to lie?" she countered. "You're not going anywhere unless I allow it. What do I gain by persuading you of anything?"

"I have no idea," he admitted. "I don't know why I'm still alive, come to that."

"Oh, that's a story," she said. "I'm not sure you're ready to hear that." She paced over to the table and ran a finger along the edge of his shield. "Care to tell me who enchanted this for you? I haven't seen anything this elaborate and well-crafted in a long time."

"That seems like something it would be better for you not to know," Donabal said. "They did me a great service, and I'd rather not repay them by sending a fire-breathing, unstoppable foe to their door."

"I don't want to kill them, fool. I truly admire the work, and it's been a long time since something really captured my attention." She considered for a moment. "How does this sound? We trade questions, swear an oath to be truthful, and that we won't use what we learn against the other, unless we agree on a course of action afterward."

"What oath would bind you?" he asked. "You're far more powerful than any simple mortal, to be held by words." He had no idea what a dragon's sense of honor was, or if they had any, but it didn't seem a wise point to bring up.

"Even I have a heart," she said. The woman moved out to the opening and came back with the vial he'd seen earlier. She tilted it slightly, letting one careful drop fall out. "I swear on my blood that I will answer your questions truthfully, take no violence against those we speak of unless we both agree, and offer you safety for the length of our discussion." The drop hit her arm, glowed a vibrant purple, and then disappeared. She looked back up at him. "If you agree to that last part, I will let you down while we discuss things."

"Where are you going to get my blood?" he asked, not sure he wanted an answer. By way of reply, she moved her hand to his face, and he felt a sharp pain as her nail flicked across his wound there. She held the nail in front of his face, blood in the slight curve. He nodded, and she dripped it on to his forehead. "I swear to answer your questions truthfully, to take no violent action against those we discuss barring agreement, and to offer you no violence while we speak." From the corner of his eye, he could barely see the flash of gold light from where the blood had landed on his skin.

"Close enough," she nodded. "Don't try and be clever and exploit some kind of gap left by your words. Intent matters more than phrasing with such oaths." She gestured, and the manacles popped open, releasing his wrists and ankles. He nearly fell but caught himself in a lurching shuffle step forward. She backed up and raised an eyebrow at him. "I'd just as soon you not fall on me," she said.

Now that he was free, rubbing his wrists with his fingers, he was becoming aware of other needs. A red flush rose on his cheeks, and he looked at her. "Do you have... ummm… I need to…"

She waved a hand at him. "Yes, yes. Go out of here, move three openings to the right, and you should find what you need. Meet me in my study when you've… attended to yourself." She walked away at a brisk pace, and he followed, glancing to the right, then back at her. He saw the furniture he'd noted before and deduced that to be her destination, then hurried himself to the opening she had indicated. With a grateful moan, he took care of a rising need and then took a quick moment to inventory his wounds. Whatever she had done with her touch had not simply eased his pain, all his bruises were gone, his limbs moved freely, and the aches he'd been worried about had gone. The only wound he still had was the cut on his cheek she had just reopened, and even that barely hurt.

Feeling a bit more composed, although still not happy at wearing just the padding from his armor, he crossed the floor to the study she had indicated. She sat in the chair at the desk, and another, which he would have sworn wasn't there before, was placed nearby. The vial of brilliant red blood sat near the center of the desk. "I'll ask first," the woman said as he seated himself.

"Why should you get to begin?" he asked.

"Who came into whose home with the intent to kill them?" she asked mildly. He flushed and felt an ever-growing confusion. He actually was starting to like her, and that wasn't at all right. She hadn't Glamoured him, he was almost positive of that. Had he been that wrong from the beginning of this quest? "That's what I thought," she said at his look. "Now then, who did the work on your shield?"

He could feel the mild pressure of the oath in his head, along his veins. It wouldn't compel him to speak the truth, but it would certainly punish him if he didn't. Donabal shivered at the feeling. "Ossric du Monfort of Duradan," he answered truthfully. "He lives in a gray tower to the west of the city's main gate." A random thought struck him. "I know not to ask for your True Name, but what should I call you?"

She chuckled. "That's your first question?" She shook her head and got a faraway look in her eyes. "Davina will do." Her attention returned to him. "I'll consider that merely courtesy, and allow another question."

"What did Lord Golland want from you?"

That seemed to catch her by surprise. She drew in a breath, eyebrows raised in thought. "I suppose any agreement between he and I would be considered void when he didn't fulfill his obligations." She tapped her fingers on the desk for a moment. "His wife had given him two daughters. He isn't getting any younger and was desperate for a son to carry on his name, title, and legacy."

"You can do that? Make a woman pregnant?" Donabal asked, surprised.

She arched an eyebrow at him. "No, that's his job. I can, and did, prepare a potion to ensure that the end result of their night would be a male offspring." She chuckled. "I suspect they both rather enjoyed the process."

Donabal flushed red again, and she laughed. "Surely the mighty warrior has been with a woman? You know what passes between lovers?"

He waved a hand at her. "Yes, I know. I mean, yes, I've had lovers. Isn't it your question?" he added in a transparent attempt to change the subject.

Still chuckling, she asked, "Where did you hear about the maiden hair for your spear?"

"There's an old woman who lives in a small village at the northern end of the Artemus Wood. She's justly renown as a storyteller and collector of old tales. I learned a great deal from her. Her name is Fialla." He paused. "You won't hurt her? I know we swore the oath, but she's a remarkably kind woman."

Davina's face softened slightly. "Your concern does you credit. I won't hurt either of them, even had we not sworn the oath. We live a long time, and something new and interesting becomes rare as the years, and decades, pass. I will visit these people and learn from them."

"What are the Servitors?" he hadn't meant to ask the question, but the words came out of him at a rush.

She frowned. "I don't know what you might have heard about them, but here is the truth. Dragons are creatures of powerful magic. Our mere presence causes some things to happen, gives power to emotions that linger after death. A particularly evil person who comes after us with ill-intent changes them over time." She shrugged. "The one you fought was another of Golland's would-be assassins. He came with greed in his heart and murder on his mind. We fought, he lost, and the magic worked its change on him."

"Because you didn't kill him," Donabal added, and she nodded.

"Why did you go to such lengths to kill me? You gathered stories, paid I have no doubt a great deal of gold to enchanters for your arms and armor, and I won't even speculate what you offered the maiden for her hair." Her look made him flush again, and she laughed, then returned to her question. "Was I such a threat that you spent what, at least a year of your mortal life traveling and preparing? Mortals live such short lives," she added in a wistful tone.

"I…" he tried to order his thoughts. "I didn't do all that to hunt you. Some of what I did was years before I knew of you. I hunt monsters. I slay creatures that prey on the innocent and those that can't fight for themselves."

She rubbed her chin and then her eyes widened. "Wait, are you the one that killed Garanth the rock troll?" He nodded, and, to his relief, she smiled. "Foul creature. You did the world a service by ending him."

"Why am I still alive?" The question had been bothering him since he regained consciousness, and the vow they'd both sworn made him feel that this would be the safest time to ask.

The smile fell from her face. "That is a matter not generally spoken of. Although I don't suppose you'll be able to take advantage of the information." She pondered, lips pursed, fingers tapping on the desk again. "What do you know of how dragons come into the world?"

He shrugged. "Eggs. Everyone knows that." His eyes widened. "Do you mean… to… mate with me?" his voice rose to a near squeak.

She scowled at him. "Would that idea be so appalling? This form is comely, for a human." Davina dismissed whatever he'd been about to say with a wave of her hand. "That's an impressive amount of ego and being wrong in just two sentences. I'm not going to mate with you. That's not why you're alive. And there is no such thing as a dragon egg."

He looked at her, jaw hanging open, embarrassment giving way to shock. "What? But… everyone knows… many have died trying to capture… and you say they aren't even real?"

She let out a snort, small wisps of vapor coming from her nose. "Pardon me for not feeling guilty about people dying trying to steal our young so they could either kill or enslave them."

"Then… how… I mean, where…?" Donabal floundered, not even sure what he meant to ask.

"Listen closely, little human," she said, her voice suddenly much deeper and radiant with power, resonating around the stone walls. "Dragons create other dragons. They study humans who seem worth the effort, who show promise, who display a measure of skill, or fortitude, or determination far above the rest of their kind. Like, for example, a mortal with no powers, who doesn't cast magic, but pits himself against powerful beings over and over with little more than weapons that have a few tricks ensorcelled into them and raw talent."

Donabal felt his stomach lurch. Surely, she couldn't mean…

"Then, the dragon tests the mortal further, making certain that the being isn't simply benefitting from an inflated reputation or a lucky happenstance once upon a time. If they show the skill needed, and enough character that the dragon in question isn't worried they are going to unleash some a great horror on the world, then they can proceed."

"The stories about dragons rampaging and killing whatever they find…" Donabal started.

She shrugged. "Even we aren't infallible. When we make a mistake that great, we take steps to end the threat, and then that dragon isn't allowed to attempt a new creation for a hundred years or so. More, if the damage is particularly egregious."

"But…" was as far as he could manage to protest. The words just weren't forming.

"Was there anything else you wanted to ask me?" she prompted.

"No…" his voice trailed off, mind whirling with shock.

"Then our discussion is at an end, is it not?"

"It… is..." he managed, then the importance of his words hit home. "Wait…"

"For what it's worth, this won't hurt you." She paused for a beat. "Unless you're evil. Then I guess I get another Servitor."

Time felt as if it slowed around Donabal. The air seemed to thicken like jelly. Davina picked up the vial. "This will change your life," she said as she removed the top and, as she had for the oath, carefully tilted the vial, letting one drop spill out. Her other hand moved with a speed he couldn't have hoped to match and took hold of his hair. Donabal's head was forced down, his strength not able to resist hers. The drop fell on the back of his neck.

"With my own blood, spilled by your hand, I offer the chance of new life," Davina intoned. "May your transition be smooth and without pain."

The blood didn't exactly burn, but it felt extremely warm on the back of his neck. Donabal still couldn't move, and he wondered what kind of spell she had used on him. Not that it mattered. The deed was done. Warmth suffused his entire body, spreading out from where the drop had fallen.

Davina walked out to the center of the cavern, easily carrying the immobile warrior.

"Rest. You'll need it," she said. He saw her form swell and shift, the red scales appearing, wings sprouting from her back, claws at her fingertips.

She picked him up in a surprisingly gentle grip, and he felt her scales against his cheek. They were smoother than he expected, warm, and with a strange texture along the edges, as if many small pebbles clung there. The world went black, and he lost all track of everything.

He had no idea how much later it was when he woke up. He was in a bed. Groaning, he sat up, moving easily now. Whatever spell the dragon woman had used on him had faded. He was dressed in simple, slightly worn clothing, so at least he wasn't just in the padding still. Donabal went out into a hallway and down a flight of stairs, to a common room that could have been in any of countless inns and taverns he'd spent a night or more in. Behind the bar, an older woman with gray hair smiled as he came in. "Your friend said you'd had a rough time of things. She paid for your room, and your mount is in the stable. Feeling better?"

"Yes, thank you," he said, trying to get any clue where he might be from her accent, the furniture, even the smells of the food. Nothing stood out to him. He walked over to the door. "I'll just go check on my horse,' he said, and ducked outside. Nothing familiar or distinctive came into view. It was a nice looking village of decent size. Glancing up, he saw the sign above him, "The First Foothill." So at least he was still in the lands of Nianosa, going by the script. Glancing down the street, he saw a road that led to mountains in the distance, partially obscured by fog. Was he on the other side of the range he had found Davina in?

Faser was in the stable, contentedly munching some hay. The horse whickered softly in greeting, and then went back to eating. "How'd we get here? And where are we?" Donabal muttered.

He went back to his room, telling the innkeeper he'd be down later for a meal and a drink. In his room, he went through his pack and his possessions, finding everything he had brought with him, and a small pouch of gold coins. He sat on the edge of the bed and examined his patched, but clean, travel cloak. In the pocket, he found a note.

"We'll meet again. You'll know how to find me. And maybe we'll give mating a try after all." It was signed with a large, florid D. He sat there, rereading the few words, and tried to work out what he was supposed to do next. Distractedly, he scratched the back of his neck. He froze as his fingers found something hard, but smooth, warm to the touch, with a pebbled edge. He tugged, but it didn't move. Somehow, if he had the ability to see behind himself, he was sure it would be a bright red.

Now what was he supposed to do?

Cinders in Sindre

By Kristina Barnes

John sat in the lobby staring at the bullet points in front of him. Knuckles white from his grip on the notebook and face pale from the bad feeling in his gut, he barely got halfway through a sentence before having to start it over. Squeaking from the secretary's chair as she swayed absent-mindedly from side to side kept creeping its way in his head, breaking his focus. She sat hunched slightly at her desk, chin in her palm, looking at a floating magazine. Occasionally she would flick the index finger of her free hand, and the magazine page turned. The light blonde curls dancing on her shoulders with each sway, the ones that charmed him when he first saw her, now only added to his frustration.

He lowered his head, base of his palms on either temple, fingertips interlaced above his head and stared wide-eyed at the notebook that now lay in his lap. He took a breath and tried to shut out the world. Splashing came from the fountain, and he closed his eyes. No good. He could feel the serpent watching him.

"John," he imagined it calling him, "Coins John. Bring me coins."

Nope, okay, time to get some air. He'd imagined voices his whole life. Which was fine when he was six. Hell, it was a superpower when he was six. He was never a bored only child. Now it invaded him. A punishment for wishing to wield magic like the heroes of generations past. How badly he had wanted to grow up and perform magic in the dragon slayer's arenas. Anything really, as long as he had magic.

Tim, his childhood friend, said the arena was a front for the night sweepers. Every time John saw him the conversation went the same way. Tim would exchange social niceties for as long as he could stand to, the running record was three minutes, and then he'd get a crooked smile, brush his red hair to the side, and say "They operate just under Sindre citizen's radar. They stalk their routes for weeks before making opportunity grabs. Once they make a grab, they abandon the route for a few months before a new crew picks it back up." He'd usually pause here and run his hands over his always black attire.

"They're the arena heroes. It's not magic or makeup, that's really what they look like. Old breeds. The dragons they fight are the people they steal off the streets." After a few beers he'd talk about the meal deliveries Sindre citizens receive. "They're one of the main tactics. The sweepers use them to keep tabs on the city and remove dissenters."

Sindre citizens, for the most part, agreed that the night sweepers were a government operation with vastly exaggerated rumors. Nothing to fear. But John had never met anyone without magic that went out after the unofficial curfew after which the night sweepers supposedly operated. Most of their friends distanced themselves from Tim, but John never could.

Tim had been his best friend. Tim had been normal until the night Mina ran away.

Tim said he was at his window. That he heard the hooves of the minotaur and then saw its horns. Goblins surrounded her. They chased her toward the minotaur. He grabbed her by her midsection and poof. They disappeared. All official reports say she ran away, but that's all they said. No evidence one way or the other.

John paced around the lobby behind where he had been sitting. Through the broad windows, a few people he'd passed in the halls but never really got to know, shared a smoke break. Two men in button down shirts walked the gravel trail. The man with half a horn on his forehead and elongated chin and nose was moving his hands all over the place while his companion nodded. *There's a good drinking game, take a shot every time this guy nods,* John thought.

Charlie, another elf descendent, sat on a bench with his calling stone. Probably trying to rack up last minute sales to secure his place in the company merger. Not that Charlie had anything to worry about. He didn't come back from his lunch break one day to find a super cryptic meeting memo on his desk. So far, he'd only heard of four people getting one. Lucky them.

The sun reflected a bright red billboard in the distance behind Charlie. It blinded John for a moment. He blinked hard and then rapidly. Once his eyes adjusted to the glare, John read it. "FIREBALL STARTERS - Cast fire The Wiz way! Just squeeze, it's as easy as one, two, three. Get yours today." The Wiz, a young man in a very long gray hair and beard wig, wore a blue cloak with silver stars. He held the flaming ball in one hand and blew fire at a dragon with the other. John hated those billboards. He loved pretending to cast fireballs into his fireplace though.

He moved his fingers along the spiral of his notebook he held at his side. His performance over the last two months, all of his major accomplishments, his resume-level best qualities listed in little bullet points in case he blanked and needed to talk about himself, he had all of it prepared in there, just in case. He sat back down to try reviewing it again. He got a few pages in and started feeling confident. That's when a loud whoosh and thunk interrupted him. He snapped his head back up in time to see the floor-to-ceiling boardroom doors swing open.

Ezra, an up and comer young elf on the sales team, ran out with smoke billowing behind him. He crashed against the couch across from John and tipped it over, rolling off the back of it as it fell just as another fireball came flying out. This one bright blue with white at the center, growing as it passed.

It's going to hit the secretary, John thought.

"Don't." he imagined the serpent say.

It's going to hit her and she's just sitting there, swaying and reading her magazine. It was a long shot, but if he moved fast enough, he could go around the side and tackle her out of the way. The fireball was about one foot away from her and he was two. He was going to get hit, she probably was too, but his feet kept moving and so did he. Just before the edge of her desk he leapt. It was too late to move them both out of the way. He was going to take the hit. The thing looked like it would melt right through him. *I'm going to get melted for some girl that doesn't have the sense to move out of the way of fire. And these are going to be my last fucking thoughts - great.* He closed his eyes.

And then it happened. He hit hard and fell back on the floor. Except he didn't feel any burns. It had to be the adrenaline, or he was already dead. *Well, at least I died quick,* he thought. Then he thought of Freckle, Speckle, and Spot. The havoc they would wreak in his absence. Once he had lost track of time at Tim's. He slept on Tim's couch rather than risk the night sweepers - not that he had admitted that to Tim. In his absence the heads had managed to work together long enough to chew through the drywall and visit the neighbors. Their table was full of deliveries for a brunch party they were throwing, and the heads helped themselves. What would happen this time? He felt the stir of habitual anxiety he had developed around his complete inability to maintain any control over his home's wellbeing or his hydra's behavior. He pushed at the anxiety, fighting it back down until he remembered he was probably dead, and none of it mattered. The hydra could eat anything it wanted, and it wouldn't affect him now. The weight lifted, and he sunk into a calm peace, waiting on that inevitable light to follow to whatever's next.

But then he smelled smoke and stomach-turning waves of burnt hair.

He opened his eyes. Unless the afterlife looked a lot like the lobby's ceiling, he was still alive. He was on his back on the floor, still in front of the secretary's desk. The air around her desk had a bright blue tint, right where he jumped. Where the fireball would have hit was the same bright blue light but now fading as ashes dropped from it to the stone floor below. He propped himself up on his elbows to see her standing. She was looking down at him. Her mouth wide in shock and amusement. She covered it with her hand and laughed. A soft, not unkind laugh, but it still stung a little more than the pain in his back.

"Are you okay?"

"Who, me? Oh yeah, I'm great." He pushed himself to sit upright. His flop of honey-warm colored hair stuck to the side of his face. His low ponytail long lost in the commotion. "Just had to get my daily dose of running into spirit shields before lunch."

She laughed again, this time she didn't cover her smile. "And here I thought you were worried about me. Well, it's always nice to have a hobby." She looked over at Ezra who was still on the floor with the couch, patting his hair where the flames had been. He winced whenever he accidentally brushed against the long tips of ears. He was bald between them, as if the fire had been set right there on the top of his head and even though it didn't eat its way down the rest of his hair, it certainly took a bite of his ears. "That must have been an awfully small fireball he hit you with. I think he likes you." She laughed again.

John and Ezra met eyes. What kind of madhouse dystopian company bought out H&Z Homegoods? He could leave right now.

"Sisko," A man called from the boardroom.

John got up off the stone floors. He could turn around, walk through the lobby, pass the four story water fountain, go right out the front door, and never look back. He could bum around for a loan and open his dream bakeshop with George as a very involved mascot.

Ezra shook his head, "Don't do it to yourself man, just quit."

Or he could get laughed out of every bank and loan shark's office in town. He could search the help-wanted ads and settle into another mediocre cubicle. If he was lucky. If not, he'd go broke, lose his apartment, and end up at the mercy of the street sweepers in their nightly raids.

He walked straight ahead.

From behind, Ezra called, "Don't believe anything he says, John. Guy's a maniac."

He should have taken his chances with the street sweepers.

A stout man in a dark suit sat at the head of the table. The only light in the room came from a fireplace to the right of the man. The gas lights overhead were switched off, and the two windows were covered with black blinds. The doors slammed shut, he thought of their own accord, until he noticed two people dressed in gray settling back into their positions against the wall. The fire's light illuminated one enough for him to note one looked male and the other female. The female had tan skin and a lion tattoo under a rolled up sleeve. From the size of her forearm alone, he'd have guessed she had an orc or troll somewhere in her ancestry.

Four more bodyguards stood two abreast on each side of the table. The only other chair was at the end of the long side of the table, just next to the head seat the stout man occupied. He would be in reaching distance of the man with the fire blazing behind them.

"Hi, uh, John, sir." He felt like a leaky faucet dripping sweat. He extended his hand to introduce himself; the man looked at it as if John had used it to wipe his ass after a particularly nasty trip to the bathroom. The man said nothing and motioned to the chair. John pulled the chair out and winced at the loud scrape of the leg against the floor. The dark room would usually be comforting for him, but the fire felt like a spotlight, highlighting every awkward move he made. He stumbled over his own leg as he moved to sit, and his hair bounced as he sat down too hard in the chair.

After John was seated, dwarfed by the massive un-cushioned chair, the man said, "Quite the theatrical heroics earlier. Do you make it a point to rescue distress-less damsels often?"

"No, uh," he cleared his throat, painfully aware of how dry his mouth was, "I work in product design, in the kitchen department. Mostly I work in baking equip-"

"What a waste."

He couldn't see the fire directly, but would have sworn that it flared up, hungry to reach him. "Just a taste," the fire begged in his mind.

"I'm actually quite good at it, sir. My products aren't the highest selling in the department, but my latest -"

"Home goods and fools' comforts. These are treasures not worth obtaining." He brought his hand up and flexed it so that his fingers were spread out and straight up. "There are more delights in this world than its complacent men can know. Dragons own the skies, yet men think it wise to hide in skyscrapers. They are chickens decorating their coops to forget that foxes roam just outside." Thin streaks of fire shot from his fingertips and illuminated a dragon's head mounted high on the wall. As the sparks came back down, more mounted heads were made visible. There was one, three rows down from the dragon, that bore the pointed ears and short face of a goblin. Goblins, with the exception of rumors like Tim's account of the night Mina disappeared, hadn't been sighted for hundreds of years and were thought to be extinct. Two rows down from that, he saw pale skin and fangs. Some had horns, others had scales, plenty had fur, but the flames shared little else of their details. "We live in a world that is not our own. There is no more noble a pursuit than to seek its ownership."

John opened his mouth, and no words came out. He closed it and cleared his throat again. The silence between them drew on. The fire crackled like the tik tik tik of too many seconds passing.

The man offered nothing to ease the rush of silence. And so finally John said, "But we, or the chickens, still need to eat. Selling products that make making food easier for money to buy food is still a relevant pursuit. And, not to completely miss your metaphor, the only dragons left are in the arenas. If the world belongs to anyone, it's us. Maybe more you magic guys than us, but still."

The room brightened and the details of the man's cold face came into view. He had hard lines and a thin mouth shadowed under stringy black hair long enough to cup either side of his face. John's skin reddened, and he was sure this time that the flames had risen out of their fireplace. In his peripheral they were fingers outstretched to run their nails along his skin, only an arm hair's length away.

"My grandfather had a magic like yours. Not exactly the same, but closer than mine."

"Magic like mine? I don't have any -."

"No?" The stout man leaned back in his chair. "Then you're in good company with three fourths of the population, aren't you?" He held eye contact without blinking and continued, "Why is that? That we went from magic under every rock, in every crevice to," he held an open hand out in John's direction, "this." He closed his fingers starting with the pinky in quick succession and pulled his hand back down in front of him on the table.

"As the ages passed -" today was not John's day for talking uninterrupted.

"As the ages passed, magic faded. Dragons became fewer and farther in between. Heroes died off and were bred out of the gene pool. Yes. Surely. That makes the most sense." He leaned forward over the table. "It makes perfect sense that magic has changed. It would make no sense whatsoever to believe the definition of and access to magic is what has changed."

He stood, and John tensed as the man walked behind him. He continued forward, pacing in the large room. "I will show you your magic. I will teach you what my grandfather spent his life mastering. But you will further my magic first. One gain for another. Deal?"

Was it possible? That magic could remain, not spirit shields, not purchased tricks, but real magic. Could he possess it? That his life didn't have to revolve around daily commutes and cubicles? "I…" But one gain for another. And the bad feeling in his gut that hadn't softened as the day went on. "What magic do I have? And what could I do to further your magic?"

"Deal or no deal?" The man stood facing the doors.

"I - what's the price?"

The two body guards pulled the door open. The man said nothing. He waved his hand over his shoulder and the two bodyguards closest to the fireplace stepped closer to John. "Good day then."

"Wait, wait. Alright. Deal,"

The man turned as the body guards shut the doors. The corners of his lips turned upward, wrinkles reached his eyes, but the cold intensity of his gaze remained. He held up his hand, palm facing inward, and slammed it shut in a fist.

Flames sprang from the fireplace. A thousand little flame eels with black eyes swam through air at him. John jumped out of his chair with enough force to knock it over. He kicked it at the flame eels, for all the good it would do, and ran for the door.

The man, still between him and the exit, was covered in coiling flames. As John moved towards him these flames took shape as others had. Their sharp-toothed and burning-tongued mouths snapped at him from both sides. The bodyguards hadn't moved. *Maybe I'll get lucky,* he thought. He turned on his heel. One step forward. If he could get enough air, he could land in a roll and maybe that would be enough time to bolt for the door. *Thanks for the heads up, Ezra,* he thought, *Real persuasive, excellent job on the details. 'Guy's a maniac' was the best you could do sales-man-of-the-month? Well hat's off to you, man.* On the second step, he planted his front foot and pushed down hard. *And head's off to me if this doesn't work.* He was doing it. He was in the air, now just to land on the table and keep moving -

With a loud smash, black flowered through his vision. Throbbing in his head tore past the adrenaline-fueled numbness he'd felt earlier. Warm wet dripped down on his head. Between the black spots of his vision caving in on him, he could make out the stone floor and dark liquid. Above him, the edge of the table continued to drip blood from where his head hit. Warmth had wrapped itself around his previously extended ankle and now crawled up his leg. A shadow darkened the dripping blood and hands, they felt like hands, landed firmly on his shoulder. Another pair under his head. They began to pull him upright, and he could swear he heard a lion roar in his ear. It made him think of all the reports of visual and auditory hallucinations people had when they were dying. The dark caved in on him once more.

Somewhere miles away, the stout man's voice, low and raspy like the crackling fire, said, "No, don't move him." The hands let him back down and receded. Darkness pulsed in his vision.

Warmth moved under his shirt. Drunk with dizziness, he snapped his chin down to see bright orange streaks glowing through. He began to pull his arms up, flailing at the flames. But they dug in, crawling up and up and up. They were on his neck and, though his air flow was not restricted, he choked. He gasped for air and wrestled with the fire eels. He kicked his feet and rolled over. Bright light in rhythm with the pain flooded him as his wound touched the stone.

The eels made it to his face. While he gasped for air or tried to scream, he wasn't sure what his body was trying to accomplish at this point, the eels made it to his mouth. They crawled in and slid their way up, not down his throat, but up. He missed the other version of feeling choked. He heaved and kicked. And then somehow, some terrible how, they were behind his eyes. Pain gone. Fear gone. Like they had never existed. He was gone.

John stood at eye level with a worn wooden table. A wood burning stove warmed the house against the crisp cold that invaded it. An old man sat at the table, wrinkled knuckles raised and fell as he kneaded dough in a pile of flour. John looked up, black hair fell into his eyes. He brushed it away. He felt love and curiosity. Then he heard his voice say, "But *how*? How do you put the magic in it, Pop?" Young and high pitched, his voice had a hint of raspy crackle as it drifted from his mouth.

No, not my voice, he thought, *a voice I know.* He reached back in his mind for a name and found nothing. The more he tried to concentrate, the more he had glimpses of memories with Pop. Were they his? They felt like his.

"It's not about putting magic in. Mooney. It's about uncovering the magic that's already there. Helping it find its way to the surface, and give it a little push to shine."

Mooney asked to help, and Pop let him. He passed him dough, and Mooney worked it like he was shown. "Am I doing it, Pop?"

"You're doing great." He passed Mooney the biscuit cutter once he flattened his portion of the dough. "You're doing a great job. But the magic, it's not so much about what you do. It's about what you feel. What do you feel, son?"

Mooney had the urge, the ever present urge, to do two things. One was to tell Pop that he was not his son. He was his grandson. Surely it wasn't that hard to tell him and his dad apart. Somewhere in the background John wanted to explain that 'Son' was a term of endearment, but as quickly as the awareness came, it left, and he was Mooney again, feeling perplexed at his grandfather for confusing a child with his father. The second urge, a compulsive and stinging urge, was to lie. "Of course I feel it, Pop. I'm good enough. I have magic too. I'm good. Like you." the urge wanted to say.

So he did. "Of course I feel it, Pop. I -"

"Feel what, Mooney? What do you feel?"

Well, crap. "It, Pop. The magic!" He pushed the biscuit cutter around on the dough. He wiggled it around from side to side, but the dough didn't break.

"Good. Good, son, that's great. What does it feel like?" He placed his hands on the dough around where Mooney struggled with the biscuit cutter. "Like this," he turned his wrist in the air so Mooney could see the firm spinning.

"I feel... uhm…" And for a moment they sat together in the sounds of the cabin. Rain fell on the tin roof, and wind sang past the windows. They cut biscuits from the dough, reformed what was leftover, and made more.

Mooney teared up, a scared helplessness drew up rage that mixed and meshed until they were one in the same. It formed a bubble in his throat, and he had to hold his breath to keep the tears back. The fire crackled, and two flames spit out toward him. The flames said - flames didn't speak. He learned that when Jillian pushed him off the swing and said "Only dragons and monsters hear flames, you liar." But still he heard them, and one said, "I feel hungry. Feed me some and I'll cook it for you." He wanted to. The exchange, the power, all of it he wanted to indulge, but mostly it was the hunger.

He knew that hunger; he had never not known it. The other flame twisted around the first, brushing Mooney's skin with its heat and said, "Tell him. It's okay. Tell him." The warmth of the fire's brush wasn't just heat. It was like the warmth in a hug, or the warmth that rose in his cheeks when Layani laughed at one of his jokes in class. It was the same hunger and joy he felt when he let the flames out to play in his room one night. The night he learned how hungry fire really was. The last night with his parents before they sent him away to live with his grandfather.

So he told him, but he was careful. He told his Pop that he felt hungry. That cooking the biscuits could help him with that hunger. "And that's my magic," he said.

"What a simple magic," Pop smiled. They put the biscuits on the wire rack in the oven. Pop used a dish cloth and pulled back when the flames licked at him. Mooney did neither.

"What does it feel like for you, Pop?"

"For me it feels like whispers. Plants whisper to me, and I can whisper back. I can ask the grains to heal when I knead dough. Or I can ask the trees to grow their branches in a certain direction. And they ask things of me too."

The memory faded. The words and the cabin drifted away. The stone floors of the boardroom returned. John jolted up to his feet and steadied himself against the table. He reached up to the wound on his head and found dried blood and warmth, but no pain. No gash.

"Fire is always hungry. It wants to eat whatever is in its path, but with a little direction, a little negotiation, a bit of my grandfather's whisper technique, and the fire will eat only what you ask it to."

"What was that?"

"That was the day a new mother lost herself creating new life. And my grandfather brought her back from the dead with a baked apple."

It was two months before he cursed the mob that came for Mooney. John remembered it like it was his own. He was in the school cafeteria.

Jillian pranced around him, that stupid lion necklace bouncing on her chest. "Liar liar, dragon's fire." He could hear her sing. "If you're not a liar, then you're a monster. That's why your parents didn't want you anymore, right? Because you're a freak with fire." The other kids joined in. He didn't mean to. He just lost control. The fire burning in the kitchen screamed as loud as the children mocking him. He needed it to stop.

No one was killed, but it didn't matter. The mob formed that night. Their yells echoed through the hills. They came with stakes to stop the monster.

John remembered hiding in the cupboard, black hair glued to his face from tears. His knees drawn into his chest, huffing in breaths and feeling like he was getting none of the air. The click of the opening cabinet. His grandfather's hand on his shoulder. His hairy arm sliding past him to grab a jar of poppyseeds. He could smell the comforting dry flour that apparently stuck to his grandfather after so many years of working with it. "Don't move, son. Stay here until their voices are gone. Even if I don't come back, don't come after me." But Pop came back. And the next morning the yard was filled with poppies and a pile of stakes.

But those weren't John's memories. He hadn't been transported this time, but the memories felt like his own while he had them. He looked at Mooney for an answer.

"That will happen. They will fade as the vision did. You will be left with yourself. Your own memories, your own life. The only way for you to tap back into my grandfather's secrets is to feed my flames."

"How?"

"The arena. We want the arena," the coiled flames around his wrists flared up.

John made it home just before the unofficial curfew set by the night sweepers. They both heard voices. Mooney in the abstract, his grandfather in whispers. *Maybe I don't imagine the voices,* he thought. He opened his front door, and the sounds of struggle pushed the day's events out of his mind for a moment. He shut the door in slow motion and tip-toed through his living room to the kitchen. It was much more enjoyable for him to catch his miniature hydra causing chaos than it was to walk in on the aftermath.

Freckle, Speckle, and Spot were on his kitchen table. Freckle and Speckle bit at the delivery box where the city's meal deliveries appeared. Spot sniffed at the box and then turned from side to side and dive-bomb bit at the other two heads, quickly returning to sniffing the box when Freckle or Speckle looked up to see which head had pecked at them. Then, seeing Spot busy, they would bicker with each other, leaving Spot free to nip at the box. After a moment they would notice Spot's nipping and return to their heist until Spot started the process all over again. John stood at the table across from them for a good ten minutes before any of the heads noticed him. Speckle saw him first and took a casual sniff then turned away like the box was no big deal, turning to nip at the others when they took too long to catch on.

"Oh yeah, real smooth cover there boys," John said as he sat and dispersed the food. Roasted purple and yellow carrots, broccoli, and baked kraken strips for him, worm kibble and a few shrimp treats for the hydra. Freckle and Spot dove for the shrimp. Speckle grabbed at the shrimp in the other two heads' mouths.

"The arena", Mooney had said. "We want the arena." How he was going to get Mooney the arena was a mystery. He rolled his carrots around with his fork. It didn't matter how. In whatever way Mooney wanted him to get the arena he had to do it. Mooney was his only chance to connect with that piece of himself that had always been there but just out of reach.

The hydra's tilted their heads - none of them in sync - "Why isn't he eating?" popped into John's head. Then, "Maybe he doesn't want it, maybe… us?" He pictured Freckle when the words came through his mind. He threw a carrot in the air towards Freckle and all three bit after it. He had the slight urge, the inkling of the magic he felt with Mooney.

While the heads pulled the carrot from one another he took a breath to put himself back in the feeling he had when Mooney's school fire broke out. He concentrated on what it felt like to have words pop in his head and believe completely that they came from Freckle. And then he said, "Which do you want, Freckle?"

They stopped. The heads looked at each other. Then Freckle tilted his head at John again. "All. Me, all."

"You have to pick one."

"Purple. No, kraken. Purple kraken." He lifted his head up above the others and sniffed. He chomped the air and took one more big sniff before settling his head back down. "Kraken."

John tried with the other two and ultimately landed on the same answer, though Spot requested a cupcake and then all he heard was cupcake for the next few minutes. Spot squinted when John said there were none, but eventually relented. He set three pieces of kraken aside on a plate. "One for each of you. And cupcakes next time they come."

The heads yipped in victory, which of course, devolved into nipping at each other.

"But no cupcakes for any of you if you fight or steal anyone else's kraken. Got it?"

They nodded. Speckle first, then the others.

He pushed the plate to them expecting chaos. He expected that this conversation was just a big delusion, and he had finally snapped. But the hydras did as they agreed. Despite his excitement the bad feeling remained in his gut.

He picked at his plate while they ate and then cleaned up. He spent most of that time being bombarded with "Cupcake?" "Cupcake!" and explaining that the next time they got cupcakes, yes. The hydras had him show them that no cupcakes had appeared in the delivery box about eighteen times and then they settled down.

In the quiet, his thoughts returned to the arena. "We want the arena." And to the night sweepers. Their base of operations, according to Tim, was the arena. What if Tim was right? He was right about magic. And there was the goblin head on Mooney's wall. The consensus is that the sweeps are exaggerated or rumors altogether, but how many people actually bothered to test that? He never had. Had Mina?

Rattling came from behind him. He was halfway through Freckle's name when he realized they were curled up in his recliner. Freckle poked his head up, didn't see food, and buried himself back under Speckle and Spot. The rattle came again. Someone was turning his door knob side to side. He heard the creak as whoever it was pulled the door knob toward them, shaking the door. Was it someone escaping the sweep? Or the sweepers?

He'd never had to put in a special request anywhere for delivery when he had dinner company. He hadn't sent in a form when he stopped eating pork, pork just stopped showing up in the deliveries. How did the sweepers know? All thought of deliveries coming from anywhere else disappeared. And if they knew that, then what else did they know? They knew he was getting close. They knew what Mooney had asked him to do. They knew and they were here for him.

The door shook again, and he dashed to his end table drawer. The door kept shaking. He pulled out a fire starter. The door stopped shaking. The knob twisted again. Tools clinked as the door knob moved side to side. He fumbled with the wrapper. Clink, the lock twisted into place. He yanked the wrapper off. First squeeze. The door opened. Second squeeze. Footsteps. A black boot and gray pant leg came into view from the door. Third squeeze.

"Oh good, you're up." She was still in all gray, sleeves rolled up past her lion tattoo. "Hey, are you good-"

The fire had started in his hand. He jumped and tossed it at the fireplace.

Kind of.

"Yeah, nope, all good here, just," The flame ball bounced off the edge of the fireplace onto the floor. He kicked it in, "just settling in, getting a fire going. You know, regular Tuesday." He stomped out the remaining embers on the wood floor, "Regular Tuesday stuff happening over here."

The lion tattoo roared. He hadn't imagined it earlier.

She shut the door, walked over, and sat on the edge of the recliner next to the hydra. She said hello and ran her fingers down the hydra's back.

"So you're one of Mooney's bodyguards?"

She laughed, coarse and harsh "Yeah, we're his bodyguards as much as you're a dragon slayer. It's Jill, by the way." She held out her hand, and they shook.

"Okay, great, very helpful. What are you then?"

"We're you." The lion on her forearm roared again. She put her index and middle finger on her inner arm, just above the elbow and a large ball of yarn fell down to her lion. The lion caught it and began to bat it back and forth. He chased it in circles around her arm and for a moment she stopped to watch him. "Not like, actually *you*, we're like you. We made the deal, or our versions of it, and we awakened to our magic." Spot lifted his head and eyeballed the lion playing with his yarn ball.

"Cool, so once I keep my end, if I survive my end," the bad feeling in his gut had only grown since yesterday, "he'll show me his grandpa's memories and then order me to stand around him in half-lit rooms to scare or singe employees of companies he acquires? Sounds great."

"I doubt it. You have to actually be useful to help him with new discoveries. Your pal, the elven sales guy -"

"Ezra."

"Ezra, whatever, if you weren't on the support team Ezra would be dead, not singed and scared."

Spot lunged at the yarn ball. He recoiled and shook his head after hitting her skin and not finding a ball. He tilted his head at her. She pet him, and he nipped at her fingers.

"Wait, so what hap-"

"Mooney offered him magic, and he ran just like you did. Just like most of us did. Except he couldn't handle the memory share. Mooney pulled back, but the guy went haywire. We were trying to pull him back out, ground him in this reality to keep him from going full on batshit, and he charged at Mooney. Mooney's flamelocks, the coils on his wrists, flared up, and then it was just a matter of damage control." She put her index and middle finger on the table the same way she had on her arm. Ink drizzled down and created the image of Ezra charging Mooney. The flamelocks charged Ezra back then chased him around the room while Mooney and the support team pulled at the air beckoning flames away from him.

"We got as much off of him as we could before he made it to the door. And we got about half off the other coil before it made it out to the lobby. Then Mooney stopped us. He put real shields under that spirit shield shit and there you go."

"I guess that explains why they rebounded me so hard."

"Rebounded you? They should have torn you up. That's why Rhea was laughing. You're lying on the ground trying to act cool when you should have been shredded up. It's why Mooney was so sure you had magic. That's why we didn't have to waste half an hour playing up the coy investigator act."

He had more questions, hundreds more, but she pulled a drawstring pouch from her pocket and placed it on the small table between them. She pulled out a blue calling stone, a vial of what she called 'light em up' powder, and a glass jar holding one of Mooney's flamelocks, and a couple other tools she explained how to use and when. She helped him put the flamelock on. She went over the plan with him again.

He knew what to do. He had no clue if he could pull it off. Proof. Proof for magic, that was the deal. Proof that rumors about the night sweepers didn't even brush the surface of what they were really doing. Maybe Mooney and his goons were crazy. Maybe John was too frightened of the night sweepers to really let himself believe that Mooney and Tim could be right, that the rumors could be true, but the itch to feel his magic was too strong. He was on the brink of knowing a part of himself that had hidden just out of his reach. He had to try.

Before the sun cleared the horizon, way too early in the morning, John was at Tim's door. Freckle chewed at his harness while Speckle and Spot nipped at each other over a dandelion growing through a crack in the sidewalk. He dropped the hydra off, "in case I don't make it back," he'd told Tim. Tim took the leash with one hand and left the other in his black jeans pocket. He asked John what was going on.

He gave Tim as few details as he could get away with. In the end, John told Tim he was going to the arena to do something that he had to, that Tim couldn't talk him out of it, and that he promised his hydra cupcakes. Freckle, Speckle, and Spot perked up at cupcakes. They nipped and yipped at Tim's feet.

Tim said, "Sure, anything for you, man."

John wrapped Tim in a one armed hug and walked off. It was the last moment they would spend together.

John walked into the arena with the crowd. He knew he blended in just fine, but he felt like a walking red flag. The spotlight feeling returned. He was aware of the muscles in his face and couldn't position it to feel natural. His steps were too far apart. He was too purposeful in his attempt to look casual. The guards, rumored to use magic and makeup to look more like their wild ancestors, glared at him. They knew. They were the night sweepers and of course they knew. One in particular, a hunched man with gray flesh, locked his red eyes on John's for a moment that stretched out way too long. It was only a matter of time before they picked him out of the crowd. And who knows what they'd do with him then.

He followed along with the crowd through the shops that lined the halls to the stadium proper. Advertisements for the show were spread out every few storefronts. *"Watch the heroes rise." "We slay so you can play - We've kept Sindre safe for hundreds of years. Come see it live. Tonight!"* He rounded the narrow curve between shops and walked into the foyer opening. Straight ahead and down a corridor to the left is where he would find the doors that lead to the hero's chambers below the arena.

A band of bards dressed in the attire of yore played in the twenty foot space between the stadium entrances. *"Can our heroes keep the dragons away?"*

John stood in the crowd gathering around them. A stocky girl with thick dwarven hair threw coins in their case. A little boy pulled at his mother's sleeve in the direction of the toy store. Decent foot traffic moved through the space.

"Who will claim victory and who will be slain?"

Two guards were stationed at the entrance to the corridor. One by the entrance that had a clear line of sight to the corridors. Rotation would come in a few minutes. He'd have about eight seconds to slip in. The long guard would have a different rotation schedule. John would need to use the crowd as cover or just get lucky. He drifted through the crowd. The little boy who had been pulling on his mother's sleeve darted in front of him. She apologized while chasing after her son. John said it was no problem and kept moving.

"The monsters that slumber in dungeons below"

The guards looked around the area and then started moving away. John scanned the area. The other guard whose line of sight he'd be in was helping a red headed man in a black shirt, get lucky it was. Go time.

"In the end will Sindre belong to hero or foe?"

John used the mix Jill had given him the night before on the locks. The whirring insides went quiet, and he pulled the door open. The creak of the door was too loud. It was deafening. But no one came running and screaming after him. That spotlight feeling must have been in full effect. He stepped into the shadowy chambers. All he had to do was make it to the prep room and set up the powders. This was easier than he thought it would be. He looked over his shoulder down the dark hallway. Then the hallway got darker. And then there was nothing.

He woke up in chains on cold concrete. His head ached in rhythm with his heartbeat.

"Your accomplice is dead." said the ghoul that had made eye contact with him earlier. He was smiling, blood dripping from his mouth. He wiped it with the back of his hand then licked it off with a sharp tongue. "Don't want to waste that."

His stomach turned. He heaved and it caused him to curl his legs up, nearly into the fetal position. The smell of the ghoul's rotted flesh wasn't muted by magic down here. He took a few labored breaths. "I don't have an accomplice. I don't know what you're talking about. I just got turned around, thought this was a themed bathroom entrance -"

"He smelled like you. He certainly distracted Tazriel long enough for you to slip down here to the 'bathrooms'. But by all means, go ahead. Relieve yourself. You won't live long enough to do it any place nicer than this." With that the ghoul left.

John tried to stand but the chains were bolted to the ground. He fell and busted his jaw. Blood gushed in from his lip, and this time he threw up. Accomplice? One of Mooney's guys? He shrugged it off and patted his pockets. Doing so pulled the chain cuffs against his wrists and left bright red rub marks on his skin. Empty. All he had left was the flamelock.

If he had backup, it was gone now. He pulled at the chains, hoping the bolt would come loose. Nothing. He whispered to the flamelock like Jill had showed him, "Burn the chains. Metal for you, freedom for me." and got nothing in response. He was at their mercy. At least he'd had the foresight to drop off Freckle, Speckle, and Spot with Tim.

Tim. Red hair, black shirt. An accomplice who distracted the guard with red hair and a black shirt. No. It had to be a coincidence. *Tim wouldn't follow me here,* he thought, but he knew it was a lie as soon as he said it. That's the first thing Tim would do. Try to help. Anything for answers in the sweepers den. Anything for his best friend John.

He cried in the darkness. It reminded him of young Mooney holding his breath to suppress the tears. He leaned into that feeling, tapped back into the feeling of power brimming just beneath the surface. He remembered calling to Freckle. He focused everything he had on the flamelock. The way it felt embedded in his arm. The sickly warmth of the flames crawling up his throat before the vision came. The flamelock grew warm. He whispered and it rose up through his palm, snaking its way to his fingertips.

The scrape of metal on concrete shut him up. Four guards came in with the ghoul, including Tazriel. Tazriel said, "Last words? Smart move, but it's too late for that now." he tossed an orb on the ground. It rolled to John's leg, bumped it and stuck.

But John had the flamelock. John had his own magic too. "It's not too late for shi -" Bright yellow light erupted from the orb. The light sunk into him like razors. It dripped beneath his skin, and it felt like his bones were breaking. Cracking, rearranging. He was being ripped apart inside and out. He didn't know if he was screaming. The pain, the light, it was all too loud. He longed for the relief of unconsciousness. And finally it came.

He awoke to bright lights ahead. He was being pushed, zapped forward towards a screaming crowd. Hearing footsteps that were too loud. Feeling a body that was too heavy. Hard to walk in. He tried to speak, but his mouth couldn't form words. Instead he heard himself roar. "The dragon enters!" the announcer yelled above the crowd as the arena came into John's view.

The hero, a blonde elf in polished-to-shine armor, cast his spear at John. It bounced off his scales and the crowd booed. Then he brought his hands together over his head, "May the lightning of Sindre strike you down." The crowd cheered and stomped in the stands.

John dodged where he could, but the bolts kept coming. He was exhausted. Sick of pain. Sick of this. He just wanted to go home and get his hydra a cupcake. He wanted to mourn his friend. He didn't want to be facing death just to answer the call of magic in his bones.

The more he focused on that, the more hits he took. But the more he felt like himself. He could feel the flamelock in his paw. It rose and he felt himself shake. Another hit from the lightning and he was on the ground. The crowd went wild in the distance. He held onto the flamelock. Onto his hydra. His humanity.

And then he screamed. Just like last time but without the yellow light. His bones broke and his flesh bubbled apart. Somewhere in the distance he heard panic in the stands. The announcer urged people to leave, but it was too late. They had seen and couldn't unsee. Where there had been a mighty dragon now stood a dying man.

The elf raised his bolt to strike him down one final time. The flamelock leapt from him and did what flames do best. It devoured. Soon he was surrounded in flames. From the stands, Mooney sent them one after another. They wrapped themselves around John as they had done in the boardroom. A lion, first a black ink outline, came to life in the stands. It leapt from the last row of chairs down into the arena, a trail of blood dripping down leading back to Jill. Her eyes and the lion's matched the crimson trail following the lion through the air, and while her body gave small jerks here and there, the lion responded with the full movement. It landed on the elf's shoulder, claws curled, jaws wide towards the elf's neck. The elf tried to spin to face the lion. He tried to send a bolt at the lion's face, into its mouth. But Mooney's flames were upon him. As they devoured the elf, they devoured his magic.

John's vision flowered. He fell to the ground and swayed to the patterns exploding in the black of his vision. Relief would come. Darkness, unfeeling nothingness would come and sweep him away. But as the darkness grew within him, he found the nothingness was alive with a pulsing intensity. He could feel the lion, satisfied by the blood it drew from the elf. He could feel the eternal hunger of the flames, the desire to grow itself overwhelming him. John did not see the flames brighten or the lion strengthen, he didn't see his eyes when he finally stood and reopened them, but Mooney did. And Mooney smiled.

The bolt came out as a crackle, fizzing instead of burning with heavenly power. The lion, and to a much smaller degree, Jill, jerked its head back and shook. Then it pushed its weight into the elf, dragging them both to the ground. The flames dug their way into the elf. And the lion feasted.

Mooney sat at John's kitchen table. He shared pieces of his cupcake with the hydra's heads as John directed which head each bite should go to. "Ready?"

John nodded and the flames reached out for him.

Penitent No More

By Michael Morton

As the incantation faded from hearing, a thick gray mist replaced Maleck's view of the Tribunal Hall. The solid stone floor beneath his feet disappeared, and he looked around to see that the mist encompassed them completely. There was a moment of stomach-lurching vertigo, and his vision cleared, revealing a different hall. This one was plain, with simple iron wall sconces holding unembellished mage lights. There were no gorgeous tapestries or elaborate portraits on the walls. More importantly, the courtroom, the judge, and the Law Mages were gone. Instead, there were three men standing there, dressed in mail and bearing weapons.

The middle one, with long gray hair and a harsh visage enhanced by an old scar cutting from his left temple to the corner of his mouth held out an iron rod tipped with a red crystal. It emitted a brief flash, and Maleck felt the iron band around his neck grow warm.

"Penitents of Alsera, you have been sentenced to Cornerstone Tower for your crimes. Your Collars of Contrition are now active. If you travel more than one hundred yards from this tower, it will end you. If you betray us to the creatures of the Madness, it will end you. If you fail to complete your sentence, it will end you. If you cross the Iron Mages, it will end you. I am Enoch, Tower Marshal, and you will obey me in all things."

Maleck touched the narrow iron collar with his fingertips, but the warmth was already fading. When the Law Mages had fitted it on him, it felt uncomfortable and filled his nostrils with the heavy scent of iron. Now, it was like a heavy weight on his neck, threatening to suffocate him.

He looked over at those who traveled with him to this place. Three other men and two women stood grouped around him, all in various stages of stunned disbelief. At the time, the judge's sentence of twenty years at Cornerstone was just words, but this plain hall and Enoch's speech drove the true impact home. He swallowed and vowed not to disgrace his family by soiling himself on the spot.

"Here, you will defend humanity from the threat that comes from the Madness. You will serve twenty years in this Tower defending the people and society that you chose to wrong. If you survive, you will be free to rejoin civilization."

Enoch motioned the other two warriors forward. "Not all fight but all will serve. Danag is the Training Master and Julius is the Quarters Master. They will determine where you will be placed."

Maleck and four of the others were selected for combat roles. Pero had belonged to the Watch, but he'd been more interested in both the bribes he could take and the beatings he could administer in his official capacity. It was his bad luck that the drunk he'd beaten to death had a highly-placed family. Serge was a gang member with multiple tattoos and claimed to have killed his way to the top of his gang. He was caught with illegal drugs and killed three of the City Watch before being subdued. Samara drugged an entire dinner party, intending to rob them blind but had misjudged the dosage and killed half of them. Yeddiah was a barbarian of the northern wastes who had killed seven men in a drunken tavern brawl. Maleck only admitted to being sentenced for murder and left it at that.

They were all killers, and none of them were prepared for what awaited them.

Cornerstone Tower was a squat, square block of ugly gray stone, placed to defend the sole outlet of the ravine that housed the Madness. The tower itself was eight stories tall and over a hundred feet tall on a side, but the rocky walls next to it towered another fifty feet above the structure. The walls of the tower were built as close to the rock walls as the designers could make it, but that still left a ten-foot gap. A wide, deep moat surrounded the tower and an awful smell emanated from it.

"The Iron Mages dump their failed experiments into the moat. The acid in there gets rid of the remains for them and provides another layer of defense for us." Danag stood off to one side, letting the new arrivals get their fill of the scene beyond the Tower.

The empty space beyond stretched for over a hundred yards, arrow straight. The hillsides were seamless and unnaturally even, as if a giant trowel had smoothed them over. At the distant end, hovering in mid-air about fifty feet off the ground was a swirling cloud, motion visible even at this distance. Black and silver lightning lanced through the clouds at unpredictable intervals, but there was no accompanying thunder. It was difficult to judge how big it was, but it seemed to be half the size of the Tower.

"Get a good look at it. You'll learn to hate it sooner or later." Danag spat into the moat, but his face was flat and expressionless. "Once you hate it, you can stop being afraid of it and the things it spawns. Creatures whose only desire is to kill every living thing. Spirits in the mists that get inside your head and possess your soul. You'll face all that and more in your twenty years here."

Samara looked back and forth between the tower and the ravine walls. "I don't see any defenses out here."

The scarred Marshal nodded. "If there's an attack coming, we fight from inside the tower. We don't fight outside ever. If you're outside and the alarm sounds, run for the door. Fast. Or you'll be left outside and torn to pieces."

A loud crack sounded from above and mild cursing followed it. Seconds later, a metal rod hit the ground in front of the tower. Looking up, they saw several figures on a nearly-translucent, gray floating disk about ten feet across, hovering in mid-air next to the tower's roof. They were wrestling with something, trying to get it from the roof to the disk.

Maleck shaded his eyes with his hand. "Are those… Iron Mages?"

"Aye. They have the top two floors and the first floor. Times like this when the Madness is quiet, the mages go and study it with their devices and spells. When the Madness erupts, they use what they've learned to help fight it."

Serge snorted. "Heh. What'd they do to get stuck out here?"

Danag stared at him until the other man looked away. "Nothing. They compete for the privilege of coming here and studying the Madness. To them, it's a great honor to be here."

They stared in disbelief as the mages finished transferring their device and then steered the disk out towards the black cloud at the other end of the gorge.

Maleck watched as Danag put the others through their paces on the training field behind the tower. The flat, grassy area was incongruous next to the massive stones of the tower and especially out of place compared to the swirling darkness at the other end of the canyon, just a few hundred yards from the Tower. The Training Master had led them out here past several working parties of other Penitents as they cleaned and repaired previous damage. In several places, it was obvious the walls had been breached and then rebuilt. Maleck wasn't sure he wanted to know what was capable of smashing foot-thick stone to rubble.

They would all be tested on their skills and assigned to the Front Rooms. Located on the side of the Tower that faced the ravine, these were where the defenders fought the horrors spawned by the Madness. As they warmed up, they were taunted with warnings, catcalls, and descriptions of lurid deaths by the old hands. Danag said nothing about this treatment, his face blank as he waited for them to be ready.

Samara was the next to last to be tested. The slender woman made no attempt to match Danag's strength, instead ducking and weaving in and out of his strikes. She didn't appear to have much formal training but was quick on her feet and had a keen sense of just how far to move to avoid a strike. As with the others, the Training Master called a halt and nodded for her to step over to join one of the waiting sergeants from the Front Rooms.

Motioning to Maleck to join him, he paced back to the center of the field. He asked the same question he asked of everyone else. "Have you any weapons experience?" His tone doubted it was true.

"Aye. I've had training on the blade, both sword and saber. I can wield a shield and lance in formation. I've also done some bow work, hunting mostly."

Danag cocked his head. "Those are noble's weapons…" he trailed off. Maleck stared back at him, a silent challenge in his eyes. The older man sighed. "And it matters not. Take up the sword and buckler, then. If ye do know your way around them, then maybe you can survive the Front Rooms longer than the others."

Their bout started out cautiously, each man feeling his way around his opponent. Danag was as quick as Maleck's former trainers and knew most of the tricks they had taught him. His strokes were economical but strong, lacking the training field finesse the younger man was used to. Still, Maleck was able to go for several minutes before Danag landed a touch, which was longer by far than any of the others. Calling a halt, the Training Master nodded. "Front Rooms for ye. Second floor, Yor's squad. And could be you'll survive longer than most, if you can keep yer head about yerself."

Later, the five newest Penitents sat in a rough circle gnawing on the coarse black bread, spicy sausages, and strong cheese that constituted lunch. Samara wrinkled her nose at most of it but there was nothing else, so she ate sulkily. "I dined on nothing but the best dishes back in the capital. Pastries so delicate they melted in your mouth. Spices from the eastern isles. Exotic fruits and berries in cream."

Yeddiah had already eaten most of his and was eyeing her portion. "Beats lye-soaked fish and whale blubber."

Serge bit into a sausage and bread sandwich, smacking his lips. Crumbs trailed into his scraggly beard. "Better'n rootin' trew garbage piles or waiting' fer trenchers from them uppity nobles." He eyed Maleck as he said the last.

"Likely you are correct, Serge," he said with forced friendliness. "Still, if we are to die here, I too would prefer a better meal selection."

The rest of them glanced past the Tower at the canyon beyond. Pero shuddered and wiped the grease from his fingers on his expansive shirt. His chest was massive, but the years of soft living had given him a gut to match. Julius had been hard-pressed to find him a uniform shirt that fit. "Ain't right, ain't fair, ain't proper. Them Iron Mages, who do they think they be? Using us folk in their war with the Madness."

The rest cast uneasy glances with each other, except Maleck. *We're already consigned to this gods-forsaken place; what else could be done to us? Still…* "Pero, be careful. While I doubt the lofty mages in the tower penthouse would deign to notice such as us, Marshal Enoch can. And I daresay Danag would have more than words for you."

Snorting, Pero pushed at him again. "Danag. You be his little pet, ain'tcha? Made his day to find a real fighter amongst the lot of us. Well, you're in the Front Rooms, same as us. What'd it get you?"

Samara saved Maleck from answering by throwing a heel of bread at the former Watchman. "Moron. If you used your mouth for more than stuffing your face, you'd learn a thing." She looked around the group. "Second floor, center. If you listened to what the old-timers were saying, you'd know it's the hardest hit spot. Always. Danag didn't do him any favors putting him there."

No, he's like a smith. Putting the iron where the fire is hottest to see if it can be turned into steel. "It gets me where I need to be, Pero. The only way to survive this is to learn from those who are still here. I intend to survive my twenty years and get back to my house and family. I suggest you also seek out those who have made it this far if you want to survive as well."

The large man snorted in disgust. "You suggest! Fancy words from a snot-nosed brat like you. You say you're here for murder. Who'd ye kill, some beggar that wouldn't get out of your way fast enough?"

Maleck looked around at the others. Most looked uncomfortable, but they were still interested in the answer. *No secrets out here for long. And I need all the allies I can get.* Finally, he looked Pero in the eye. "I killed, murdered in cold blood, an Iron Mage."

Pero began to sneer but Maleck's expression made him pause. He glanced at the others, who looked on with various expressions of disbelief or shock.

"You can ask Marshal Enoch if you wish. An Iron Mage had taken a fancy to my youngest sister. They can marry, you know. Most don't because they're too involved with their wizardry, but some choose to live a more normal life. At first, we thought it was a great honor."

He looked up into the sky for several moments. "Then he took her against her will and used his magic to do things to her. She won't speak at all to this day. She just sits for most of the day, stroking a doll and staring out the window. When we pressed for charges, we were told that the Iron Guild would handle things. And the next day that… person was free and walking around. And my father would not allow us to speak of the issue after that."

Looking around the group, the young noble saw he had their full attention. "I stalked him for seven weeks, learning his habits and patterns as I would for a stag in the woods. I took him by surprise one night when he was alone, observing the stars. A bag over his head laced with a soporific made it easy to take him to a private room in one of the best inns. The kind where they don't ask questions for those with enough money. A few hours of work and I left him with his manhood, if you can call it that, in his mouth and his throat slit."

"Once he was found, my family would be the obvious suspects. To save them from repercussions, the next morning, I turned myself into the Watch. And now I'm here with you." Maleck looked down, the hard crust of bread in his hand squeezed into a ball. Looking up, he saw their expressions ranged from Samara's look of shock to Pero's satisfied smirk. "But make no mistake, when my twenty is done I'm leaving without a look back at this place."

Danag left Maleck's assignment to the last, and so the young man saw how the others were welcomed. Some squads had jeers and rude quips for their newest Penitents, while others gave them little notice at all. Pero was in the room next door and Maleck watched his attempts to garner goodwill fall upon uncaring expressions and turned backs.

Sergeant Yor greeted him with a nod and motioned a thumb towards a bunk near the back. "That's yers. Rest of the squad is on drill, so stow yer gear and I'll show you your place."

Drill was taking place in their Front Room. They were so named because these series of defensive fortifications faced down the canyon that led to the Madness. It was a square room about twenty feet on a side, built with solid stone and brick. Three metal shutters, all open, revealed archery embrasures through the outer wall. A rack of windlass-cranked crossbows and several racks of sword, axes, and other weapons lined the back wall, and bundles of bolts sat in barrels in the center of the room next to sturdy wooden tables.

The rest of the squad paused in their motions as they entered, unloaded crossbows in their hands. There were eleven of them, in three groups. The center group only had three people and the sergeant motioned for him to join it. "This here's Maleck. You'll be number four center. Your lead is Pascoe."

The center team watched with bored expressions as Maleck joined them. Pascoe was a lanky man with long dirty-blond hair that hung about his face. He grimaced and said, "Right, here's how this works, Four. I'm One, Cyara is Two, and Jorn is three. We rotate through the center window, shooting at them bastards as they close on us. Your job is to make sure the bolts are ready for us as we cycle back to reload. Always have a spare bow ready in case one of us has a problem or someone goes down and you need to step in. Something gets in, you kick over the table and hide behind it while we get organized."

"I can hold my own in a fight, Pascoe."

"That's One to you, newbie. Just try not to get underfoot, get in the way of the others, or get one of us killed. Mind your place and make sure you have clean pants waiting for you. If you live." The rest of the team smiled mirthlessly at that last.

Maleck said nothing in response. He wouldn't try to gain favor like Pero had, with jokes and obsequious behavior. Nor would he ostracize himself by ignoring their instructions. He just nodded and said, "I won't run. I will fight."

Pascoe stared at him a moment longer and then turned away. The others either smirked or rolled their eyes and turned back to the drill. While they worked, Pascoe described the various threats they faced from the Madness.

"We get a lot of flying things. Bat wings, bird wings, creatures that just float. They come and try to block our view of the ground, so the big'uns can get close. Those will smash through the walls, and not just the ones down on the ground floor. Most can climb or jump really high."

Cyara laughed. "But they all bleed and die, newbie. Don't worry none about that. We kill'em as they come and keep you safe."

Pascoe smirked. "That's right, kid. Do as you're told, and we'll keep you alive."

Jorn looked over with a sly expression. "But you gotta watch out for the soul stealers. They'll eat you from the inside out and take your body for their own."

"Aw, now Jorn ain't nobody here who seen one of them. Last guy who did finished his twenty years ago."

"Maybe he finished it, Pascoe. Or maybe something finished it for him!"

The crew laughed, a shared joke that excluded Maleck. But he only nodded and continued with his work.

That night, as the newest member Maleck was assigned to the mid-watch. He was alone in their Front Room, responsible for readying the crossbows if the alarm went off. He wasn't sure what that would be, only that Pascoe had said he would know it when he heard it.

"Them Iron Mages, they be up there," he pointed at the ceiling, "watching the Madness. Some say they're studying it. Others say they're trying to figure out how to close it 'cause they opened it in the first place. All we know is that they can see somehow when an attack starts. So listen and be ready. We haven't been attacked in four days so it could happen anytime now."

After an hour of inspecting every part of the room and the weapons, Maleck became bored. It was quiet in the room, and there was no noise from outside, not even animals. The wind stirred through the canyon every so often, carrying with it a faint metallic smell, like rust. He gathered his courage and stared ahead, trying to make out the dark on dark of the tear in reality.

He thought maybe he could see some movement when a noise from below caught his attention.

By standing on his toes and peering down through the top of the embrasure, he could see movement down below. Slowly, a lone figure walked with a stiff gait in front of the tower. He couldn't make out any details, only that it was carrying an axe and wore mail.

"That's Selkirk. On his nightly patrol."

Maleck jumped at the voice behind him. Jorn stood at his shoulder, dressed in a simple shirt and breeches. He held an earthen jug in his hand, the smell of strong liquor emanating from the neck.

"Nobody mentioned anything about going outside at night. And Danag said we don't fight outside."

"Oh, we don't, boy. They do." He pointed with the other hand.

Several more figures stalked through the night, in the same stiff gait that Selkirk used. They were spread out across the frontage of the tower, beyond the moat. Selkirk had stopped to look up at the moon. A low moan carried forth from him and one arm reached out for the pale disk in the sky.

Jorn took a drink and stared out the window, hatred plain on his face. "Them mages say you don't remember your life before you get raised. I say they're lying."

Selkirk's face was illuminated by the moonlight, and Maleck could see the massive rent in his skull where something had nearly caved in one whole side. The desiccated lips issued another moan, this one full of longing as the undead warrior gazed upwards. The iron collar on his neck hung loose around the shrunken flesh.

Jorn took another swallow from the jug. "Twenty years, boy. One way or another, we all serve twenty years at the Tower."

Six days served

They waited in the dark, hands gripping the stocks of their crossbows as the weird cries rang out into the night, echoing across the canyon walls. The rest of the squad looked unworried, Maleck thought, but his heart was hammering in his chest and his throat was dry. He had to watch and learn if he was going to survive and get back home.

Sergeant Yor was watching the approaching swarm through the ceiling-mounted periscope, though how he could make out any details in the darkness was beyond him.

"Alright, boys, they're just about..." He was interrupted by the heavy twang of bolts being loosed from the upper floors. "Let 'em have it!"

The two Penitents on either side of the three embrasures flung open the metal shutters while the third at each window brought his crossbow up to fire. The heavy strings twanged as they released, nearly in unison.

Screeches of pain came through the narrow firing slits as the number two man in the team, having recovered his crossbow, stepped up to fire. The first man stepped back several paces to wind the crossbow and claim a steel bolt from the table. Number three was waiting for two to fire, while Maleck as the number four, the spare, ensured the table was supplied with bolts.

It was like a dance as the Penitents cycled through their firing routine. Fire, step back, wind, load, and step forward. A steady cacophony of screams came from outside, some in rage but most in pain. The scene in this room was being repeated on all five floors of the tower. From the roof a steady rain of mage fire, lightning, acid rain, and freezing cold fell upon the creatures of the Madness, taking its dreadful toll. And still they came.

Minutes into the attack, something smashed into their embrasure hard enough to spall rock back into Cyara's face as she fired. Her bolt hit something right away, and green blood spurted into the room from her target. Where it landed on stone, nothing happened. But where it landed on her leathers and on her skin, smoke began to rise, and she began to scream. The stink of sulfur filled the air.

Yor grabbed Maleck by the collar and yelled, "Grab the bucket of natron!" as he ran to Cyara.

Maleck stumbled to the back wall, his gaze on the screaming woman as she swiped at the burning blood and only succeeded in smearing it across her skin and hands. He found the bucket of grayish material and hauled it over to Yor, who held Cyara down by her shoulders as she struggled and screamed. The rest of the team dodged around them, keeping up their steady fire into the night.

"Smear it over her wounds!"

Doing as instructed, he grabbed handfuls of the powder and started with the worst burns first. The ash bubbled and hissed as he did so and Yor commanded him to put more on. He worked quickly, covering her wounds as thoroughly as he could. The acid on her wounds burned his hands as he did so, but he ignored the pain as she writhed under his hands. All the while the screeching and screaming from the outside continued, as did the metronomic twangs of the crossbows.

She passed out at some point in his work, for when he looked up her eyes had rolled back into her head. Yor motioned to the back wall. "Lay her there. The medics will take care of the rest. And then grab your weapon and get on the line."

The young Penitent gasped as he dragged her limp body to the back wall. His hands itched and burned, and he saw his fingers were red and slightly swollen. Pushing the pain aside, he studied the room, waiting for his chance to join the fight. Now was his chance to show them he could fight.

Grabbing the spare crossbow, he loaded it and stepped up into the embrasure to fire. The dark night strobed with reds, whites, and greens of magery, highlighting the swooping, leathery-winged creatures in the air and the muscular, talon-fingered monstrosities on the ground. Without thinking, he raised the weapon to his shoulder and fired at a nearby flyer. Before he could step away, Pascoe shouldered him aside to take his turn.

Maleck lost track of the time as the attack continued into the later hours of the night. The repetitive cycle of loading and firing numbed his brain, and he only remembered bits and pieces of the battle later. At one point, something large and with far too many limbs covered all three embrasures with its body, its tentacles questing into the room. Yor ordered the shutters closed and then called the room above via the speaking tube. Long seconds passed as they struggled to hold the shutters closed against the hammering from outside. All at once, the stink of tar filled the air, splashing onto the creature and the walls around it as the squad above them poured it out through a funnel. Small rivulets of the stuff found its way through seams in the shutters and Yor yelled for them to back away.

Then the squad above them dropped lit torches down and ignited the tar on the creature.

It burned in place for several long seconds. The keening moan of the creature's pain was a deep, basso howl that vibrated the stone. The burnt pork smell of roasting monster flesh filled the room. Finally, they heard it detach and fall, its keening moan fading away. When they went to reopen the shutters, they had to wrap spare cloth around their hands to protect themselves from the heat.

Outside, the night was as hellish as before as they continued their dance of bolts.

The next morning, they cleaned up the mess from the battle. Debris was carted off, walls were rebuilt, wounds were tended to. The most serious of the injured received magical attention from an Iron Mage. The screams from the patients during the healing process were often more agonizing than the initial wound.

Serge was standing next to the moat, staring at the swirling rift in the ravine. His face was slack, as if all emotion had been drained away. He bore some minor injuries but seemed to have come through their first battle relatively unscathed. Physically, at least.

"What gives, Serge?" Maleck walked up next to him, trying to see what the former gang member was looking at.

"He's gone."

"Who's gone?"

He gestured at the rift. "Yeddiah. Damn fool was in the same room as me. Wall got busted open and he charged, frothing at the mouth with an axe in each hand. Something grabbed him and carried him away."

"Well, he might be out there in the ravine. Maybe a search party…" Maleck trailed off as Serge shook his head.

"Enoch already sent a team. They found nothing. No blood, not even the axes. It's like he never even existed."

One year served

They found out why the rest of the tower wasn't around when they had first arrived. The arrival of new Penitents from the capital coincided with the Ceremony of Completion and most of the tower inhabitants spent the day celebrating. For it was on this day that sentences were considered completed for those who had arrived twenty years before.

All save those on sentry gathered in the open meadow past the Training Fields. An Iron Mage in the rust-red robes stood off to one side. Marshal Enoch walked to the center of the semi-circle of Penitents, wand of office in hand, with Danag and Julius a pace behind.

"Lars. Betha. Redrigo. Stand forward."

The three stepped forward to stand in front of him. All carried the look of experienced warriors, with scars aplenty to prove it. Surprisingly, they stood nervously in front of him and the mages.

"You have completed your sentences as Penitents. You have given twenty years to pay for your crimes, and now begin a new phase of your life. On one hand," Julius stepped forward, three bags of coins jingling in his hand. "You can choose to return to the society you protected for so long. You will be transported back to the capital and receive one hundred pieces of silver to start a new life."

A small murmur ran through the assembly. Maleck had learned that not every year had living people who had completed their sentences. There were always the dead that had served twenty, though.

The mage stepped forward, hands hidden inside the folds of the robe. Enoch waved at the mage. "Or you can take the mithril collar and become a Protector. Choose, then; silver or mithril."

Maleck whispered to Yor. "What's a Protector?"

"They remain here and fight, by choice."

A cold shiver ran through Maleck as Lars stepped forward immediately. "I choose silver."

Enoch nodded to Julius, who gave the man a bag of coins. Lars clutched the small purse like it was gold and stepped to the side, where the mage tapped his collar with a steel rod. The collar clicked open, and Lars removed it quickly, handing it to the mage like it would bite him.

There was a long pause while the crowd watched Betha and Redrigo. They both stood in silence for several long moments. Betha turned her face to the sky while Redrigo stared into the distance. Then, almost simultaneously, they both said, "Mithril."

The Iron Mage walked over to them and withdrew red-gloved hands from the robe. In each hand was a silvery-white U-shaped collar bearing an emerald. Both warriors stood stock still as the mage fitted the mithril collars around their neck. There was no lock or other fastener. The metal flowed into itself, completing the circle around their necks. At the same time, the iron collars rusted away, crumbling to dust.

"What does it mean to be a Protector, Yor?"

"They will never leave the Tower, and most don't want to. They choose where they fight and aren't limited to a Front Room. No one questions their decisions. They will defend against the Madness for the rest of their lives. But if they fall, their bodies will be buried with honors and no hand of necromancy will touch them. Their names will be etched into the Great Hall back at the Capital as Defenders of Humanity."

"But, why choose this? Why not take the silver and leave?" *That's what I'm going to do.*

"Lad, some can't leave. Either the fighting has changed them too much, or it's been too long since they left and there's nothing there for them. Lars, he'll be going back to a city where everyone thinks he's dead. Family will be gone, and friends moved on. He'll know nobody and have nothing but his silver. Most of them that take the silver wind up back here within a year as a Penitent again or drink themselves to death."

Maleck stared at the two newest Protectors with distaste. *It won't be like that for me. Father knows I'm not dead and the rest of the family will be waiting for me when I get back.*

That night was the other half of the Ceremony of Completion. Again, the living Penitents and Protectors gathered in the meadow. This time three Iron Mages stood in the center of the formation with a small iron pot simmering over an open fire. Enoch stepped forward, Julius and Danag at his side.

"Fellow warriors, tonight we honor those who have completed their sentence in death. Twenty years have passed since they stepped through the mist and now, we give them rest."

The mages began to chant, a low-voiced unintelligible murmur that nevertheless raised the hairs on the back of Maleck's neck. As the chant began to rise in pitch, smoke began to rise from the ground. Figures started to become visible through the haze. One by one, several undead Penitents stalked forward to stand in front of the fire, called by the magic. All bore signs of extreme use; severed limbs and heads reattached with sturdy twine, rents in their armor, eyes and ears torn away.

Enoch raised his voice to be heard above the chant. "Now, brothers and sisters, it is time to bid our comrades goodbye. Say what you need to say and be quick!"

One by one, people separated from the crowd and walked to the gathering of the undead Penitents. Some just clasped a hand or patted a shoulder, while others embraced an old comrade. Maleck could only watch, horrified as the living bid farewell to the undead.

Finally, when all had said their piece, the mages' chant changed tone and rhythm, rising and becoming commanding. The mist swirled around the undead warriors, forming separate streams around each. As the chant reached fevered pitch, the smoke swirled faster and faster and a green glow began to emanate from each undead throat. The mini-tornado spun into the sky, pulling a torrent of green sparks forth. A shouted command from the mages caused the mist to disperse, and the green sparks shot into the sky.

There was a collective sigh from withered throats, and they collapsed to the ground like puppets with their strings cut. The desiccated flesh rapidly decayed, turning to dust and left bare bones behind. These were in turn swallowed by the earth, leaving behind their iron collars, which the mages reclaimed.

Three years served

The exterior wall of their Front Room exploded inwards, spreading debris across the floor, peppering them with rocks, and leaving a gaping hole three feet across. A massive beaked head poked inside, screaming defiance. Cem spun from his embrasure and shot it point-blank in the eye. Clear fluid spattered him, and the creature bucked and heaved in pain, pulling more stone away from the wall. The rest of the squad were reaching for their swords and axes when a hooked talon reached through the enlarged hole and speared Cem in the upper thigh. He screamed in pain and terror, but it was mercifully brief as the talon yanked him backwards, slamming his body into the wall. His skull shattered like cheap crockery, leaving a bloody smear behind.

There was a crashing sound in Pero's room next door, followed by people yelling. Maleck ignored that and darted forward with a short spear, executing a lunge and thrust to spear the creature in the other eye. The point went in deep, and he hoped he had gotten to the brain. The weapon was yanked from his grip as the head disappeared back through the gap, the body falling lifelessly to the ground. Quickly, he backpedaled, not wanting to be caught next to a breach. Cyara handed him an axe as he reached the line in the center of the room. Pascoe and Geff still held loaded crossbows and were aiming at the gap, waiting. The rest of them formed a rough semicircle, axes and blades at the ready.

Something slammed into the interior wall from the next room over and new screams joined those they had heard before. Dust flew and shattered brick spilled into their room, opening up a crack nearly five feet across. They barely noticed the damage as a massive paw with jagged claws appeared in the exterior hole in their own room, grabbing from below. Pascoe and Geff fired in unison, and twin crossbow bolts sprouted from the paw. A pain-filled howl rose from outside, but the paw heaved, and another appeared next to it. However, the damaged stone gave way and the second paw struggled to find a new grip.

They charged as the creature blindly searched for something to grab on to.

Maleck was first there, whether by dint of speed or from the others hanging back a pace. *Are they slower, more cautious, or just letting the new guy take the risk first?* He swung the axe into the first paw as its mate found a more secure grip. Bones crunched under his blow and red blood spurted out, but the creature did not lose its grip. As he stepped forward to wrench the axe away, he glanced downward. He wished he hadn't.

A massive man-shaped creature with the head of a wolf looked up at him. Jaws slavering and teeth bared, it growled deep in its throat as it heaved itself upwards into the gap. Hot breath washed over him as Maleck threw himself backwards, pulling the axe free as he went. The rest of the squad darted in to land their own attacks, an avalanche of blows that spread blood and gore everywhere but failed to prevent the wolf creature from gaining entrance to the room.

Bleeding profusely, with one arm hanging by shreds of flesh, it ignored its wounds to leap at the nearest defender. Geff died with his face torn off, despite burying his spear in the creature's chest. Maleck rolled to his feet and came in low, swinging the axe at its knee. Yor followed with a high strike on the damaged shoulder a second later with a mace, crunching bone and toppling the creature onto its side as the damaged knee gave way. It still managed to slash Maleck across the chest, leaving four bloody furrows.

As one they pummeled it then, taking full advantage of their superior position. It finally died when Yor landed a massive overhand blow on its head, stoving in the skull and sending it into convulsions. Still, it had managed to bloody all of them in the short time before it died.

They turned to defend the gap once again, but the night sky lit up with actinic glare and thunder sounded. The Iron Mages had loosed their lightnings upon the enemy, having apparently judged that they were sufficiently bunched up. The smell of ozone filled the air as the near-continuous rumble of thunder assaulted the ears. The din was loud enough to even drown out the sound of the dying creatures at the base of the tower.

Several long moments later, after the lights had faded and the thunder was a mere echo in the canyon, it grew quiet outside. No screams of Maddened creatures came from the dark night outside. The only sounds they could hear was their own breathing and faint weeping through the wall of the adjoining room.

It was later the next day when Maleck learned two things. First, Yor was being promoted to Floor Captain, in charge of all the Front Rooms on this level. This meant Pascoe was now in charge of their room, and to his surprise, Maleck was made leader of his team.

The second was that Serge was dead. Yor offered to let him go say goodbye before the Iron Mages took him to be raised, but Maleck declined. He preferred to remember the tattooed man as he was, not as he would become.

Five years served

The dull rumble of thunder sounded across the training yard. Everyone paused for a moment, eyes tracking towards the canyon beyond the tower. Gray clouds were building in the distance. Activity resumed, although with a more determined pace. The beginning of the storm often signaled the rise in activity that would lead to an attack, although it sometimes took days for it to happen.

Maleck noticed that Pero was still staring at the ravine, and the next rumble of thunder caused him to shiver. He walked over to the other man, whose face was pale and sweating under the heavy beard. "There's time, Pero. Hours, maybe even days before they come."

Pero swallowed heavily. "I can't. I can't go back and face 'em again."

"Yes, you can. We'll be there with you, Pero. We'll all be there, and we'll face them together."

"No. No, no, no." He took an involuntary step away from the nightmare he saw in his mind's eye.

Laying his hand on Pero's shoulder, Maleck attempted to arrest his backwards movement. "It'll be alright…"

"No! It'll never be alright! We fight and we fight, and we die and then they still make us fight! It never ends!" The other man shook off his hand and continued backing away, his shouts causing others to turn to look at him.

The young noble took a step forward, but Yor laid a hand on his shoulder, mimicking his earlier attempt on Pero. "Let him go. He's had it. This place breaks many people, and it's broken him."

"But he's going to get too far away from the tower. His collar!"

"Lad, no matter how far he goes, Pero will never be able to get too far away from this place. His collar now becomes his solace."

They all watched as the former Watchman turned and walked deliberately away from the tower. A long minute passed and then his collar began to glow white. A high-pitched tone sang through the air. Pero screamed but continued walking. His steps began to falter but he doggedly kept taking step after step. Several seconds later, the collar exploded with a loud crack. The now-headless body staggered a few paces and collapsed to the ground, blood fountaining into the grass.

Maleck looked away. Around him, everyone else went back about their business. "We should try to get his body."

Yor nodded at the corpse. "No need. The Iron Mages, they don't wait."

He looked up to see the body and head disappearing into the ground. Soon, Pero would be back on duty, his head stitched back on and undead body patrolling the grounds outside the Tower.

Seven years served

Maleck dangled his legs over the edge of the moat, a flagon of ale in the grass next to him. The wind blew gently through the gaps between the tower and the ravine walls, stirring his hair and bringing the scent of the prairie grass with it. It had rained on and off for several days, and while the ground was damp to sit on, at least the smells from the moat were muted.

He heard the squish of footsteps approaching from behind him.

"I know it's you, Samara."

"Of course you do. I know better than to try and sneak up behind anyone here. At least, not without reason." She sat next to him, her own flagon brimming. "Health, Maleck."

He picked up his flagon and raised it in her direction. "Not sure that's the right toast for this place."

She sipped and made a face. "Why can't someone who knows how to brew a decent ale get sent here? No, you're probably right. But what should we toast to, then? Death to the Madness?"

"Death to the Iron Guild, more like it."

She glanced upwards with a shudder. "Don't even joke about something like that."

"Wasn't joking."

"Maleck…" Her voice trailed off. "Everyone knows you hate them. Frankly, everyone is amazed they haven't done anything to you by now."

He set the flagon down next to him. "I'm not worth their time. What would they do, send me to the Tower? Put me in a Front Room? Besides, even if they kill me, I'm still here for years yet. What do they gain by doing anything to me?"

She turned to look at him, hair blown across her face by the wind. It wasn't as pretty a face anymore, with a long scar tracing from left ear to chin. Part of her scalp near that ear was burned away too, and no hair grew there anymore. But she looked stronger than she had when she'd first arrived. "Maleck, you don't get it. It's not just your animosity to the mages. The newer Penitents look up to you. The older ones are impressed by your skill and leadership. You actually care about what happens to people here. No one has ever done that before, beyond what was needed to survive."

He shrugged. His goals were no secret. "I do what I need to."

She reached out and touched his shoulder. "No, you do far more than that. You do what you think needs to be done for all of us, not just yourself. Most people here don't think beyond living to the next day. And they'll take their silver, if they live, and drink and whore it all away and return here to die. None of them think about those that come after them. This whole construct is perpetuated by a refusal of any of them to do anything about it after they return."

"Samara, I'm taking silver and leaving here when my twenty is done."

She gave him a measuring look. "Maybe. Or maybe you'll take mithril and become Tower Marshal. Think of what you could do as Marshal."

He glared at her, ire rising. His voice rose in pitch in his response. "I said, I'm leaving here, Samara!"

The former thief leaned back on her elbows, a slight smile on her face. "Are you trying to convince me, or yourself?"

Ten years served

Maleck and Sylla eased quietly into his Front Room. The clouds hid the sun for the most part, but thin sunbeams came through the mostly closed shutters. The faint noises of drill and work parties came from outside but for now, they were alone in here.

Both of them had traded their duties for this time together. It wasn't romance or love but basic need that brought them both together. With a male to female ratio at the tower of more than four to one, the women could have their choice of who to partner with. There weren't rules against it, only that it couldn't interfere with your duties and there was no partnering within the same Room.

Sylla worked in the kitchens, which was ironic given that she burned down her restaurant to collect on the insurance. It was just her bad luck that the fire spread out of control and killed twenty others in nearby buildings. Still, no one at the Tower cared what you had done on the outside to earn your sentence here; you were here and that was it.

After they had finished with each other and were drowsing in the blankets, she asked, "You keep talking about going back. Why?"

He stared at the ceiling for several long moments. "I've been taught, had it drilled into me that I would take my place in society and continue our traditions. My family is well placed and generations old. At first, I was going to go back and fulfill that heritage. But after being here, seeing what the Iron Mages are like… what they did to my sister… I'm going back to reign them in. They have too much power over us with the threat of the Madness." He rolled over to look at her. "They could use soldiers and mages from the army, not convicts. People who view it as their duty to protect, not those who've been compelled to be here."

She smiled. "Your eyes light up when you talk like that. That's the first real passion I've seen in anybody besides hatred for life here." Rolling out of the pallet, Sylla walked to the other side of the room and stood next to the shutters. The sun was still shining through them, although the beams were more horizontal now and dimmer. They silhouetted her body as she looked out through the shutters. Thin streamers of mist passed back and forth through the light.

"It's all the same for everyone else. They talk about what they hate here, what they would do to survive here. But no one talks about changing this place." Her voice was soft, but it carried in the quiet room. "You have a goal besides just surviving. Most of us can't see beyond our twenty."

Her nude form was dappled in sunbeams and mist swirled past her into the room in thin streamers. Something in his heart stirred, and he was shocked to realize that he didn't want to quash it. *It wouldn't work outside…*

She opened one shutter a bit more, the well-oiled hinges making no sound. "I'll be back before you. I only have seven years left. Maybe…" her voice trailed off.

Maleck laid back and looked at the ceiling again. Maybe. *Maybe I'd come by her restaurant and get a great table and excellent food, but the gap back there is greater than anything here.* Sylla said nothing more and he was ashamed to be grateful at the quiet. Perhaps she was waiting for him to answer. He could hear her breathing speed up, starting to come in gasps. He hoped she wasn't going to cry. Neither of them needed that.

The screech of metal tearing reverberated through the Room. Maleck jumped up as Sylla turned to face him, holding one of the shutters in her hand. The sunlight had nearly disappeared from behind her, but it still cast her in shadow. And in that shadow, her eyes glowed red. The mists swirled around her body, concealing her form and blurring her motions.

She charged him, swinging the shutter like it was made of nothing. Glowing red strands emanated from her back and head, trailing into the mist surrounding her. As he ducked behind a table, he faintly heard the Tower alarm sounding.

Sylla, or whatever was possessing her, seemed to be lost in rage. She/it smashed the shutter down on the table, but it was sturdy oak and resisted collapse. Maleck rolled under the table, towards her and bowled into her legs. He was surprised when she didn't go down, and even more surprised when strong hands grabbed him by the shoulder and thigh. The pressure from her grip was excruciating but short lived as she threw him across the room with an inhuman scream. He crashed into a crossbow rack, taking several to the floor with him as he fell. Something popped in his back and pain screamed up his spine.

Maleck struggled to gain his feet, his nerves screaming in alarm as she stalked towards him. They both turned as the door to the Room crashed open and Pascoe charged in, yelling, "Attack! Some sort of posses-," he cut off as he saw the two of them.

She reacted before him, charging and latching her hands around his throat, driving him into the door jamb. His hands gripped hers, trying in vain to gain some room to breathe. Face purple, his struggles began to grow weaker and weaker.

Maleck staggered over to the other wall and grabbed an axe from the rack. Stepping forward and swinging with a mighty grunt, he buried the axe in Sylla's back. His back spasmed and the axe dropped from nerveless fingers.

She collapsed like a puppet with its strings cut and so did he, body and mind numb. It prevented him from thinking about what he'd just done.

Fourteen years served

Enoch had completed his sentence years ago and Maleck couldn't remember which Marshal this one was. Several had tried to replace the stolid warrior, but the succession of faces and names were a blur to him. They were all just 'Marshal' to him. And the Marshal was talking to him.

"Pascoe recommended you as Floor Captain before he died. Yor said as much as well before he was, well, melted."

Maleck only nodded. *Six years left.*

"You know, many of the others look up to you. Being in the center Room is demanding ,and you've lived up to the challenge with honor."

The no-longer young man gave him a flat stare. "There's no trick to staying alive. You just have to want it more than anything else."

After a few moments, the Marshal turned away. "Well, yes. Still, you've done good work surviving and teaching the others." He paused, eyes searching the blankness on the other man's face. "Have you considered… what you'll do at twenty?"

Maleck considered the question, eyes finding the mithril collar on the man's neck. There really didn't seem to be any other answer to give, though. It was the mantra he repeated year after year. "I'm going back. I have my family and a House to return to, and I'm going to challenge the policies on running this place. The Iron Guild has had free reign for far too long."

The Marshal looked around with a quick glance and then nodded nervously. "I see. Well, if you change your mind…" His words trailed off and after a moment he walked away.

The new Penitents watched with wide eyes until Maleck turned back to them. "Well? What are you gawking at? Act like that in a Room and you'll be dead. Get those weapons up! Let's see what you remember!"

Twenty years served

The Marshal stepped forward into the semi-circle of Penitents, the Training Master and Quarters Master next to him. Maleck listened to them recite the words he had heard every year since. Beside him, Samara waited in absolute stillness. They were the only two left alive from their year group. Pero, Serge, and the others would get their turn later tonight. Her time in the tower had taught her the value of patience and forethought, he thought. *I wonder what my time has taught me?*

"Will you take silver or mithril?"

Samara stepped forward immediately. "I choose silver. I'm done with this place and its crappy food."

As she accepted her silver, she turned her back on the Tower and the rest of the Penitents. *She never changed. I think she was even more eager to leave this place than I was.* As she stepped aside and all eyes turned to him, Maleck had a strange thought. *Am I eager to leave? Silver or mithril, what do I want? I thought I knew.*

He looked down at his hands and the old scars of the acid burns from Cyara and other fights. The scars on his chest from that wolf creature pulled at his chest every time he turned his head. His body was a history of scars, twenty years' worth. All for the Iron Mages and the Tower.

No. Not for that. Looking around at the gathered Penitents, he saw those from his Floor watching him with expectant eyes. His Floor had taken the least casualties of all the Floors since he'd become Captain. They were his people, and the thought made his chest tighten. Taking the silver meant leaving them behind.

He looked at the waiting Iron Mage with the mithril collar.

And stepped forward.

"I choose silver." He turned to the crowd. "Not because I'm done with this place. But because I'm going back to change this place. To bring the Iron Guild to account for what they've done to us and all those who came before. I'm going back for you."

The Raven and the Crow:
The Orb of Raia
By Michael K. Falciani

Seated at a table on the far side of the common room of the Box and Rum gambling house were five men pitted against one another in a game of chance. Three had already folded their hands while the last two eyed one another warily.

The younger of the pair was a tall man, built with the lean muscle of an expert swordsman. He wore a dark green cloak and leather bracer on his left arm that marked him as a hunter of the forest. He sat with his hands folded one over the other at a table of worn pine. Displayed in front of him were seven playing cards stacked neatly in a pyramid design, each facing upward. Three at the bottom bore the twin skulls of the horde, denoting their rank. The man's dark eyes glanced down at the trio of cards that marked the strength of his hand. A card depicting a green vial of poison lay between two bestial images. One displayed a set of fangs while the other showed the claws of a wolf. He had a single card remaining. It lay face down, waiting patiently for the man to play.

"I'll wager a dozen eagles," the hunter said, giving his counterpart a smile. He pushed a stack of triangular coins into the middle of the table and leaned back in his chair.

"Ahh Zedaine," came the lilting brogue of the dark-eyed smuggler sitting comfortably across from the big hunter. "You think to force me from the game?" The smuggler shook his head. "I've already got four champions showing," he boasted. "That's an 'Iron Company,' and I've still another card left to play. I will not withdraw in the face of your triple horde."

Boldly the smaller man shoved a pair of circular coins into the middle of the table. Their gold luster gleamed brightly in the candlelight next to a heaping pile of silver.

"I'll see your bet, and raise you a talon," the smuggler said, doffing his cap and drinking from his earthenware mug.

Zedaine's face soured as he glanced to his right at the man sitting between the two remaining players. With a lean build and sharp eyes, anyone who looked at them for longer than a heartbeat could see he and the hunter came from the same blood. The man to Zedaine's right had folded his own hand early in the contest and now sat watching the end of the game.

"Kildare, I need you to stake me," the hunter said softly, nudging his sharp-eyed sibling.

Kildare batted his brother's hand away in irritation. "This is your mess, Zee. I'm not cleaning it up for you. Either fold your hand or dig deep and play on."

Zedaine stared at Kildare, his eyes hard. "Fine, I guess I'll have to tell Blade that you cost her twenty in gold to bribe your way out of the stocks yesterday."

"Shut up!" Kildare snapped. "You know damn well that was necessary. Why in the hell would you bring that up now?" he questioned, flashing an angry look across the table.

Zedaine frowned, "Dodge and his boys aren't going to say anything, are you lads?" he said, gesturing across the table to his opponent. "After all, we're going to be working with them."

"I'll take it to the grave," Dodge said, tipping his flat cap reverently. "If you play out the hand, that is."

Kildare turned his glare to Dodge, his eyes as hard as steel. "You might be the finest middleman in Gallanse, but I'd think twice before threatening me," he warned.

Dodge managed a look of resentment. "Me, threaten my new associates?" he questioned, placing a hand over his heart. "Of course not! I'd at least wait to see if you could cover your brother's bet before any threats were issued."

Kildare stared at the man for a long moment. Shaking his head, he reached down and dug a hand into his money pouch. Looking balefully at Dodge, he flipped a gold coin on the table where it spun for a few seconds before falling with a metallic clang.

Looking back at his sibling, Kildare sniffed in disapproval. "You have long odds brother. There's but a single horde card in play, and it's one chance in four that it lies in front of you."

"You worry too much," Zedaine laughed, clapping Kildare on the back.

"Idiot," the elder sibling grumbled. "Do you *ever* consider the odds?"

"I leave that to you," Zedaine replied with a grin.

Kildare shook his head. "You're impossible," he retorted, taking a drink from his mug, draining its contents.

The elder brother turned his head over his shoulder and raised a hand. "I'll take another," he shouted to the serving girl behind them.

"Hoping to drown out the pain of loss?" Dodge quipped, taking another drink from his own mug. Wiping his mouth with a cotton sleeve, the weasel-faced man raised an eyebrow toward his opponent.

"Your play lad. Let's see if lady luck favors you a bit longer."

Nonchalantly, Zedaine reached forward and casually flipped his last card.

It showed the image of a dark-haired woman staring up at them, a pair of white eyes resting beneath the twin skulls of the horde.

"Damn," Kildare swore, looking at his brother, impressed. "You *are* lucky tonight."

"Fortuitous, to say the least," Zedaine admitted with a smile. Looking up at Dodge, he cocked an eyebrow. "Might I present you with the Raging Horde, four skulls strong."

Dodge's two companions, powerful men, peered at Zedaine in confusion.

"What's that you said?" the first asked, his vapid face covered in a red beard.

"How do you mean?" Zedaine asked.

"That word," the other chimed in. "Fortuidness—what's it mean?"

"It means serendipitous," Dodge answered, looking at his men with a sigh.

Neither registered any understanding.

"Coincidental. Unanticipated…haphazard," the weasel-faced Dodge continued.

"It means he got lucky," Kildare put in, looking sharply at the smuggler.

"What?" the smaller man asked innocently. "I may be street—it don't mean I'm not a learned man."

Kildare frowned, saying nothing. Instead, he leaned back in his chair, and scratched at his chin.

Dodge finally looked down at his opponent's cards, tipping his cap toward Zedaine. "A fine hand to be sure, especially this late in the game. What's your play?"

Zedaine folded his arms in front of him. "I'm out of coins, I call."

Dodge nodded and reached downward. As he touched his last card with his fingertips the middleman broke into a toothy grin. "What say we wager a bit more?" he asked, glancing at the elder sibling.

Kildare shot Dodge with a cold look. "I'm not interested in vesting more money."

"Come on Kil," Zedaine encouraged. "I've already beaten the odds."

"There are two champion cards left, the mage and the bard," Kildare reasoned. "Either could be lying in front of your opponent. That's two chances out of three. You'll need the kiss of Arianal herself to dig yourself out of a hole that deep."

Zedaine's eyes flattened. "You owe me," he said softly. "For that time in Tal-Mur."

Kildare's brow furrowed in confusion. "What the hell are you talking about? *I* saved *your* ass in Tal-Mur."

"Oh yes, that's right," Zedaine replied thoughtfully. His face brightened. "I can owe you one."

"You owe me dozens already!" Kildare snapped angrily. "Here," he grunted in disgust, tossing Zedaine his money pouch. "Bet whatever you want. Just leave me enough to get drunk, you sod!"

Zedaine snapped the pouch out of the air and rummaged inside. "By Chara," he gaped in wonder. "How much do you have?"

Pulling out his hand, the big hunter plopped a fistful of circular gold coins, into the middle of the table. "That's fifteen talons!" he gasped in awe.

"By the gods…what the hell is wrong with you?" Kildare sputtered, his voice strangled in outrage. "Don't bet it all!"

"The wager's already in the pot," Dodge pointed out, his eyes filled with avarice. "The bet is made."

Kildare looked apoplectic. His face turned a hue of red none of them had ever seen.

"It'll be fine," the big hunter assured him. "Here comes the serving lass Kil, have another drink on me."

"You boneheaded idiot!" Kildare fumed. "You had better win, or so help me, you'll wish I was back in those stocks!"

The serving girl, a buxom lass with a round face and sparkling blue eyes, set a fresh mug of ale in front of Kildare. "That'll be three obols," she said, her eyes twinkling at the downtrodden face of the elder sibling. As she leaned forward, all five men at the table could not help but ogle at her enormous bosom. It was mere inches away from Dodge's beaming countenance.

"I'll be with you in a moment, lass," the smuggler said to the girl, his nose twitching in excitement.

"Let's get this over with," Kildare muttered darkly, giving the girl a nod of thanks as he wet his lips on the rim of his mug.

"I agree," Dodge said, reaching for his last card.

"Just a second," Zedaine warned, his voice low. "Aren't you forgetting something?"

Dodge scratched at his whiskey-colored facial hair, looking closely at the two brothers.

"What's that?" he asked.

"You need to call the bet," Zedaine said evenly. "Else you forfeit the pot."

"Funny thing," Dodge replied, scratching at his goatee. "I don't have the gold to cover the bet *on* me at the moment."

"What?" Kildare growled, his eyes narrowing dangerously.

"I *could* have my men run halfway across Lower City to collect it and then bring it back to the Box and Rum, or—you can take my word for it, and I'll flip the card now… a gentleman's agreement, if you will."

"That's a whole lot of trust for a man we barely know," Kildare stated darkly.

"I'm not a 'man you barely know,'" Dodge answered, looking insulted. "We are boon companions, you and I—set to work together on the morrow. Besides, the city of Gallanse is my place of business. Should I somehow lose the game, you and your brother will come by first thing in the morning, and I'll pay my debt."

Zedaine flashed a quick look at Kildare.

"Alright," the younger sibling said, extending his hand across the table. "A gentleman's agreement."

"Done then," Dodge concurred, reaching out, shaking Zedaine's hand.

The big hunter nodded and sat down, his eyes resting on the final card laying in front of his opponent. "The play is yours."

Dodge gave him a knowing smile and turned the card face up.

His surprise was absolute when he saw a faded image depicting a blue crown, a castle card.

Dodge had lost.

"Fortuitous," Kildare sniggered into his mug.

The brothers woke an hour before dawn. Quietly, they descended the staircase from their chambers on the fourth floor of the Box and Rum. The stale odor of spilled ale permeated the air of the now empty common room. Like shadows, the two warriors slipped out the front door into the fading darkness of the night.

A quarter turn of the hourglass later, they arrived outside a run-down building sandwiched between a butcher's shop and a cobbler's shoddy stand.

They were not the first to arrive.

Outside the building were three figures, standing at the doorway. One of them, a well-muscled warrior, knocked firmly as the brothers moved close. Movement could be heard from inside the shop as the faint light of a candle spilled onto the street through a crack in the door. After a quick word, the opening widened and the trio walked inside, the brothers a step behind.

"He'll be with you in a minute," grunted the man who had let them in. Kildare recognized him as the same bearded brute who had been confused at the table last night. Without another word, the stocky warrior ambled past a display case made of glass. Moments later, he disappeared through a doorway at the back of the building.

"Nice of him to leave us in the dark like this," Zedaine muttered, his voice irritated.

"I agree," croaked the shortest of the trio.

They stood in silence for a moment until a single word broke the stillness.

"*Gerskah.*"

A bauble of green light appeared, floating above the head of the shortest of the trio. He wore the hand sewn garb of a tribal spellcaster, a gnarled wooden staff in his hand.

"That's better," a diminutive man breathed, his wrinkled face coming to light in the glow of his magical creation.

"You're a shaman," Zedaine said, looking down at the caster in curiosity.

"I am," the man rasped, giving the hunter a look of suspicion.

"You seem surprised," Kildare added, watching the man carefully.

The magicker's wizened face relaxed a fraction. "I did not think to find anyone in this land wise to shamanistic magic."

"We've run across a few in our travels," Zedaine replied. "They are never dull, that is for certain."

"You must be Karn," Kildare guessed, nodding in introduction.

"I am," the shaman croaked roughly.

"You are the Raven and the Crow," a second man guessed. He was short in stature, though taller than the first. He stood a fist over five feet and carried a hand-crafted lute slung over his shoulder.

"That's us," Zedaine quipped with a smile. "We're famous."

"More like *infamous*, if the tale-tellers speak the truth," grumbled the last of them. Taller by a finger than his lute toting companion, this fellow sported a trident-shaped goatee, its dark hair flecked with silver. He carried a curved blade at his waist, along with a brace of knives strapped across a leather bandolier that crossed his chest.

"Don't mind Gavakyn," the second said with a wave of his hand. "He was born angry." He extended his hand toward Zedaine, his manner friendly. "Name's Jax. I'm a bard of little renown."

Zedaine took his hand, giving the man a warm smile. "I'm Zedaine, or Crow, if you prefer. This is my brother, Kildare, though he often goes by Raven."

"A pleasure to meet you both," Jax said, putting his hand out to Kildare.

The elder brother absently shook it, looking warily at Gavakyn. "Interesting weapon," he nodded at the man's curved sword.

"It's a machete," the powerful warrior replied, drawing it, holding the blade out for Kildare to inspect.

"They have similar weapons in Valasca," Zedaine murmured, eyeing the blade expertly.

"Not like this they don't," Kildare breathed, looking at Gavakyn in awe.

"What do you mean?" Zedaine asked, narrowing his eyes.

"That's a mythic steel blade," Kildare answered, raising his eyebrows.

"Indeed, it is," Gavakyn acknowledged, putting it away.

Kildare stared closely at the powerful warrior in front of him. "Interesting accent you have," Kildare noted, his gaze carrying slowly to all three. "I've not heard it before."

Gavakyn glowered at Kildare and made to speak. A hand from Jax halted him.

"The world is a big place, master Raven," the bard explained. "Even one as well-traveled as you could not hope to have seen it all. What is important is we work together at the task before us. Only with cooperation can we achieve our goal."

"What goal is that?" Kildare asked. "Our employer was none too specific in revealing the details of this mission."

Jax glanced to the shaman.

"I'll explain when our guide arrives," Karn rasped, sitting in a chair located against the wall.

"Sorry for the delay lads," came a voice from the door behind the counter. Stepping forward was Dodge, who glanced up at the green light floating near the chipped ceiling. "That's a neat trick," he mumbled, walking underneath it.

"Dodge is the guide?" Kildare asked skeptically.

"Top of the morning to you too," the smuggler murmured, tipping his cap toward Kildare.

"Our gold?" Zedaine asked lightly.

Dodge put up his hands defensively. "Being gathered as we speak," he replied. "Fifteen talons, as agreed."

Zedaine grunted in satisfaction.

"Now that we are all here," the diminutive Karn rasped. "I will begin."

The shaman leaned forward in his chair, his rasping voice sounding throughout the room.

"Somewhere underground, located on the outskirts of this city, is the remnant of an old temple. It is thousands of years old and was once home to an ancient being."

"Who?" Kildare asked, looking intrigued.

Karn shook his head. "I know not what she was called in these lands, but in the old days, she was known as Raia, the mad goddess."

"That does not sound promising," Zedaine quipped.

"Why are we looking for this temple?" Kildare queried, ignoring Zedaine.

Karn made a gurgling sound in the back of his throat. "There is an item there, a stone of enormous power. The three of us have been sent to find it and prepare ourselves against a great evil yet to come."

Kildare and Zedaine looked at one another, exchanging a confused glance.

"What evil?" Zedaine asked.

"One that has already touched our lands," Gavakyn answered gruffly. "We three have taken an oath to retrieve the item Karn has spoken of, or die trying."

"What's this then?" Dodge interrupted. "I was hired by the dragon sage to lead you to the temple I stumbled upon. I'm not interested in risking my bleeding neck for some, mystical…magical, artifact of the gods."

"You will do what we hired you to do!" Gavakyn growled angrily.

"Easy," Jax said, placing his hand on Gavakyn's shoulder. He looked back to Dodge.

"We have been told that you know the routes around the city better than anyone. We need you to lead us to the temple."

Dodge's eyes were a bit wild, but he managed to keep his cool. "That was more than a year ago. Never been back, never wanted to. The place was…" he trailed off, his eyes tightening, as though he were reliving a memory he'd rather forget.

"Was what?" Karn hissed, rising from his chair.

"It felt evil," Dodge answered, giving an involuntary shiver. "I'm not the bravest of men, I'll admit—but I've stared down death enough times to know I'm not a coward either."

He paused and looked at Kildare and Zedaine, a tinge of horror in his eyes.

"But that place…I've no shame in saying—it terrified me. Blade only told me I needed to lead you to the entrance. I didn't sign on for any more than that."

"That's all we ask," Jax said gently. "I would not have you risk more than you wish to. The three of us, however, have no choice."

"We have seen what the evil you spoke of can do," Gavakyn cut in. "There is no running from it. If unleashed, it will kill every living thing on Quasa."

"What's waiting for us down there?" Zedaine asked, all vestiges of humor gone.

"We don't know," Karn answered.

"Bullshit,' Kildare snapped. "If it was a simple task, Crow and I never would have been hired on."

"Why do you say that?" Karn asked, furrowing his brow.

Kildare snorted. "My brother and I are among the deadliest warriors on the planet, and our employer knows it. Here you are, three strangers, speaking with an accent I've never heard, hailing from parts unknown. One," he continued, pointing at Gavakyn, "a fighter, wielding a blade of mythic steel. My gut tells me he's as good as we are with that weapon and still, that's not enough."

The elder sibling shifted his gaze to Jax. "You, with your open demeanor—you have been rubbing the back of your pack since we met. You claim to be a bard of little renown, but I'm worldly enough to know that the lute strung on your back is imbued with magic—enough to bring down a bolt of lightning and have enough power left to lay waste to this building."

"And you," Zedaine cut in, nodding at Karn. "Your bauble of light has given you away. Most casters use a white light to illuminate the darkness. Those that are more advanced will use red or yellow—but you cast a green sphere, a color only a master would use. If I had to guess, I'd say the three of you are the most powerful of your kind, from wherever shores you call home."

"So, the question remains," Kildare continued, looking at them all, "what's waiting for us in that temple? What foe is so powerful that a deadly blademaster, a powerful bard, and a master shaman need the help of two of the finest warriors in the world?"

A heartbeat of silence pulsed through the room.

"Aye, what they said," Dodge added, puffing out his chest, shuffling over to stand next to Kildare.

The elder sibling gave the middleman a sidelong look and rolled his eyes.

Jax blinked twice in rapid succession and gave the brothers a toothy smile. "She said you were smart," he murmured, pulling a pack off his back.

"Who?" Zedaine asked, in confusion.

"The dragon sage of the Rhone, your employer," Gavakyn offered, nodding in approval.

"Blade?" Zedaine guessed, turning his lips in a frown.

"Aye, why so surprised?" Jax asked. He was untying a bundle that had been strapped alongside his pack.

Kildare snorted. "She's not exactly one to rain compliments upon us."

"She spoke highly of you both—Dodge as well," Karn croaked, laying his staff on his lap.

"That still doesn't answer my question," Kildare pressed, his eyes intent. "What is waiting for us down there?"

"We don't know for certain," the Karn began, tying a sprig of holly to his staff. "Could be nothing…or it could be a coven of undead."

"That's a lie," Kildare growled, stepping forward. "The three of you could handle that without us. What are you hiding?"

None of them answered right away. Instead, Jax pulled out two bundles wrapped in wool cloth. Unwrapping the bundles revealed a pair of swords, three feet in length and made of metal as dark as ebony.

"Shadowsteel?" Kildare gasped, his voice stunned.

"By Jora…where did you come by that?" Zedaine whispered, his voice echoing his brother's surprise.

"They are treasures of my people," Karn answered, pinning a bracelet with three feathers to his staff. "I am surprised you have heard of shadowsteel. It was thought the knowledge of forging a shadowsteel blade was lost ages ago."

"We have read enough ancient tomes to know what these are," Zedaine answered, as Jax handed the two swords to the brothers. Each stared at the dark metal blades in reverence.

Kildare's visage turned to suspicion. "There is only one enemy shadowsteel was forged to fight."

"Aye," Gavakyn confirmed.

"What enemy is that?" Dodge blurted, completely in the dark.

The room lay quiet for several heartbeats.

"Demons," Kildare answered, his voice deadly quiet.

The six companions ducked out the back door of Dodge's establishment and made for the outskirts on the northern edge of the city. An expert scout, Zedaine had taken his customary position at the front alongside Dodge, while Kildare walked behind the rest, his eyes searching for any signs of trouble.

They made their way out the northernmost gate and Dodge immediately cut to the east. For the first mile, the terrain was spacious and easy to navigate. After a quarter turn of the hourglass, they entered the confines of a forest known as the Wildwood. Once inside, their movement slowed somewhat as there was no set path to walk upon. They climbed several hills and their corresponding gullies over the next mile. As they moved, Dodge slowed even further, picking his path more carefully.

"What were you doing out here?" Zedaine asked, wiping a line of sweat from his brow at the top of an arduous climb.

"Had a…disagreement with a…city guardsman," Dodge panted, taking a drink from his waterskin. "He seems to have thought…I cheated him…in a game of…cards."

"Did you?" Jax asked, taking a moment to catch his breath.

Dodge put his hands on his knees, the waterskin dangling precariously between his fingers. "Course not," he answered, flicking his eyes quickly at Zedaine.

"I take it the guard was none too happy," Kildare guessed, not even out of breath.

Dodge shrugged. "He grabbed a few of his friends and chased me out the north gate. They stayed on my heels, following me all the way here into the Wildwood."

The smuggler pointed down into the next gully, which was flat and covered with leaves at the bottom. "I took solace in a small opening I found in the rocks. It led into a tunnel I hadn't expected to find. I brushed my tracks away and masked the entrance as well as I could before making my way down the tunnel. It turned into a corridor after a bit and opened into what looked like an underground temple of some kind."

He paused, speaking slowly. "That's where I sensed the evil of the place." He shuddered at the memory. "I turned around and came back here, waiting until dusk before stealing my way back to the city."

"The guards?" Zedaine asked.

Dodge smiled. "One of them fell and broke his leg trying to get down. They had to return empty handed. I hear they still keep a look out for me." He gave a knowing grin. "Course I used a different name back then."

"What name was that?" Gavakyn asked.

Dodge smiled. "The Stoat."

Picking their way carefully, the six of them made their way down the gully in good order. They had to make allowances for Karn, as the shaman was older than the rest. While strong and fit, he lacked the dexterity of his youth. With the help of Gavakyn and the assistance of Kildare, they finally reached the bottom.

"This is it," Dodge gestured at a small opening in the rock.

Jax strode over to the opening and placed his hands upon the stone. He mumbled a brief incantation under his breath. "Yes," he whispered. "I can almost hear it."

"Hear what?" Zedaine asked quietly.

"A resonance," Kildare answered, looking at Jax.

The bard smiled. "You feel it too," he said. "You have the calling."

"So I've been told," Kildare admitted.

"You could be a true bard, if you gave yourself over to it," Jax said, moving away from the opening.

Kildare gave him a short look and shook his head. "Maybe one day, but not now."

Dodge removed his flat cap and held it in front of his chest. "Well…seeing as how I've got you here, my task is finished."

He doffed his cap and gave them all a short bow. "I'll take my leave of you. I wish you all the best of luck."

"Wait," Gavakyn argued, frowning at Dodge. "You're just going to leave?"

"Course I am," Dodge answered, his face draped in a smile. "I've done my part, haven't I? Taken you to the temple entrance."

"You agreed to take us to the temple!" Gavakyn snarled.

Dodge placed his cap back on his head and touched his fingertips to his chest. "And I've done that," Dodge replied. "This is the temple entrance. It will take you right where you need to go."

"Coward," Gavakyn accused.

Dodge gave him a smile. "Well, I'm no hero, that's for certain. I'm a businessman—if there was coin to be made, I might be tempted to stay."

He gave Zedaine a *particularly* innocent look.

The younger sibling sighed. "I'll let you keep the fifteen talons you owe us if you stay," he drawled.

Dodge blinked and stepped forward. "The way narrows a bit at first, and then widens further in," he instructed, stepping through the entrance.

Kildare frowned at his brother. "Those are my winnings you just gave away."

Zedaine gave him a winsome smile. "Did you really think he was going to pay?"

Kildare frowned as Zedaine ducked in after Dodge. "I hate you sometimes."

The passageway led underground, sloping steadily downward. Kildare would have guessed they had walked a mile before the hall began to level out. As they moved, the air became thick with moisture. The dripping sound of water on rock echoed from somewhere in front of them.

At nearly a half turn of the hourglass, the stone passage opened into a large chamber. They had made a descent of at least three hundred feet from the tunnel's entrance. The room was dark, illuminated only by the green bauble of magical light Karn had conjured upon their initial descent. With a wave of his hand, the shaman sent the luminescent sphere into the room and amplified its power.

The magic sphere floated high above them, revealing a huge room, nearly two hundred feet long and half again as wide. Spaced evenly throughout the chamber were six stone pillars, each carved with intricate patterns of ivy and creatures of fey.

Overriding the serenity of the temple's fixtures was a pulsating feeling of rot and evil.

"I see what you mean," Jax said, pulling his lute off his shoulder.

"About what?" Dodge asked, his face pale.

"The feeling of evil," the bard answered, putting his fingers to strings. "It's like a dark layer of filth clinging to the air. It should not be so. This was a holy place of Raia, a benevolent creature, loved by our people."

Kildare felt it too. A pervasive fear that threatened to inundate his soul.

Jax began to play, his fingers plucking expertly against the strings in an upbeat melody that resonated with hope. Almost immediately, the spirits of the others lifted, as the oppressive evil of the room dissipated under the magic of the bard's melody.

Minutes passed. When the song finished, the others stared at Jax, a touch of wonder on their faces.

"It won't last," the bard said, slinging the lute back over his shoulder. "Let's get our business attended too."

The group stepped into the room and walked forward. In the middle of the chamber, concealed from their view at the entrance, lay a pedestal, the face of a beautiful woman etched upon the front. On top of the pedestal lay a half dozen polished gray stones.

"Is that what you are looking for?" Dodge asked quietly.

"Perhaps," Karn answered, moving forward, his staff in his hands.

"Let's find this stone of yours and leave," Zedaine said, his voice uneasy.

"Aye," Kildare echoed, his eyes searching the rest of the room. "Even with the power of Jax's song, this place reeks of malevolence."

"Something has come and tainted the temple," Jax said, his voice low. "I sense only a feeling of anger and hate.

"Jax," Karn rasped, beckoning the bard forward. "Work your magic quickly. Crow and Raven are right. We should leave this place as soon as we have what we came for."

As he spoke, the shaman peered closely at the runes etched on the side of the pedestal.

"Quickly now, else some ill fate befalls us," Karn whispered absently.

Jax pulled a hand-crafted drum from around his waist and moved in front of the pedestal. He loosened his fingers a moment and slowly began to beat upon the taught sharkskin leather that made up the head of his instrument.

As he played, the resonance he had sensed outside began to fill the room. It amplified and a high-pitched vibration became pronounced, enough that all six members of the group could hear it. A ringing began to emanate from inside the platform. As Jax played, the half dozen stones atop the pedestal rolled off, falling with a crack to the rocky ground. The sound of grinding rock split the air, as another stone, this one glowing with a pale blue light, rose from inside the pedestal until it came to rest in front of them.

"Is…is that it?" Dodge asked, dumbfounded.

"The Orb of Raia," Gavakyn whispered fervently. "Take it bard, while we still can."

Kildare, engrossed in what he saw, felt a cold permeate the air around them. "Something is not right," he muttered, his hand going to the hilt of his shadowsteel sword.

"Grab the damn thing and let us leave this place," Dodge begged, inching toward the exit.

"Yes," Jax agreed, stepping forward, reaching his hand out toward the blue stone.

"Wait," hissed Karn.

"What is it?" Kildare snapped, his eyes going hard.

"This temple has been desecrated," the shaman read, looking intently at the runes. "This here is written in an old tongue," he pointed at the writing. "I cannot make out much, but it warns of the coming of Urak should the stone be removed."

"Who is Urak?" Zedaine asked.

"A demon lord of great power," Karn answered. "An enemy to Raia."

"Leave it where it is," Dodge begged, licking his lips. "I'd rather exit this temple with my life intact."

"We cannot," Gavakyn growled, drawing his blade. "Without the stone, our lands will be engulfed in darkness."

"Gavakyn is right," Karn barked, nodding at Jax. "Take it bard—the rest of you ready yourselves."

Dodge began to walk backward from the room. "I think it's time I say goodbye. Best of luck to you."

He turned around and nearly sprinted from the chamber.

"Remind me to have a word with Blade the next time she sends us on a suicide mission," Kildare snarled, tearing his shadowsteel blade from its sheath.

"If we survive," Zedaine quipped, flashing a smile at his brother, mirroring his actions.

"Ready?" asked Jax, licking his lips in nervous anticipation.

"Pull the damn thing," Kildare snarled, his eyes hot coals of rage.

Jax reached forward and grabbed the stone, placing it quickly in his deepest pocket.

For a moment, nothing happened.

"Could we be that lucky?" Zedaine asked, his voice hopeful.

The air began to shimmer in front of them.

"We never are," Kildare groused, his grip on the sword tightening.

Without warning, a flash of light exploded from the space above the pedestal. Magical sparks shot outward. They stood rapt with attention as a reddish gray light swirled in the air above the pedestal.

It was a portal to another world.

Leaping through the magical vortex came a creature, manlike in appearance, save for the bat wings on its back and the thick horns that curled back and down around its skull. In its hand it held a barbed spear of polished obsidian, the haft made from a dark mineral lined with white stone. A black gorget of metal encircled the creature's neck, protecting it from the top of his throat down to the middle of his chest. Matching bracers cast in the visage of fiery hounds were clamped on either wrist. Around its waist was a belt of dark metal, its center fashioned in the shape of a human skull. Eyes, the color of the setting sun, looked down upon the mortals beneath them, burning with an unholy anger.

The demon lord Urak had come.

"Who are you, that would stand against me?" Urak spat.

It was Karn who answered.

"We are the champions of this world, here to cleanse this place of you and your foul kind," the shaman rasped, his voice amplified in the temple of his forebears.

The demon lord smiled, revealing a row of white fangs. "I have waited many centuries for those who would trigger the magic your goddess left behind. Instead of calling to her, it has opened the barrier between our worlds."

Urak's eyes changed from a burnished orange to a fiery red. "I will not let a handful of subspecies thwart the will of the Rage King! I will…"

"Shut your goat-faced mouth!" Kildare roared, running forward, swinging his sword at the demon.

Urak, taken by surprise, managed to parry the blow as a shower of sparks rained down upon them from his spear. The demon, inhumanly fast, countered, forcing Kildare back into a defensive position.

"Where did you come by a shadowsteel blade?" Urak snarled, his voice tinged with both anger and curiosity.

"You will find we are full of surprises," Kildare spat, dropping into a low fighting crouch.

"As am I," the fiend retorted, beckoning his hand behind him.

With a roar, six demons shot through the swirling gateway and attacked in a fury.

Dodge was far from a coward, but he did not see the sense of staying in an underground temple destined to be attacked by a ridiculously powerful creature from another world. Moments after he left, the smuggler from Gallanse heard an insidious voice coming from behind him.

He picked up his pace immediately.

Reverberating down the hall, he detected the distinct bark of Karn's voice, ringing with authority.

Against his better judgement, Dodge slowed his speed before coming to a stop. He cast a quick look behind him and listened as the booming voice of the bard echoed through the corridor. From the steely clangs inside the chamber, he knew a fight was raging.

"I must be out of my bleeding mind," he whispered, drawing two of his knives. With a quick breath of determination, Dodge stole back down the corridor from whence he'd come.

"Leave Urak to us!" thundered Gavakyn, racing forward, his mythic steel blade in hand.

Karn leveled his staff, and shouted words of power.

"*Sep nyal za Angnar*!"

A burst of green flame shot from the shaman's staff striking the demon full in the chest.

Urak grimaced in pain but was able to spin away from the attack and engage Gavakyn with his spear.

The stocky warrior parried the spear and swung his mythic steel blade, drawing a line of blood along the demon's arm.

Urak, glanced at the wound and shot forward, attacking with fury.

"Right side!" Kildare shouted, moving in that direction to cut off three of the demons that had come out of the portal. The first, a jackal faced creature wielding a long handled khopesh, lashed out in fury, thinking to take Kildare by surprise.

The crafty warrior expertly parried and returned the attack with a lightning riposte that took it through the heart. The jackal faced demon barely had time to register its surprise before falling, its green lifeblood pumping onto the ground.

The other two demons hesitated, seeing how easily their comrade had been dispatched.

"Come on you hell spawn," Kildare taunted, goading them forward, flicking the blood of their fallen comrade at them with his sword. "I'm no easy meat."

The two demons, one with the face of a feral cat, the other with the countenance of a human woman, lurched forward to attack.

On the other side, Zedaine had downed a demon of his own, slashing it viciously across the throat. A creature with a ram's head lay dying on the ground. The big hunter was currently engaged with a fearsome beast, a snarling hound the size of a horse, steeped in fire. Further to his left, Jax had engaged another of the demons, this one sporting the visage of a bull. The two were locked in combat, Jax proving to be surprisingly adept with his iron shod quarterstaff.

Eyes locked on his target, the bard swayed away from his combatant, inhaling deeply.

"*Brak'dur*!" he bellowed.

The power of his voice smashed into the bull faced demon, stunning the creature in its tracks. "Crow!" he shouted, cutting in front of Zedaine, engaging the big hunter's foe.

Zedaine, knowing Jax could not kill the creature with his staff, sidestepped across the space between them and thrust his shadowsteel blade through the creature's heart. The bull faced demon slid to the ground and joined its companion in death.

"Zee!" shouted Kildare, his voice glacier cold.

The younger sibling looked over at his brother. Kildare was engaged with two of the remaining demons. An expert swordsman, Kildare was back on his heels, fighting for his life. The two creatures in front of him were big and fast, both with a greater reach than Kildare.

It was only a matter of time.

Zedaine moved to assist his brother, when two more demons bound out of the entrance.

"Shit," Zedaine swore, turning to engage the enemy. "We need to close that portal!" he shouted to Jax.

"I know," the bard answered, his staff whirling in defense at the hound in front of him.

"Do something fast!" Kildare shouted, swaying away from a claw that managed to win past his sword, slicing open his shoulder.

The blow was enough to jostle Kildare off balance, knocking him to the floor.

"Raven!" Jax shouted, his stomach turning to ice.

The feline demon loomed over Kildare, intent on the kill.

"No!" screamed Jax.

Out of nowhere, a steel knife flashed in the green light of the shaman's magic and slammed into the demon's eye.

The cat faced creature staggered backward, howling in agony.

Kildare, realizing he'd been saved, scrambled to his feet, and attacked with an all-out offensive against the human faced demon. Sword whirling, within moments it was down, blood oozing from a deep wound under its armpit. The first monster, still reeling from the knife in its eye, he dispatched a moment later with a quick thrust to the heart. Kildare glanced back to see the beaming face of Dodge standing near the entryway.

"You're welcome!" the smuggler quipped, tipping his cap in Kildare's direction.

Kildare snorted with dark humor. At that moment, Karn let out a burst of green fire from his staff. Urak countered with a white mist of force. The demon's power proved too much, and the shaman was tossed away from their magical duel. Karn flew backward, smashing to the ground, coming to rest in a daze on the floor in front of Dodge.

"Get him up!" Kildare roared, racing to the other side of the room, slashing at the haunches of the hound-like demon facing Jax.

Taken by surprise, the creature shied away from this new adversary, and the bard smashed his staff over the canine skull, shouting words of power.

"*Bree nok*!"

The demon's head exploded under the strength of Jax's magic, splashing him and Kildare in a wave of green blood.

"Aid Gavakyn!" Kildare shouted, wiping the gore from his face, leaping to assist his brother. "Leave these last two to us."

Jax nodded, seeing Gavakyn was being pressed backward by Urak despite his incredible skill with his machete.

Quickly Jax unslung his lute and strummed out a high-pitched chord.

"*Enon nelhnal!*" the bard shouted, glaring at the demon.

A yellow bolt of lightning shot from his lute, slamming into Urak. The demon lord let out a howl of pain, its skin charred black from the blast.

Gavakyn, gaining a modicum of respite, thrust his hand forward and unleashed a magical attack of his own.

"*Htasn sntemu*!" he cried out, his voice hoarse with exhaustion.

A dozen, foot long icicles shot from his hands, burying themselves in Urak's chest and legs. The demon lord screamed again, more loudly than the last time.

"Enough!" the demon shouted, thrusting his own hand forward. A whip-like chord made of black and green energy appeared, lashing out at the attackers in front of him. Both Jax and Gavakyn were knocked down, thrown backward to where Dodge had successfully gotten Karn back on his feet.

"I have toyed with you for too long already," Urak shouted, raising his wings behind him. With one powerful billow, he ascended above his attackers.

"*Dey Zegal*!" Urak screamed, unleashing a jet of orange fire toward them.

Desperately, Karn raised his staff.

"*Daan Lokba*!" he countered, blocking the flames with a blue shield of energy.

For the span of several heartbeats, the shaman managed to hold the fire at bay.

"He is too strong!" Karn gasped, his shield faltering.

"Get up!" implored Dodge, scrambling over to the unconscious Gavakyn.

A moment before the demon fire broke through, Urak lost his concentration. The maniacal Zedaine had cast caution to the wind and leapt from what remained of the pedestal, landing on the demon's back.

"Die you whoreson!" the big hunter roared, swinging wildly with his shadowsteel blade. The keen edge of the sword bit into one of the batlike wings, causing Urak to shout in pain, forcing the creature from the air. The agile demon grabbed hold of Zedaine's collar and cast him off with supernatural strength. The big hunter crashed with a meaty smack against one of the temple pillars located behind Dodge. Zedaine managed to crawl to his knees but could only grimace in pain as he attempted to clear his head.

"It is high time to end your miserable lives," Urak stormed, his body covered in a bounty of wounds. "Not one of you can stand before me."

"We will see," came a voice from behind him.

Blood dripping from his shadowsteel blade, Kildare stepped between the demon and his prey.

Urak snorted. "You?" he taunted. "A single human?"

Kildare's eyes roared to life, as he wiped the blood from the wound on his shoulder. "Yes," Kildare spat. "This human will thwart the will of an immortal demon. Your quest to enter this world ends here."

The fire surrounding the demon flared to life. "Who are you to threaten me?" he sneered.

Kildare dropped into his fighting stance. "I am the Raven, the deadliest warrior this world has ever known."

Urak narrowed his eyes and surged forward with his spear.

A shadowsteel blade was there to meet him.

"Come on!" Dodge begged, trying to rouse his companions. Karn and Gavakyn were both unconscious, while Zedaine was stunned from his collision with the wall. Only Jax seemed alert, though his ankle was folded at an odd angle beneath him and could bear no weight.

"Help me," the bard grimaced through clenched teeth.

The smuggler looked at Jax, his eyes widening in surprise.

"What the hell?" he stammered, his voice shocked.

"What is it?" Jax asked.

Dodge licked his lips nervously. "You look…different."

Jax glanced down at himself, knowing the illusion that had hidden his true features was gone.

"I will explain after," he grated, his ankle throbbing with pain.

Standing next to Dodge, was a creature he had only heard about in legends.

Jax was a dwarf.

Shaking himself out of his momentary reverie, Dodge maneuvered himself underneath Jax's arm and helped him to his feet.

"I need my lute," the bard insisted, hopping forward, each movement excruciating.

"I have it," Dodge answered, scooping up the lute from where it had fallen.

"Get me close," Jax muttered, inching forward. "By Kruk," he gaped, seeing the titanic battle play out in front of him.

"What's wrong?" Dodge grunted, struggling under the bard's weight.

"I thought Gavakyn to be the greatest warrior I'd ever seen," Jax said. "Now, I'm not so sure."

As he spoke, Kildare launched a new attack at the demon lord. Urak was fighting like mad to defend against the lightning quick warrior in front of him.

Kildare had moved inside the reach of the demon, who could not use its superior size to its advantage. The shadowsteel blade was wet with new blood as wounds on Urak's chest and bicep bled freely.

"Come on you bastard," Kildare taunted, scoring another hit on the demon's hip. "I thought you were going to end our miserable lives. I've seen ninety-year-old whores with more fight than you, you horned toad bastard!"

"Insolent human!" thundered Urak, taking a monstrous swipe at the darting Kildare.

"Missed again, you son-of-a-bitch!" Kildare retorted, hammering another thrust into Urak's ribs, snapping the bone underneath the creature's skin.

"This is close enough," Kildare heard Jax say from behind him.

Get that portal closed, Raven thought. While he did not show it, the earlier wound to his shoulder was beginning to ache. He suspected the cat faced demon had injected some kind of poison into him when it had landed its blow. Soon it would impede his ability to fight. For now, he had to keep Urak's attention on him and away from the others.

Goading his enemy, Kildare spoke again. "*You* are a demon lord?" he spat. "What are you the lord of? Cleaning dung? I've fought baby chicks that put up more of a fight!"

Angry as he was, Urak was not stupid. He had caught sight of Jax, who was beginning to play his lute. As the first notes sounded, the demon knew the bard was trying to close the gate.

"No!" shouted Urak, thrusting forward with his spear, simultaneously racing past the human warrior in front of him.

Kildare parried the attack and lashed out again, scoring a deep cut upon the demon's hamstring. Urak dropped to one knee, hurling his spear at Jax with all his strength. Dodge, acting on instinct, stepped in front of the bard and closed his eyes knowing he was about to die.

He heard a ring of metal striking stone and felt a blur of wind whip past his ear.

"No!" Urak shouted in disbelief.

Dodge opened his eyes to see the demon looking behind him.

Standing unsteadily on his feet was Crow, his arm extended in front of him as he'd thrown his sword in the nick of time, knocking the spear off course.

Jax struck the last chord of his melody and everything inside the temple came to a standstill.

Urak began to rise in the air, the portal drawing him into its swirling maw.

"It is not possible!" the demon lord roared, his voice sounding in disbelief.

"I told you," Kildare mocked as the demon floated past him. "You cannot beat me."

"I will remember you, mortal," Urak promised, his voice dripping with venom.

"See that you do," Kildare retorted. "Next time I'll kill you."

Their eyes locked for a moment, each mirroring the hatred seen in the other.

"We will see," Urak managed, before disappearing into the portal.

With the demon gone, the swirling vortex vanished, and Kildare slumped to the knees.

Focusing his strength, he stumbled over to the rest of them, using what little energy remained. Casting his gaze toward Jax, Kildare's eyes peered at the bard.

"You are a dwarf," he surmised.

Jax nodded and gave Kildare a friendly grin. "Aye laddie, Gavakyn is too."

Craning his neck toward the others, he managed to make out the form of Karn laying on the ground. There was pale, sallow skin covering his wizened face.

"A goblin," Jax said, answering Kildare's question before he could ask it.

"How?" Kildare asked, grimacing in pain. "You're creatures of legend."

Jax waved his hand. "I will explain later," he answered, once again playing his lute. "Let's see about neutralizing that poison in your shoulder and healing our wounds."

Kildare was about to argue, but the pain in his shoulder made him swoon. The last thing he heard before passing out was Dodge, speaking with Jax.

"Seeing as how I did more than I promised, is there a way we can renegotiate my cut?"

It was hours later when the six emerged from underground and stepped into the late afternoon sun. Their wounds had healed, thanks to the curative nature of the bard's song. Jax had played his lute for more than an hour. At the end of that time, even his dislocated ankle had popped back into place and was quickly on the mend.

Jax had needed a few hours of rest after his medicinal administrations, as he was no longer a young dwarf. While he slept, Gavakyn and Karn relayed to the others information about their distant homeland. Located thousands of miles across the Ariath Ocean, the dwarves made their home on the island of Rahm. Their sallowskins counterparts lived only a few miles away on their own island called Garthan-Tor. The two nations had been at war for generations but had found an uneasy peace over the last eighteen years as the threat of demon invasion had united most of them together.

The brothers had many questions, as dwarves existed only in ancient tales around the countries of the Crystalline Sea. The dwarf and the goblin answered what they could in the brief time they were allotted.

"Where will you go now?" Zedaine asked, rubbing at the back of his neck.

"Blade has booked us passage to a place called Dagor," Karn croaked, as he cast a new illusion upon himself and his companions.

"A question, if I may?" Kildare asked.

Karn nodded.

"Why the subterfuge?" Kildare frowned. "Why not just show us who you were when we met?"

It was Gavakyn who answered.

"Our folk left these lands eons ago," he replied gruffly. "Through powerful magic, we were able to contact the dragon sage, but we feared most folk would not take kindly to seeing races thought to be long dead."

"You're probably right," Zedaine mused. "Humans can be biased, racial bigots—even with one another."

"Word will get out," Kildare warned. "Not through Zedaine and I, but eventually, your secret will come to light."

All eyes turned to Dodge, who held up his hands defensively.

"I'm not saying nothing," he said. "What happened in that temple is liable to give me nightmares for the rest of my life. Don't you worry bout old Dodge. I just as soon forget the matter entirely…as long as I get paid, mind you."

"Altruistic to the end," Zedaine joked, clapping his hand on Dodge's shoulder.

"I don't know the meaning of the word," Dodge sniffed solemnly.

Upon arriving at the docks, the trio from across the seas took their leave. They boarded a sturdy looking cutter moored at the harbor that was planning to sail at dawn.

"These belong to you," Kildare said, handing the shadowsteel blades over to Jax, who took them graciously.

"You two fought well," Gavakyn replied, clasping first Zedaine's hand and then Kildare's.

"So did you," the younger sibling said with a smile. "I had not thought to meet swordsmen as good as we are."

"I did my best," Gavakyn responded. "Urak was unlike any foe I've ever faced."

"He was as deadly as the come," Kildare agreed, clasping the dwarven warrior's hand.

"May your journey end in peace," Karn put in, giving them a crooked smile.

"Yours as well, shaman," Zedaine replied with a nod. "Stay out of trouble."

"Hmmpt," Karn snorted. "Not likely."

Zedaine chuckled as Gavakyn and Karn boarded the ship. Jax lingered a moment longer.

"You have the gift, should you ever choose to pursue it," he said to Kildare. "There are few on Quasa born to work bardic magic."

Kildare looked at Jax, his face tight with regret. "Perhaps one day," he replied. "When my life is less…complicated."

"Find me," Jax said warmly. "I will teach you."

"I'll hold you to that," Kildare said.

"Dodge, Crow," Jax said, clapping both on the shoulder before boarding after his companions.

"Good luck to you, bard," Zedaine said with a wave.

They watched as the trio disappeared below deck.

"I never thought to see the day when dwarves and a goblin would walk beside us," Zedaine said in wonder.

"Nor did you think of the trouble they'd bring," Kildare replied wryly. "Speaking of trouble," he continued, looking at Dodge. "We all would have died if it hadn't been for you. Your intervention saved us all."

The smuggler twisted his face in a knowing grin. "I did, didn't I?"

They started walking back up to the city.

"Why?" Zedaine asked. "Why did you come back?"

Dodge twisted his face in humor, preparing to give a glib answer.

"Because, despite his terrible reputation," Kildare explained, before Dodge could speak, "his deceitful ways, his below average hygiene, and his penchant for cheating at cards—Dodge is a decent man."

The smuggler looked at Kildare, a frown slowly forming on his face. "Let's not let that last bit get out, alright?"

"You don't want folks knowing you've a good heart?" Zedaine asked.

"Chara's tits! Keep your voice down," Dodge hissed, looking around to see if anyone had heard. "If word gets out I've gone soft, the thieves and cutthroats of the city will take advantage now, won't they?"

"They won't hear it from us," Kildare snickered.

"Good. Life's hard enough on the streets as it is." His face soured as he looked at Kildare. "You were wrong, by the way. About two things."

"Oh? What's that?" Kildare asked.

Dodge ran his hands down the front of his brown tunic. "My hygiene for one. I took a bath not a week ago."

"My mistake," Kildare replied, suppressing a smile.

"I don't cheat neither," Dodge continued, tugging unconsciously at his sleeves. "That kind of thing can get you killed in Gallanse."

Kildare put a hand on the smuggler's chest, halting all three of them in the middle of the street. "Then how do you explain this?" he asked, flipping a card from his pocket. It depicted the smiling visage of a black thief, a champion card from their game the night before.

"Where did you get that?" Dodge gasped, looking at Kildare in surprise.

Kildare leaned in and spoke softly. "From inside your sleeve before your final play last night."

Dodge opened his mouth to speak, but the look Kildare gave him froze his tongue in place.

"A word of advice, Stoat," the elder sibling said. "If you are going to cheat, make damn sure you're the smartest person at the table."

The swordsman relaxed a fraction and handed the card to Dodge. "Thank you for saving my life today. I will not forget it."

Without another word, Kildare walked away, making for the gaming house.

"By Duorn," Dodge muttered, watching Kildare leave.

"I wouldn't be too upset," Zedaine offered, clapping Dodge on the shoulder. "Those talons I plunked on the table last night—they were lead coins painted gold. Even if we'd lost, we would have won."

"How's that?" Dodge asked, miffed at being fooled.

"It was never about the money," Zedaine answered. "Kildare and I wanted to get a read on *you.* If you'd done anything we did not like, we never would have allowed you to accompany us."

Dodge raised an eyebrow. "So…cheating last night…that was ok?"

Zedaine laughed. "Not really, but it the great scheme of things, it was understandable."

He leaned in close toward Dodge. "You were not condescending toward your men, even though you could have been. We could see that they respected you. That's when we knew."

The big hunter tossed Dodge a pouch that jingled with coins. "It's all there. The fifteen talons Blade promised. I added a bit for your trouble."

Zedaine winked at Dodge. "Don't spend it all in one place."

With that, the big hunter set off at a jog, catching up to his brother.

Dodge watched him go. Looking down, he loosened the drawstring and opened the pouch. Inside were at least thirty talons, their gold luster visible in the light of the setting sun.

"Fortuitous," he said with a smile.

As the sun began to set, Karn moved above deck to stand next to a figure cloaked in blue robes.

"You found the orb?" the figure asked, pulling back her hood to reveal a handsome woman with dark hair.

"Yes," the shaman answered, reaching into one of his many pockets. Karn pulled out a metallic stone, appearing glossy black in the reddish hue of the setting sun.

"A shadowstone as payment, as we agreed," the goblin rasped, handing the oval shaped sphere to the woman.

"My associates?" she asked, pocketing the stone inside her robes.

Karn gave the woman a soft smile. "Better than I would have dreamed possible," Karn admitted. "Where did you find them? They are no run of the mill mercenaries."

The woman gave him a crooked turn of her lips and waved away his question. "I'm glad they were able to help," she answered, pulling her hood back over her head. She took a step toward the stern of the ship but stopped at Karn's words.

"The time is at hand, sage," the shaman croaked in warning.

"Do you know when?" she asked without turning around.

"Within what's left of my lifespan," Karn answered. "A year perhaps…no more than five."

"Then we have time," the sage reasoned, stepping away again.

"You should tell them what you are," the shaman advised, trailing after her.

Blade came to a halt and turned to look over her shoulder. "When the time is right, I will."

The sun set at that moment, and twilight came to Sapphire Bay. Karn heard Blade take two more steps toward the bow of the ship. The cutter shifted momentarily as though a great weight pressed against it. Looking up, the goblin saw a creature of legend ascend into the darkening sky.

Karn let out a wonderous sigh, as he watched a dragon disappear into the night.

Made in the USA
Columbia, SC
23 May 2023

16959148R00214